DEAD MAN'S HAND

LORRAINE BARTLETT

GAYLE LEESON

ACKNOWLEDGMENTS

My thanks go to the members of the Lorraine Train: Amy Connolley, Mary Ann Borer, Debbie Lyon, Linda Kuzminczuk, and Rita Pierrottie for their continued support.

Cover by Wicked Smart Designs

CAST OF CHARACTERS

Katie Bonner: owner-manager of Artisans Alley, the anchor on Victoria Square

Ray Davenport: former homicide detective and owner of Wood U on Victoria Square

Rose Nash: jewelry vendor at Artisans Alley and Katie's friend

Nick Ferrell: co-owner of Sassy Sally's B&B on Victoria

Seth Landers: McKinlay Mill's only attorney and Katie's friend

Don Parsons: co-owner of Sassy Sally's B&B on Victoria Square

Moonbeam Carruthers: owner of The Flower Child gift shop

Andy Rust: owner of Angelo's Pizzeria and Katie's former boyfriend

Brad Andrews: Noted chef, hired to manage Tealicious tea shop

Carol Rigby: Monroe County Sheriff's Office detective

Nona Fiske: owner of the Quiet Quilter on Victoria Square

Vance Ingram: vendor at Artisans Alley and Katie's second-in-command

Gina Solero: gambler

Connor Davis: owner of The Flower Patch florists and part-time gambler

Jamie Seifert: Seth's significant other, medical examiner, murder victim

Gabrielle Pearson: owner of Calexia Industries

atie Bonner squirmed in her seat under the glare of a maniacal clown. Her friends, Nick Ferrell and his husband, Don Parsons, enjoyed embracing Halloween and making their bed-and-breakfast, Sassy Sally's, look spookily festive for their guests, but this particular decoration was creeping her out.

Shifting a Pirouette chocolate-filled wafer cookie in her mouth as though it was a cigar, Katiee tossed a blue candy-coated chocolate into the pile in the middle of the table. "I'll see your yellow and raise you a blue."

Because of the hand she'd been dealt, Katie felt pretty confident. In their current mode of exchange, yellow candies were worth a hundred dollars; blues were worth five hundred; reds were worth a thousand, and greens were worth a hundred thousand. Other colors were to be eaten as they were removed from the bag. So far, Katie was up three hundred and forty-two thousand. Too bad that, unlike poker chips, these candies couldn't be redeemed for currency. Oh, what she could do with three hundred thousand dollars! Images of buying, renovating, and developing the abandoned warehouse behind Victoria Square played in her mind.

As though reading her thoughts, Seth Landers said, "If the Merchants Association partnership is planning to buy that old warehouse, they need to make an offer. I got word yesterday afternoon that a developer from Rochester has been looking at the property."

Smiling, Katie said, "I was just sitting here counting my candies and deciding how I'd renovate that place if this was real money."

Seth grinned. "I could tell."

"I'll get in touch with the Victoria Square partners," she promised.

It was funny how well the lawyer-turned-pseudo-big-brother knew her. She was glad Seth's partner, Jamie Seifert, had been able to attend that night's poker game. Even though the couple had been together for over a year, she hadn't had the opportunity to get to know Jamie as well as she would have liked.

Knowing Nick and Don had played poker professionally, it was obvious Jamie had studied their techniques. At last, he finally voiced it. "Guys, I've been watching you all evening, soaking up your poker moves."

"Do we have moves?" Don asked.

"It was my moves that first attracted you to me," Nick quipped.

"Not *those* kinds of moves," Jamie chided. "Katie, how long have you been playing with these guys?"

"About six months."

"You've obviously picked up more than a few of their techniques."

"I'll say," Nick said, nodding toward the pile of candy that sat before her. "I won't be getting fat on peanut M&Ms, that's for sure."

Jamie let out a breath. "Wouldn't it be awesome to win a pot like that in a real poker game in a place like Vegas? Wow, what a rush!"

Katie saw Nick and Don exchange glances, but they merely smiled.

"If I won, I'd book the two of us a luxurious vacation," Jamie told Seth.

"Good luck with our being able to schedule any significant amount of time off together," Seth said diffidently. With his busy law practice and Jamie's job in the medical examiner's office, they were lucky to spend an entire weekend together.

"I want to do it. Soon. Don't you?" Jamie persisted.

Seth shrugged. "Sure, but—"

Jamie's eyes widened as he drew in another breath and grimaced, then suddenly stood. "I'll be right back," he said and hurried in the direction of the bathroom.

Nick elbowed Seth in the ribs. "Way to go, Mr. Sensitive. Looks like you hurt his feelings."

Seth frowned. "No, I didn't. At least, I don't think I did. Jamie's had an upset stomach all afternoon." Then he shrugged. "But just in case, I'll apologize when he gets back."

"Instead of apologizing, maybe you should ask him where *he'd* like to go." Katie popped a butterscotch candy into her mouth. "I'd like to go to Barcelona one of these days. I hear it's the perfect place for someone interested in art and architecture."

"I'd love to go to Fiji sometime," Don said.

Nick wagged his eyebrows. "Yeah, the tropics are great, but how about the Black Forest?"

"What's so special about the Black Forest?" Seth asked.

Nick laughed. "Besides the cake? Kidding! Spas, vineyards, charming villages."

"What's your dream vacation spot, Seth?" Nick asked.

Seth ducked his head, the shadow of a smile gracing his lips. "Anywhere with Jamie would be heaven."

Katie felt a sappy smile settle across her features. Oh,

how she wished someone would feel that way about her. The fact that her boyfriend of almost two years had betrayed her by sleeping with another woman did not make her eager to re-enter the dating world, and so she felt more comfortable in the presence of her gay friends who were in committed relationships than in the proximity of heterosexual men. She'd feel differently one day, but probably not any time soon.

Looking around the table, Katie realized that—not for the first time—she was the only woman in the room. She enjoyed being "one of the guys," but she'd like to get closer to some of her female acquaintances. She made a mental note to invite Moonbeam Carruthers, the newest member of the Victoria Square Merchants Association, to lunch the next day.

"What are we talking about?" Jamie asked as he returned to the table.

"Where we want to go for a lovely respite," Katie said. "What's your number one place?"

"I don't know." He looked at Seth. "Where would you want to go?"

"I'd be happy at home if we could spend an entire week alone together." Seth's cheeks flushed, which surprised Katie because she didn't think she'd ever seen the man blush before. "But Hawaii would be nice, too."

With Jamie's return, their collective attention turned back to the game. Those still playing showed their cards. "Gentlemen, read 'em and weep," Katie said. As she'd anticipated, Katie won the round with a full house—three queens and a pair of tens.

With considerable grumbling, the others tossed their cards to the middle of the table while Katie dragged her confectionery booty toward her.

"Lady Luck is sure on your side tonight," Nick muttered.

Katie pointed to one of her cards. "Well, the Eagles told us the queen of hearts was our best bet," she said and smirked.

As Seth shuffled the cards for the next round, Nick casually said, "Don and I have been discussing fostering a child."

Don frowned and rested a hand on Nick's forearm. "Not now. Please."

Nick held Don's gaze, and Katie could tell a tense, silent conversation was transpiring between them. It was time to change the subject.

"So, have you all met Rose's new guy yet?" she asked.

Seth seemed delighted to hop onto a lighter subject, while Jamie jumped up to return to the bathroom. With the situation defused, the players resumed their game.

IT WAS NEARLY one a.m. when Seth and Jamie dropped Katie off in front of Tealicious and waited for her to climb the stairs to her apartment. She'd assured them she could walk across Victoria Square to her home above her tea shop, but she was secretly glad Seth had insisted on driving her once she'd realized how late it was. Okay, she'd felt just a little vulnerable during the preceding weeks. Why…she wasn't quite sure. Screw that. She knew exactly why she felt on edge—thank you, Andy Rust, for being a cad—she just felt she should feel more empowered. That she didn't brought up a lot of negativity within her.

Upon opening the door and waving goodbye to Seth and Jamie, she was greeted by Mason, her black-and-white cat. Della, her tabby, tail swishing, was too aggravated with her for coming home so late to bother rising up off the love seat.

The studio apartment was small enough so that Katie could see every wall from the front door, with the exception of the bathroom. She loved it, though. It was cozy and beautifully decorated, and in a very short time, it had become home.

Katie used her smartphone to fire off an email to the Merchants Association partnership informing them that they needed to make a decision soon if they intended to buy the abandoned warehouse behind Victoria Square. She included a poll about meeting times to see what worked best for the majority. She told them the meeting would be held at Tealicious. That was one good thing about owning a tea shop—she no longer had to scramble around to find a venue for impromptu meetings.

She had an email from Vance, her assistant manager at Artisans Alley, the anchor business that was the glue that held the whole Victoria Square shopping district together, and which she owned. Vance had rented an upstairs booth to a vendor who specialized in metal sculptures. Despite her misgivings about leasing the space to someone whose sculptures could put hundreds of pounds of pressure on a floor that was beginning to need attention, she responded with a congratulatory note. She wanted Vance to feel as though she trusted his decisions. In his brief role as assistant manager, he'd already made some decisions she'd questioned. She'd even taken the vendors' sides over Vance's on more than one occasion. Now she felt it imperative that she show him that she believed in him. Still, that much weight on aging floorboards? Hopefully, Vance had considered that and felt it wouldn't be a problem.

After slipping into her pajamas, Katie climbed into bed. Mason snuggled up on her right side and, deciding she wasn't so angry after all, Della cuddled up on Katie's left. She knew she'd regret staying up so late when her alarm rang the next morning, but despite feeling exhausted, she couldn't easily fall asleep.

For one thing, she dreaded hearing from Andy. He'd been her boyfriend for just about two years. Recently—very recently—their relationship had fallen apart. And, yet, they were both still not only members of the Victoria Square Merchants Association, but also members of the partnership some of the merchants had formed to buy property on and around the Square. Facing Andy at the meetings wouldn't be easy. But Katie was a professional—she *could* handle it.

She wondered if she should get back up and take some melatonin. As it was, she needed to get up earlier than usual to power walk an extra lap or two around the Square to work off all the candy she'd eaten that evening at Sassy Sally's. Her last conscious thought was that if she didn't doze off within the next five minutes, she'd take the melatonin.

THE APARTMENT WAS FILLED with light and Katie realized she must have slept through her alarm for it was after nine—two hours later than she'd planned to get up. After feeding the cats, she headed out for her daily exercise.

After three circuits walking the Square, Katie took a shower before heading toward The Flower Child to see Moonbeam Carruthers.

The Flower Child was an eclectic shop—fellow Square merchant Nona Fiske called it "that hippy place"—where Moonbeam sold not only bouquets of cut flowers and potted plants, but crystals, stones, tea blends, soaps, and candles. She also read tarot cards and did reiki massage. A bell above the door tinkled when Katie entered the shop. Two young women stood in front of the display case where the crystals were kept, and a man with a quizzical expression inspected the tea blends.

"I'll be with you in a second!" Moonbeam called.

As she waited, Katie wandered around the shop sampling the scents of the new candles on display.

Once she'd rung up her customers' purchases, Moonbeam apologized to Katie. "Sorry about that. It's always crazy in here on Saturday mornings."

Katie smiled. "That's certainly nothing to be sorry about, and I didn't mind waiting. I'm here to invite you to lunch."

Moonbeam's face fell. "Is it Nona Fiske? Has she been badmouthing my shop again?"

"No, of course not. I just thought it would be nice to sit and have a chat. That is if you feel comfortable closing your shop for an hour."

"That sounds great. When?" Moonbeam waved as a dowdy woman in a polyester top and pants entered the shop.

"Hi. I'm here for my tarot reading," the customer said.

"I'll be right with you." Moonbeam nodded at Katie, indicating she was awaiting her answer.

"What time would be convenient for you?" Katie asked.

"Noon. Where would you like to meet?"

Katie suggested Tealicious, and Moonbeam said she'd meet her there.

As Katie walked to Artisans Alley, she hoped it wouldn't rain that day. Although it was a beautiful sunny morning, the sky was beginning to darken to the west. A storm was definitely brewing.

CHAPTER 2

*K*atie entered Tealicious at a few minutes past noon, surprised to see Jamie at a table in a back corner. He must have gotten over his upset stomach, otherwise, he wouldn't be out to lunch. Since he was seated at a table with a well-dressed, dark-haired woman with whom he was deep in conversation, she didn't go over to say hello. Instead, she sat at an empty table near the door and waited for Moonbeam, hoping she'd make it before the heavens opened up. A rumble of thunder rattled the windows. It sounded as though the storm was going to be a bad one.

Katie threw a look over her shoulder. Jamie and the woman leaned in over the table, as though speaking quietly so that they wouldn't be overheard.

Weird.

Soon, Moonbeam came through the door in a flurry of color. She'd thrown a purple, yellow, orange, and blue poncho on over her jeans and sweater, and carried a red umbrella.

"That's a beautiful poncho," Katie said, after waving Moonbeam over.

"Thank you. I got it in Peru." She took the seat across from Katie. "So, what's new?"

"You know that eyesore of an abandoned warehouse behind the Square?" Katie asked. "Hopefully, it won't be an eyesore for much longer."

"It doesn't bother me. I burned sage in there just before the owner replaced the broken lock on the main door. I'm certain any negative energy there has been banished."

Katie knew Moonbeam was referencing the fact that someone had been murdered inside the warehouse just a few weeks before. All the more reason to give the place a makeover and turn it into something productive.

After explaining to Moonbeam that either a developer or some of the merchants might be buying the warehouse, Katie asked, "Would I sound like a crazy person if I said I thought the building deserved some happiness?"

Laughing, Moonbeam said, "Of course not. But, then, you're asking *me*—Victoria Square's resident bohemian."

Katie joined in her laughter and then said, "I'm glad everyone got the opportunity to get to know you during the Harvest Festival."

"Me, too. Even Nona peeped her head into the shop one day." She spread her hands. "She ran back out almost immediately, but it was a start."

"That's right. We women entrepreneurs have to stick together."

Before Katie could continue, the waitress arrived and took their orders.

"Have you read *Year of Yes* by Shonda Rhimes?" Moonbeam asked. "It's an excellent book."

"I haven't, but—" Katie broke off upon seeing Jamie stumbling toward the door. *What is he doing?* "Excuse me, Moonbeam." She stood. "Jamie?"

He didn't stop, nor did he turn around. He went through the door and collapsed onto the tarmac.

"Jamie!" Katie ran outside and knelt by his side.

A group of passersby stopped to see what was wrong.

"Someone please call nine-one-one!" Katie took Jamie's hand. It was clammy and his lips had a bluish cast to them. "Jamie, can you hear me?"

His eyes fluttered open. "Don't...tell...." A roar of thunder cut off his words as his eyes drifted shut again.

A fat raindrop pelted the pavement before the torrent began in earnest. She was grateful Jamie was under Tealicious's eaves.

Katie placed her fingers at the side of Jamie's neck. Thankfully, he still had a pulse, but it was weak and erratic. She removed her jacket and placed it beneath his head.

Feeling a hand on her shoulder, she turned to see Moonbeam standing behind her. "Is there anything I can do?"

"Yes. Would you go inside and ask Brad to come here?" she asked.

With a nod, Moonbeam hurried back inside Tealicious.

"Give the man some room!"

This directive was shouted by Ray Davenport, former Monroe County Sheriff's Office detective, the current owner of Wood U, and one of Katie's best friends.

"Jamie Siefert?" Ray asked. "What happened?" He, too, took Jamie's pulse, grimaced, and then gently opened one of the man's eyes.

"He was having lunch and then he came out here and collapsed," Katie said, realizing that as a former police officer, Ray probably knew Jamie from the medical examiner's office and that he was also trained in basic first aid.

"Was he alone?" Ray's thick eyebrows came together like curious caterpillars as he unbuttoned the first three buttons of Jamie's shirt.

"No. He was with a woman." Katie looked around. "I don't see her, though."

Brad was suddenly by Katie's side. "Moonbeam said you needed me." He took in the fact Jamie lay prone on the asphalt and gasped. "What happened?"

"Call Seth!" Realizing Jamie was seriously ill, Katie thought it best that Seth didn't drive himself to the hospital. "Scratch that. call Nick, ask him if he can go get Seth. Tell Seth that Jamie's sick and that he's been taken to the hospital." The local volunteer ambulance crew arrived—lights and sirens blazing—so Katie had to shout the rest of her message. "Tell Nick I'll meet them there. I'm going to ride along with Jamie."

INSIDE THE AMBULANCE, Katie sat on a bench seat next to the stretcher. The rain pounding against the roof of the vehicle could be heard over the sound of the siren. As the paramedic took Jamie's blood pressure, he peppered Katie with questions she couldn't answer.

"How was he before he collapsed?"

She didn't know.

"What did he eat for lunch?"

No idea—but she could find out.

"Had he eaten anything prior to lunch?"

"I don't know. I *do* know that he had an upset stomach last night when we were playing poker at a friend's house," Katie said.

Jamie's ominous words *don't tell* replayed themselves in her mind. What had he been going to say? Not to tell Seth about his being at Tealicious? Or the woman he was having lunch with? Or had he been about to say, *don't tell Brad I hated my lunch* or *don't tell Brad lunch made me sick?* But *had* lunch made him sick? As she'd just pointed out to the paramedic, he'd been ill the evening before. Had she—and everyone else at Sassy Sally's—missed some indication of how sick Jamie had truly been? But apparently, not even Jamie knew. Otherwise, he wouldn't have been at Tealicious.

Katie realized the paramedic was addressing her again. "I'm sorry. What did you say?"

"I asked if you're his next of kin."

Eyes widening, Katie said, "No! I mean, I've…his partner is on his way to the hospital…but he's… Jamie's going to be *fine*…isn't he?"

The paramedic wouldn't meet her gaze.

At the hospital, the ambulance's back doors were thrown open, and Katie kept out of the way while the emergency medical technicians swept Jamie out of the vehicle and into the building. Feeling bewildered, Katie walked through the ER's public entrance.

"Are you here with a patient?" the security officer asked.

Katie nodded and he handed her a visitors' sticker, which she slapped onto her shoulder. She then headed toward the reception desk. The woman she knew who'd been manning the desk the last time she'd been at this emergency room wasn't there. In her place was a man who seemed too preoccupied to notice her existence.

Approaching the desk, she said, "Hello. My friend was brought here in an ambulance, and they just took him back. May I go—?"

"Katie!"

She turned at the sound of Seth's voice. His complexion was pale, and his fists were clenched in what she could only interpret as fear. "Seth." She lunged toward him and they hugged. "We just got here. The EMTs took Jamie in back." She nodded toward the treatment rooms beyond.

"Where is he?" Nick demanded of the man at the desk.

"Are you family?"

"He's my partner," Seth said.

13

"Married?" the man at the reception desk asked him.

"Well, no, but we're engaged," he lied.

"That's not family."

"Look, I'm also his attorney."

"Unless you've got his health-care proxy, I can't give you any information. HIPAA laws—"

"I know all about that," Seth stated.

"Hey, man, show a little compassion," Nick berated the guy.

The man snorted a breath. "Let me check." He picked up his handset, called the nurses' station, and explained the situation. "Yes. I see." He glanced at the trio. "I'll let them know." Hanging up the phone, he said, "There's a team currently examining the patient. The doctor will be out to speak with you as soon as he can."

"Thank you," Seth said.

Nick squeezed Katie's hand, and they shared a worried look behind Seth's back. A *team*? That couldn't be good. Especially in light of the paramedic's *next of kin* question.

"What happened?" Seth demanded, pacing in front of the automatic double doors.

The entrance doors whooshed open, and a woman brought her crying baby into the waiting area. As she rushed to the reception desk, Nick herded Seth and Katie to a deserted corner of the room.

"He was having lunch at Tealicious," Katie said. "I met Moonbeam there, but I saw Jamie across the room. He seemed fine."

Seth resumed his pacing. "Was he alone?"

"He was with a woman. I only saw her from behind. Does he have a sister?"

Seth sighed and ran a hand through his hair. "No."

"You have no idea who this woman could've been?" Nick asked Katie. "You hadn't seen her in Tealicious before?"

"As I said, I didn't see her face, but I didn't recognize her. She was sharply dressed and appeared to be some sort of professional."

Nick looked from Katie to Seth. "Maybe she was a doctor. He was sick last night at the party."

Seth stopped pacing long enough to arch a brow at Nick. "What kind of doctor meets patients at a tea shop?"

Inclining his head, Nick said, "An off-the-books consultation maybe?"

"I never dreamed Jamie was sick enough to collapse in the street." Seth let out a groan. "He was up and down all night. I should've insisted on bringing him to the emergency room this morning, but he said he was okay and had some errands to run."

"Stop beating yourself up," Nick said. "Jamie had medical training. Had he believed anything was seriously wrong, he wouldn't have had to be *told* to go to the doctor. Right? I mean, sometimes these things creep up on you. Like low blood pressure. One minute you're fine—the next minute you're on your back looking up at the ceiling wondering what happened."

Katie placed a hand on Nick's arm. "Oh, no!"

"It didn't happen to me," he said. "It was my uncle. But it was sudden, and it scared the crap out of my aunt and cousins. But it turned out to be no big deal."

"I won't feel better until I've seen Jamie and spoken with the doctor." Seth started back toward the reception desk just as a scrubs-clad man emerged from the doors leading to the examination bays.

"Family of James Seifert?" he asked.

"Yes." Seth hurried forward. "How is he? Can I see him now?"

"I'm Dr. Adams. Come with me please."

"All of us?" Nick asked.

With a nod, the doctor said, "Yes."

He ushered them into a private consulting room. Noticing pamphlets on grief in acrylic holders and boxes of tissues placed about the room, Katie put her hand on the back of a chair to steady herself.

"Please take a seat," the doctor said.

"No, thank you." Seth's voice wavered slightly. "I want to see Jamie. I want to see him *now*."

"I'm very sorry, but Mr. Seifert has died."

CHAPTER 3

Katie felt as though she had weights tied to her legs as she trudged up the stairs to her apartment. Nick had dropped her off before driving Seth home. Don was heading across the county to pick up Jamie's mother and would meet them there. Not wanting to be in the way, Katie had promised Seth she'd see him the following day.

Upon opening the door, both cats immediately insisted they were starving, crying piteously. As she fed them, Katie realized she hadn't eaten all day. But rather than feeling hungry, she felt nauseous.

She sank onto the love seat and decided to call Moonbeam. After all, Jamie's emergency had interrupted their lunch, and she figured Moonbeam would want to know the outcome.

"Katie." Somehow, Moonbeam managed to infuse warmth, compassion, and sympathy into that single word.

"You already know?" Katie asked.

"I didn't," she said. "But now I do. And I'm so very sorry."

Finally succumbing to the tears she'd been fighting since Jamie had collapsed, Katie said, "I…I didn't mean to do this."

"Don't you worry, hon, I'll be right over."

"That's not—" Katie had been going to tell Moonbeam that wasn't necessary, but her friend had already ended the call.

By the time Moonbeam arrived, Katie had pulled herself together and put on a pot of tea. Being thoughtful, Moonbeam brought a package of shortbread cookies.

"My mom always noshed on shortbread during a crisis," she said, placing the cookies on a plate on the bistro table. "She passed the tradition down from her own mother—part of our Scottish heritage, I suppose. But I do find it soothing."

"My great Aunt Lizzie was a Scot. Do your parents live nearby?" Katie poured them each a cup of coffee.

"No, they live in California." Moonbeam sat at the table. "How is Seth holding up?"

"I believe he's in shock." After placing cups, napkins, and dessert plates on the table, Katie sat opposite Moonbeam. "Other than Jamie having an upset stomach last night and this morning, Seth said he seemed fine. He guessed Jamie had a stomach virus."

Moonbeam took a cookie and dunked it into her tea. "How did Jamie look at the hospital?"

"When we arrived, he looked much like he did when he collapsed in front of Tealicious except that his lips had taken on a bluish tinge." Shuddering, she took a sip of her tea.

"How did he look *after* he died?" Moonbeam asked.

"Nick and I didn't go in with Seth. We felt we should respect his privacy."

Moonbeam nibbled on a cookie for a moment and then said, "I have a strong feeling Jamie was poisoned."

"You mean food poison or—?"

"No. I believe he was intentionally poisoned."

Katie mulled her friend's words over before speaking again. "You don't think Seth—?"

Shaking her head, Moonbeam said, "No, not Seth. And this is merely intuition talking. But it's a very strong perception."

"Who'd want to do such a thing?" Katie asked.

Moonbeam merely shrugged.

"We need to find the woman Jamie was having lunch with," Katie said.

Moonbeam nodded. "Yes, we do."

AFTER MOONBEAM LEFT, Katie figured she had better call Brad to let him know what had happened at the hospital.

"Katie, Nick told me about Jamie. I'm so sorry." He blurted out the words as soon as he answered. "I swear the food is all fine. No one else got sick—I checked."

"I know it wasn't the food. He was sick to his stomach last night at Nick and Don's," Katie said. "Do you know the woman Jamie was with?"

"He was with a woman?" he asked.

"Yes. He was with a brunette—nicely dressed. I didn't get a look at her face."

"Meet me in the shop, and we'll go through the day's receipts. Maybe she paid for lunch."

"That's a great idea." Katie ended the call, hurried downstairs, and turned on the lights in the kitchen.

By the time Brad got there, she'd made them a pot of chamomile tea.

He greeted her with a hug and a kiss on the cheek. "This is unbelievable."

"I know," she said. "Did Nick say how Seth is doing?"

"He said Seth's doctor had come to the house and given him a sleeping aid. Seth hadn't wanted to take it, but the doc—who's also a friend—insisted that he and Jamie's mom both take one and get some rest."

She closed her eyes. "Jamie's mom. Poor thing. What's her name again?"

"Suzanne," Brad said. "She's staying with Seth tonight."

"That's good. Does she…" There was no delicate way to ask. "Doesn't she have anyone else?"

Brad shook his head. "Not around here at least. Her husband is dead, and Jamie was an only child."

Blowing out a breath, Katie said, "I hope we can find out what happened. Moonbeam believes Jamie was poisoned."

His lips tightened. "A lot of customers ate the same things as Jamie ordered."

"Not that kind of poison." With a trembling hand, she poured the tea.

"Oh, that's ridiculous. She's only trying to perpetuate her status as a—" He waved his hand. "Woo-woo authority."

"She didn't say it was a psychic vision or anything." Katie felt a bit defensive on Moonbeam's behalf. "She said it was intuition."

"Right," he scoffed, picked up his cup and took a sip. "What did the doctor say?"

"He said that in light of the circumstances, Jamie's body would be sent for an autopsy," she said. "But the unofficial cause of death was myocardial infarction."

"You know, there could be a history of heart disease in Jamie's family," Brad said. "Or it could be a birth defect no one ever knew about. That happened to a friend of mine. He was jogging, had a heart attack, and died. Turned out, he had a birth defect that wasn't revealed until his autopsy."

"I hope it was something like that, but with Jamie being sick last night at Sassy Sally's and then collapsing this afternoon…" She shook her head. "I'm afraid it had to be something else."

"Were you feeling that way *before* Moonbeam Carruthers put it in your head that Jamie was poisoned?" he asked.

"What's got you so worked up? I thought you liked Moonbeam."

He raised his hands warily. "I like her fine, but I desperately hope Jamie died of natural causes. Either way, Tealicious is going to come under scrutiny as the last place the man ate. Think about how that looks—he left our dining room, stumbled onto the pavement, and lost consciousness. Would *you* want to eat here after that?"

Katie hadn't even considered how Jamie's death might affect business. After admitting as much to Brad, she said, "Let's take a look at those receipts. Hopefully, we can find this woman Jamie had lunch with, and she can shed some light on how he was feeling before he left here."

Brad retrieved the day's receipts and divided them between himself and Katie. They checked each for the time. When they had a stack of receipts obtained between eleven o'clock that morning and one o'clock that afternoon, they began to look at credit card owner's names. Of course, some people paid in cash. Katie was praying that wouldn't be the case with Jamie and his companion.

"Here." Brad held up a receipt. "I'm pretty sure this is them. Jamie had cucumber sandwiches and almond biscotti. The woman had a blueberry scone with clotted cream." He handed the slip of paper to Katie.

"This was paid for by a credit card belonging to Calexia Industries." She took her phone from her pocket, opened the Web browser, and typed in the name. "Nothing. What is Calexia Industries?"

"I have no idea," Brad said. "But it's a start. We'll look it up tomorrow."

"I'm looking it up now, and it's a dead end." Katie rubbed her forehead. "Who has a company you can't find using a search engine?"

"A company that's a cover for something else." He covered her hand with his. "The partnership that bought Moonbeam's building—what's it called?"

"Victoria Square Merchant Association Partners," she said.

"All right. Search for that."

She did. "Nothing. There's a lot of Victoria Square stuff, but not the partnership."

"Exactly. But if you were trying to find someone affiliated with the partnership, what would you do?"

"I'd come to Victoria Square and start asking questions."

He smiled. "And that's what we'll do tomorrow. We'll find out what *Calexia* stands for or where it's located, and we'll find this woman. Heck, maybe even Seth can tell us who it is."

"I'm not so sure about that." Katie traced the fabric of the tablecloth with an index finger. "Right before he lost consciousness, Jamie said, 'Don't tell.'"

"Don't tell? Don't tell what?"

"That's just it. I have no idea."

"With all due respect," Brad said, "it doesn't matter anymore. Whatever Jamie meant, whatever secret he wanted you to keep, it's irrelevant. The man is dead, and we need to find out what happened to him."

"Of course, you're right. Would you please make me a copy of this receipt so I can show it to Seth tomorrow?"

He nodded. "May I ride over with you?"

"Sure. But—" She bit her lip. "—what should we do about Tealicious?"

"I think we should close. A man died here today. We don't want to act as though it's business as usual," he said. "Since Monday is our normal day off, closing tomorrow gives us two days to do some damage control."

Katie dropped her head into her hands. "This is terrible. Our friend—Seth's partner—is dead, and we're trying to avoid a PR nightmare."

Brad patted her shoulder. "We can't ignore it, Katie. Especially not after the fallout caused by Erikka Wiley's death."

"You don't have to remind me." She slid her hands down the sides of her face. "At the rate we're going, Victoria Square is going to get the reputation for being a murder capital, and people will avoid all the merchants."

Brad nodded. "Especially us."

CHAPTER 4

Despite a restless night filled with unsettling dreams, Katie awoke on Sunday morning to sunshine and smiled. And then she remembered the terrible events of the previous day. After feeding her cats and herself, she headed over to Artisans Alley to check out the new vendor's setup. Rose was in the vendors' lounge getting coffee when she arrived.

Setting down her cup, Rose came over to give Katie a quick hug. "I feel so bad for poor Seth." Of course, she felt bad for him. She was, after all, his biological mother. Although she'd given him up at birth, she had never stopped loving her only child. "Have you seen him?" Rose added.

"Not since yesterday," Katie said. "Brad and I are going over there in a little while."

"I'd never seen the dear boy happier, and now...this." Rose blinked back tears. "I want to go see him, but I don't want to crowd him either. What do you think I should do?"

"I'll see how he's doing and let you know." Not quite knowing how to navigate these choppy waters with Rose where her biological son was concerned, Katie changed the subject. "Have you seen the new vendor setup?"

Rose blinked. "I didn't even realize we had a new vendor."

"She makes metal sculptures. I haven't met her yet. Vance brokered the deal." Katie sighed. "I had nightmares last night that all the metal would be too heavy for that floor upstairs, so I'm going up to take a look."

"I'll walk with you." Rose retrieved her coffee cup.

"I know I'm probably being silly, but after the floor got weak earlier this month in front of Chad's Pad, I don't want to take any chances," Katie said.

"You can't be too careful, dear. After all, you're the one who's liable if anything bad happens."

Katie didn't need Rose to remind her of that. That fact became even more apparent when she saw the heavy metal already making an indentation on the wooden floor.

"Oh, no." She groaned and stepped closer to get a better look. "This stuff is going to crash through the floor and into the lobby!"

"Don't be so dramatic."

Katie whirled around in the direction of the voice to see Ray standing behind her. "I'm not being dramatic! Do you see this? Do. You. See. This?"

"I see it," he said. "And I agree that this vendor needs to be moved to a downstairs space immediately. But nothing is going to crash through the floor within seconds."

"That's easy for you to say. This place isn't your responsibility."

Ray gently placed his hands on her shoulders. "Take a deep breath. Get some oxygen into those little gray cells, as Poirot would say."

"Since when did you become a Christie fan?" Katie asked, scowling.

"And how did you know where to find us?" Rose asked.

"For years and Ida in that order. You still haven't taken that deep breath, Katie."

To pacify him, she took a breath. "Happy?"

He grinned. "Delighted."

Frowning, Rose asked, "How did Ida know where we were?"

"She was doing tags or whatever she does and saw the two of you coming up here," Ray said. "I was looking for Katie to ask about Jamie."

Lowering her eyes, Katie felt guilty about her reaction to the new vendor's setup in light of what Seth was going through. Still, this situation had the potential to be dangerous.

"Is it bad?" he asked, worry creeping into his voice.

She nodded. "He died at the hospital yesterday."

He muttered an expletive. "What happened? He seemed as healthy as a horse."

Horses were much more delicate than most cared to believe.

"We don't know what happened yet," Katie said. "They're doing an autopsy."

His eyes widened in what could only be seen as panic. "No one else at—"

"No," she quickly interrupted. "No one else at Tealicious got sick. And Jamie wasn't feeling well at Sassy Sally's the night before."

He sighed, shaking his head. "I hate this. I liked him. He was such a good kid."

"Did you interact with him during your time at the Sheriff's Office?"

"Yeah," Ray said succinctly.

"Brad and I are going over to Seth's house to check on him and Jamie's mom. Would you like to go with us?"

"No. I don't know Seth all that well. Right now, he should stick close to friends," he said.

"I agree," Rose said, her voice strained. "I want to do *something*. I just don't know what."

"None of us do," Katie said. Waving her arm in the direction of the new vendor setup, Katie turned to Ray, "Would you please speak with Vance about this? This vendor needs to be moved to a downstairs space—which means someone will have to agree to be moved. That indicates I've got to give concessions—like a much cheaper rent and lose money—as appeasement. And those floorboards need to be shored up."

"I'll talk with him," Ray said soberly.

Katie gave a low growl of frustration. "Vance knows better than this. I'll call John Healy and see when he can come by and quote me a price on repairing the floor. Man, that's going to cost me."

"Never mind that." Ray gave her shoulders a quick squeeze before dropping his hands. "Vance and I can do the repairs."

"Are you sure?"

"Positive." He winked. "You need to let Vance redeem himself."

She nodded and took in the area around them before heading back downstairs. Ray was a good man. She knew all she'd have to do was give him some encouragement, and he'd be right by her side. Just weeks ago, he'd been more than ready to take on a more important role in her life. But she wasn't ready for another romantic entanglement. Sadly, she might never be. Experiencing one doomed relationship after another was beginning to make her feel she was cursed.

IT WAS a little after ten when Brad arrived at Artisans Alley to pick Katie up so they could visit Seth. "I called the credit card company and got an address for Calexia Industries."

"Fantastic. Maybe we can go there after we leave Seth's house and find the woman Jamie was having lunch with."

"Let's hope so. We desperately need some answers." He fiddled with the visor above the windshield. "I dread this. I never know what to say or do when someone I care about has suffered a loss. All the platitudes people throw at you at a time like this seem so pointless."

"I understand what you're saying, but everyone realizes it's a difficult situation and that people express themselves the best way they can," Katie said. "When my husband Chad died, people I didn't even know came to me at the funeral home and said, 'I understand exactly what you're going through.' At first, I thought, how could they? They didn't know me, and they had no clue about my relationship with Chad or the complicated problems we'd been facing. But I soon realized they were simply expressing their sympathy. It's all any of us can do. Hopefully, just letting Seth know we're here to support him will mean a lot."

"Yeah. I hope so, too. I really hate this."

"I know," she said. "I do, too." Katie thought about the note Brad had posted in the window this morning: *Please accept our apologies for any inconvenience, but Tealicious will be closed today to observe the passing of a dear friend.* "Your message was very nice and appropriate...without implying any responsibility on behalf of Tealicious."

"Well, that's what I was going for. I struggled with the wording. It was probably my fifth draft."

"You chose wisely," she said. "I hope the majority of the partners in the Victoria Square real estate venture will agree to meet tomorrow, and we can host them at Tealicious."

"Shall I make Nona Fiske the official taste-tester, just in case?" Brad asked wryly.

"That's not funny." Katie giggled. "All right, it's a *little* funny. But you and I both know nothing served at Tealicious was responsible for Jamie's illness." At least, she prayed it wasn't.

Her cell phone rang. She recognized the number: It was her former mother-in-law/partner in Tealicious, Margo. She answered the call.

"Hello, Katie. I'm sorry I missed your call earlier. How are things?"

"Not so great," Katie said. "I'm in my car with Brad—" She

wanted Margo to know someone else could hear their conversation. "—and we're on our way to see Seth."

"Oh, no. Has something happened to Seth?"

"His partner died yesterday." Katie hadn't meant to merely blurt it out, but she didn't know how else to couch it.

Margo gasped. "That's terrible! Was it an accident? Had he been ill?"

"We aren't sure what happened." Katie glanced at Brad. "He was having lunch at Tealicious, and then he...he stepped outside the tea shop and collapsed on the asphalt."

"Brad, darling, I'm Margo Bonner. I know we've never met, but I've heard wonderful things about you."

"Thank you." Brad sounded hesitant.

"I'm sure Katie has asked you this already, but please reassure a mature lady, nothing he could have eaten at Tealicious made the man ill, right?"

"Absolutely not, Ms. Bonner. No one else at the restaurant experienced any sickness yesterday, and no one has reported anything to us today."

"And there's unfortunately always one in every crowd who'd jump on a potential lawsuit if possible," Margo said. "Still, given the fact that young woman was killed in Victoria Square only a few weeks ago, I believe we need to do some damage control, Katie. I'll be there tomorrow."

"But—"

Margo interrupted Katie's protest. "I know you're staying in a much smaller apartment now. I'll see if I can get a room at Sassy Sally's. If not, I'm sure there's a hotel close enough. Brad, darling, I'm looking forward to meeting you. Ta-ta."

With that, she hung up.

Raising his brows and blowing out a breath, Brad said, "Wow. So that was Hurricane Margo?"

Katie's spirits plummeted. "Wait until you meet her in person."

CHAPTER 5

Sunken-eyed and unshaven, with shoulders drooping, Seth looked awful. He was still wearing the now-disheveled clothes he'd worn at the hospital the day before. Katie kissed him on the cheek and hugged him, holding on for long seconds. "Good morning. How are you doing?"

Seth merely shook his head, his gaze downcast.

Moving closer to Don, who stood in the doorway between the living room and the kitchen, Katie whispered, "Has he slept?"

Don shook his head, his eyes shadowed with concern.

"I thought the doctor gave him something," Katie muttered.

"He gave him a couple of pills, but Seth must not have taken them." Don took Katie's elbow and walked her over to an armchair where a gaunt woman with brown hair streaked with gray sat. "Katie, this is Suzanne, Jamie's mother. Suzanne, this is Katie Bonner."

"I'm terribly sorry for your loss," Katie said.

Suzanne nodded. She didn't seem to be in any better shape than Seth, although she appeared to be heavily medicated. Katie wondered which would be better in this circumstance—to feel too much or not enough,

Nick brought out a tray with a fresh pot of tea and apple-crumble muffins that he'd brought from Sassy Sally's. "You need to stay hydrated." He placed Suzanne's mug on the table beside her chair and carried Seth's mug to the coffee table. Nick placed his hand on his friend's shoulder. "Maybe after you finish your tea, you'll feel like taking a nice long shower. I always feel better after I've been pummeled with hot water."

Seth turned his face away. "What's the point?"

Nick straightened and, with a jerk of his head, indicated that Katie and Brad should follow him to the kitchen.

"I don't know what to do," Nick said, sounding frustrated.

"I'm sure your being here means more than you realize," Katie said. "Have you and Don been here all night?"

"I have. Don went back to Sassy Sally's to see to our guests. He came back this morning after breakfast but will need to leave again soon."

"Why don't I take over for you guys for a little while?" She looked at Brad. "If you'd like, you can go back with Don and Nick."

"No, I'd like to stay, too," Brad said. "I agree with Katie, Nick. You should go home and get some rest."

Nick nodded, resigned. "All right. Thanks. I'll—"

A guttural howl came from the living room. Katie, Brad, and Nick hurried into the room to see Don kneeling by the couch trying to comfort a tearful Seth.

"Why?" Seth cried. "Why? Why? *Why?*"

Nick and Brad stood by awkwardly, and Katie turned to Suzanne. Tears trickled down the woman's cheeks, and she lifted her misery-filled face to Katie's. Katie bent and hugged her, and Suzanne clung to her as though she was a life raft.

Poor Jamie would never know how huge a hole his loss had left for those who cared for him most.

~

FOR THE NEXT FEW HOURS, Katie found herself puttering around Seth's home, dusting furniture that didn't need it, making a batch of rice pudding with ingredients she found in the cupboard, and mostly feeling a terrible sadness at her inability to do anything to comfort her pseudo big brother. It was with relief that she greeted Nick when he returned later that afternoon.

"Where is he?"

"Seth got up and took a shower," Katie told him, "and Brad and I convinced him and Suzanne to eat some of the quiche Brad made. Now they're both lying down in their rooms."

"Thanks for taking over earlier." He slumped onto the couch, letting the backpack he carried slide onto the floor.

"We have a lead on the woman who was lunching with Jamie yesterday," Brad said. "The credit card company gave me the address of the corporation whose card was used to pay the bill. Now we've got to see if it pans out. Seth needs answers."

"I'll go home, feed my cats, and come back to stay with Seth and Suzanne tonight," Katie said.

Shaking his head, Nick said, "I appreciate your offer, but I came prepared to stay tonight. Just let me know if you guys find this woman."

"We will." Katie dropped a kiss on his forehead. "Call if you need anything."

"I will. Oh, by the way, we heard from Margo. She'll be staying at Sassy Sally's for a few days starting tomorrow."

She gave him a wry smile. "Thanks for taking her in...I think."

For the most part, Katie had a good relationship with her former mother-in-law, but the woman could be persnickety and judgmental at times. Still, Margo would have never forgiven her had she not told her about Seth's partner; and if she could help with the PR nightmare created by yet another death on the Square, then more power to her.

Katie drove east toward the next town over. The address Brad had been given was twenty minutes outside of McKinlay

Mill. When the GPS announced they'd reached their destination, she pulled to the curb, put the car in park, and then looked at Brad.

"Are you sure we have the right building?" she asked.

Fishing a slip of paper from his pocket, he read the address and checked it against the one written on the building. "This is the place."

She frowned. "But this is an apartment building."

"Maybe the person works from home?" He opened the passenger's side door. "I'll go see."

"I'm coming with you."

They entered the building and found the apartment number —listed as a suite number—of the corporation's address.

Katie knocked on the door.

"Who is it?" The voice sounded as though it belonged to an elderly woman. Although Katie hadn't seen her face, she didn't believe the woman Jamie had lunch with had been old.

"My name is Katie Bonner, and I'm with Brad Andrews. We're looking for Calexia Industries."

"Who?" the woman called from behind the door. "This is my home. I don't know anything about any industries."

"Thank you," Katie said. "We're sorry to have bothered you."

As they ambled back toward the building's entrance, a jogger walked in, wiping his face on his sleeve.

"Excuse me," Brad said. "We're looking for Calexia Industries. We were told it was headquartered here."

Shrugging the jogger said, "Sorry, man. This is a residential building, and everyone pretty much keeps to themselves. If anyone has a business here, it's news to me."

Before she and Brad could investigate further, Katie's cell phone rang. It was Vance.

"Hi, Vance." She hoped he wasn't upset over her decision to move the new vendor to a spot on the Alley's lower level. She hadn't meant to second guess him, but he should have realized the weight of the steel sculptures would be far too heavy at the outset.

"Um...I know you're dealing with a tragedy today, and I'm truly sorry to disturb you, but is there any way you could come back to Artisans Alley?"

She frowned. "What's going on?"

"The vendors are in an uproar. The downstairs vendors don't want to share their space until Ray and I can get the floor fixed, and the upstairs vendors don't want to move—period." Vance sighed, sounding frustrated. "I'm trying to do what you asked, but they're not listening to me."

"All right," she said, irritated. "I'll be there as soon as I can."

Ending the call, she returned the phone to her purse.

Brad arched a brow. "Trouble in paradise?"

Katie merely rolled her eyes. "Is there ever anything but?"

CHAPTER 6

Katie dropped Brad off at Tealicious where he'd left his car. She parked in back and as she walked toward Artisans Alley, her cell phone rang. She didn't recognize the caller's number but took the call.

"Hi, is this Katie?" a warm male voice asked.

"It is," Katie replied hesitantly.

"This is J.P. Trammel. You consulted me on that criminal matter a few weeks back." He laughed. "Thank heavens a consultation was all you required."

"Yes, of course. How are you, Mr. Trammel?"

"I'm well. I'm calling because I heard about Jamie Seifert," he said.

Katie entered the building through the back entrance, eased into her office, and closed the door, preferring to take the call in private before Vance or one of the vendors spotted her and began railing about the floor situation.

"It was certainly tragic," she said, as she slid into the chair behind her desk.

"How's Seth?"

Knowing Seth and Trammel were friends, she decided to be forthcoming. "The poor man is devastated."

"I knew he would be. My wife and I had Seth and Jamie over for dinner the week before last. They were so happy together," he said. "I thought my wife was boring Jamie with photos from our trip to Spain, but she said Jamie had a million questions for her."

"Yeah…he recently mentioned the idea of them taking a vacation to me, too. I think he was hoping he and Seth could get away pretty soon."

"I tried calling Seth, but he isn't answering his phone," Trammel said. "Have Jamie's arrangements been made yet?"

"Given that Jamie's death was unexpected, the medical examiner is doing an autopsy before ruling on the cause and releasing his body to the family. In the meantime, Jamie's mother is staying with Seth. I imagine they'll make the arrangements together as soon as Jamie's body is released."

"Is there anything I can do?"

Katie had an inspiration. "Actually, there *is* something. Just before Jamie's collapse, he was having lunch at my tea shop with a woman. She left before anyone could speak with her, and no one appears to know who she is. Thinking she could shed some light on what might have happened to Jamie, the chef and I went through the credit card receipts. The lunch was paid for using a credit card issued to Calexia Industries."

"Calexia Industries. Hmm…I've never heard of it."

"I have the address," she said. "And, in fact, I went there today, but the location is a residential apartment building. If we could find out the name of the president or any of the directors of Calexia Industries…."

"Then you could possibly find this woman. Give me the address, and I'll look into it right away."

Katie rattled off the address. "Thank you, Mr. Trammel. I believe Seth's mind can be put at ease—at least, to some extent—

once he knows what happened to Jamie in the minutes prior to his death."

"Of course," he said. "I'll be in touch."

Satisfied that one obstacle might be overcome, Katie took a deep breath, popped a peppermint into her mouth, and tried to mentally prepare herself for the commotion she expected to find in Artisans Alley's lobby.

The scene was as chaotic as Katie expected. Vance stood among a group of vendors who looked as though all they needed were pitchforks and torches to drive him out of the village. Unnoticed by most of the assembly, Katie climbed the first three stairs to the upper level to give herself a platform from which to speak.

"Good afternoon!" she called. The crowd gradually quieted and turned to listen to her. "I apologize for the inconvenience this building's creaky old floor is causing, but it's imperative we get it fixed ASAP."

At her words, everyone started talking at once. She could hear Liz Meyer's voice over the din.

"This is beyond inconvenient, Katie. I'm paying rent on a full space, and now you and Vance are saying I have to share with someone else?"

Some people in the crowd grumbled in agreement.

Ever the peacemaker, Maddie Lyndel said, "I understand how dangerous a weak floor can be, and I don't mind sharing my booth." She smiled sweetly.

Liz scowled. "I have too much merchandise to crowd it into a smaller space."

As the vendors argued among themselves, Katie saw she needed to regain control of the situation.

"Your attention please!" She waited until the vendors quieted and gave her their begrudging consideration. "I'll waive this month's rent for all the impacted vendors while we repair the floor. And for the vendor who gives up his or her first-floor space to our new metal sculptor, you may enjoy a second month free."

Her words caused the first-floor vendors to again begin arguing. Deciding Vance had created this mess and needed to take an active role in cleaning it up, she walked down the steps, side-stepped the crowd, and left him to it.

"Katie, wait!" he shouted.

"You've got this!" she called over her shoulder. "I believe in you!"

She stopped in her office just long enough to grab her purse, then she headed for home.

After feeding Mason and Della and making a grilled cheese and onion sandwich for herself, Katie sank onto the love seat and set the sandwich and a cup of blackberry tea onto the coffee table next to her laptop. She opened it and fired it up. While she waited for operating system to load, she bit into the sandwich. Mason hopped onto the cushion beside her and looked at the food.

"You've already had yours," she reminded him.

He didn't care. He still wanted whatever it was she had. She refused to give in.

"Onions are toxic to cats," she told him.

Placing his paws on her thigh and leaning closer to her mouth, Mason indicated just how much her words fazed him.

Katie quickly ate the sandwich and took the plate back to the kitchen before checking her email. All the Victoria Square merchants who made up the property-development partnership had responded to the message she'd sent on Friday night about scheduling a meeting. Each one had confirmed his or her availability to meet on Monday evening.

Andy's email had said simply, *I'll be there*. No greeting, no niceties, no signature line. Just an acceptance of the invitation.

But, then, what had she expected? They were broken up. Had

she thought—*wanted?*—him to ask how she was doing? Tell her he missed her? Say he was looking forward to seeing her?

And how did *she* feel? She certainly wasn't thrilled at the thought of seeing Andy again, that was for sure. Oh, she'd seen him in passing—and from a distance—a few times as she was entering or leaving Artisans Alley. Every time she had, her heart had taken a nosedive and she'd looked away, wanting to avoid any awkward encounters.

Taking a deep breath, she acknowledged that the next evening she'd be face to face with Andy Rust for the first time in weeks. The fact that other people would be there soothed her frayed nerves a little, but it would still be a trying experience. She played various scenarios in her mind where he came in and saw her standing across the Tealicious dining room from him. She looked gorgeous in a diaphanous silver gown—the wind (maybe someone had opened a window or something) blowing through her hair, and an ethereal mist rising from the floor. Okay, so there would have to be some crazy weather going on. Either that, or she was starring in a music video. No matter…when Andy saw her, his heart would shatter. He'd hold his arms out to her, pleading for her to take him back, and she'd shrug and simply turn away. Or else he saw her and immediately hugged her and begged her forgiveness for cheating on her with Erikka Wiley. She would let him down gently and back away from him, leaving him standing alone in middle of the partnership crowd.

She forced thoughts of Andy out of her head. Satisfied that the partners could meet quickly without losing out on a bid for the abandoned warehouse, Katie fired off a response to the group.

I look forward to meeting with you at Tealicious tomorrow evening at six pm. In light of yesterday's tragedy, Seth Landers will not be in attendance. We can put buying the warehouse to a vote; and if the majority is in favor, can prepare a proposal to have Seth present to the property owner when he returns to work."

Katie wondered how long that would take. Based on how he looked earlier that day, it could be weeks before he was able to return to his duties at the law office.

She sighed. She so wished she could help him in some way. It crossed her mind that they might need to consider asking another attorney to handle the property bid. Although she felt guilty for even entertaining the thought, one of the other partners was likely to suggest it at the meeting, and she needed to be prepared with a response. Seth would understand if the partnership voted to use another attorney on this matter...wouldn't he?

Maybe it wouldn't take as long for Seth to return to work as she anticipated. For her, diving into work kept her sane after Chad's death. Of course, there hadn't been any mysterious circumstances surrounding Chad's death, at least that she knew of at the time. That, and her ex-boss, Josh Kimper, had only given her a week off—with half pay—to recover from the loss. If she could help answer some of Seth's questions, maybe it would help him to move on.

Katie considered calling Nick to check on Seth and Suzanne, but she decided to wait until the next morning. As strange as it sounded—even unvoiced except in her own thoughts—she'd be glad when Margo arrived. That woman always had an answer for everything.

Katie's cell phone rang and she looked at the screen, half-expecting it to be either Nick or Margo since she had them on her mind. It wasn't. It was J.P. Trammel.

"Mr. Trammel, hi," she answered.

"I've got a name for you, Katie. The person who owns Calexia Industries is listed as Gabrielle Pearson."

"Fantastic! Would you happen to have a phone number?"

"I do," he said. "Ready with a pen and paper?"

When she affirmed that she was, Trammel rattled off the number. She repeated it back to him after she'd written it on a notepad.

"That's right. Let me know if there's anything else I can do to help."

"Thank you," Katie said. "Thank you so much."

After ending the call, she immediately called Gabrielle Pearson. A warm, well-modulated female voice said, "Hello, this is Gabrielle."

"Hi, Gabrielle. My name is—"

"I'm unable to take your call at the moment. However, you *are* important to me. At the tone, please leave your name, number, and the nature of your call, and I'll be in touch with you at my earliest convenience." *Beep!*

"Hello, Gabrielle. I'm Katie Bonner and I own the tea shop Tealicious." Katie left her name and number but didn't indicate the "nature of her call." What could she possibly say? That she was calling to ask Gabrielle Pearson if she killed Jamie Siefert?

CHAPTER 7

*A*lthough Katie still clung to the fact that she was a strong, independent woman who didn't need a man in her life and required no help from anyone, she found her steps directing her to Wood U after she finished power walking around the Square Monday morning. It would be nice to see a friendly face, and Ray could tell her what he'd discovered the day before about the floor on the upper level of Artisans Alley—mainly, how much the repairs would set her back. She was already going in the hole by offering the vendors free rent for a month.

When she walked through the door she was greeted by the shiny bald top of Ray's head as he bent over the delicate hummingbird he was carving.

"Good morning," she said.

"Hey, there. Give me one second." He finished whatever intricate detail he was cutting into the wood before laying aside his project and taking off his reading glasses. "What brings you by this morning?"

"You can't guess?"

He grinned. "I'm thinking it might have something to do with that floor you have caving in."

Eyes widening, Katie asked, "Is it that bad? Really?"

"No. Vance is getting the materials today, and he and I are going to work on it this afternoon. As a matter of fact, I'm even closing up Wood U for you."

Katie arched a brow. "What's that going to cost me?"

"Nothing," he said.

She scoffed. "I'm not allowing you to work for nothing. I know that's not going to be some simple task."

"Nah! Sistering up a few boards...it's a piece of cake. But, if you insist, you could make me a home-cooked meal."

"Ray, I'm serious."

Despite his grin and the streak of mischief in his eyes, he said, "I'm serious too. Since Sophie went back to school, the quality of the grub at home has definitely gone downhill."

"You can't do that much work and be satisfied with a meal." Katie appreciated his kindness, but this was going too far. "I absolutely will not take advantage of your generosity."

"Fine. Throw in a movie—of *my* choosing."

She laughed. "All right. But if fixing that floor turns out to be more of an ordeal than you anticipate, we'll renegotiate."

"Deal," he said. "I might require *two* meals." He sobered. "How's Seth?"

Katie shrugged. "Nick says he's slightly better this morning than he was yesterday. I'm going to drive out and check on him later. I believe he'd feel better if he had some answers." She sighed. "I know *I* would."

"I imagine so." Ray ran a hand over the lower part of his clean-shaven face. "Even though Tealicious was closed yesterday, I didn't notice too many people stopping to read the sign on the door."

"Yeah. This is going to hurt our business, even though Tealicious was in no way responsible for Jamie's death," she said. "At least, I'm almost a hundred percent sure of that."

"Wait—you don't *know?*" he asked, sounding puzzled.

"I do." She closed her eyes briefly. "I truly do."

"But not a hundred percent."

She didn't like having her words tossed back at her. "There's a woman who dined with Jamie that day. Brad, Mr. Trammel, and I have determined who she is—Gabrielle Pearson of Calexia Industries—but she hasn't returned my call yet."

"And you think this Pearson woman might have had something to do with Jamie's death?"

"I don't know—I doubt it. I'd simply like to ask her whether he ate something other than cuke sammies and a biscotti and if she noticed he was ill while they talked." Katie pulled the elastic from her ponytail and shook out her hair. "This entire thing is driving me up the wall. If only I could speak to this woman and find out why she met with Jamie, if he said anything, if—"

Ray stepped closer and inspected her mane. "I like your hair loose like that. It's beautiful."

"Thank you." She realized her response sounded breathy, so she took a shaky step back.

Taking the hint, Ray stepped back to the other side of the counter, and for some strange reason, Katie felt an odd pang of disappointment.

Sliding a pen and notepad toward her, he said, "If you'll leave the woman's information with me, I'll see what I can learn about her."

"I'd appreciate that." Katie wrote down the woman's information. "Oh, by the way, Margo is arriving today. She'll be staying at Sassy Sally's for a day or two."

He let out an admiring hum. "Margo Bonner. Well, that's a nice surprise. I'll have to pick up some flowers and go say hello."

Katie turned and headed for the door. "You do that."

Ray's mocking laughter followed her out onto the parking lot. She didn't look back. Ray and her former mother-in-law had gotten awfully chummy the last time she was in McKinlay Mill.

Katie supposed they could pick right up where they'd left off. Not that she'd care.

Of course, Margo had also told Katie that both Ray and Andy were in love with her. That showed what *she* knew.

≈

AFTER A HOT, soothing shower, Katie dressed and checked her phone. She had a voice mail message. She'd hoped it was Gabrielle Pearson, but it was from Moonbeam.

"Hi, Katie. Could you please come by The Flower Child sometime this morning? It's important. Well, I *think* it's important. No, it is. It definitely *is* important. I'll see you soon. Ta!"

Katie decided not to bother Brad on his day off and went downstairs to bake some goodies for the property partnership meeting, to take to Seth, and to give to Moonbeam. In fact, she thought she could make some shortbread cookies for Moonbeam that might be almost as good as those her great aunt used to make.

Deciding that whatever Moonbeam felt was important could probably wait another hour or so, she went ahead and made the cookies, some egg salad and crab salad for sandwiches, and some blueberry scones. Seth loved her scones.

She enjoyed fussing around the industrial kitchen by herself. It was nice having all that space—along with the peace and quiet —to work. Ray's comment about not having many people come by Tealicious the day before bothered her more than she'd let on. But he was right. People were going to be wary of the tea shop now that someone had died immediately after eating there, even if the food had absolutely nothing to do with Jamie's death. Remembering that Margo had once worked in public relations, she wondered how—or even *if*—the woman would be able to restore Tealicious's image.

She boxed up some of the shortbread cookies for Moombeam and scones for Seth, and although The Flower Child was located across the Square, she drove there and wondered if she should forget about Margo and simply have Moonbeam do some sort of cleansing spell on the entire Square. She nearly giggled as she imagined Nona Fiske's reaction to *that*.

Moonbeam was giving someone a reiki massage when Katie entered the shop. A sign on the desk asked patrons to please wait patiently for assistance. Katie sniffed the essential oils samplers until Moonbeam emerged from the back room.

"Hello." The woman spoke softly out of consideration for her client.

"Hi." Katie held out the white bakery box. "I brought you some shortbread."

"How kind. Thank you." She placed the box on the credenza behind the counter. "I have something for you, too. It's why I wanted you to stop by."

Taking the long, narrow black box Moonbeam extended toward her, Katie said, "Thanks, but you didn't have to—"

"I wanted to," she interrupted. "Open it."

Inside the box was a pendant with two stones—a white and a rose crystal.

"Those crystals are clear quartz and rose quartz," Moonbeam explained. "The clear crystal is considered a master healing stone, and the rose quartz will help to bring you comfort and calm during times of grief. The pink stone will also encourage love and respect within yourself."

Katie slipped the necklace over her head, holding up the pendant to give it a closer look. "It's beautiful."

"I'm glad you've chosen to wear it. You're going to need it today." Moonbeam squeezed her hand. "If you'll excuse me, I need to get back to my client."

Feeling a bit uneasy after being told she was going to *need* a pendant that aided with healing, Katie left The Flower Child and drove to Seth's house. Don saw her coming up the walk and held the door open for her.

"Hi, Don," she said. "How are you?"

He inclined his head. "I'm feeling weary, helpless, frustrated—all the things you feel when a friend is hurting." He led her into the kitchen and took the bakery box from her. "Something that needs to be refrigerated?"

"Blueberry scones," she said.

"My favorite," Seth said, as he came into the kitchen, embraced Katie, and kissed her cheek. "Thank you for remembering...and for making them."

Her eyes filled with tears. "I wish there was more I could do."

"Coffee?" Don asked before the waterworks could start. Katie and Seth accepted.

As the three of them sat at the kitchen table, Katie asked, "Where are Suzanne and Nick?"

"Nick went home to grab a shower, and Suzanne is sleeping," Don answered. "She paced much of the night."

Seth sighed and stirred creamer into his coffee. "I keep wondering if there's something I could've done. I tried to convince Jamie to go to the doctor on Friday night, but he insisted he was fine—that it was just something he ate that had upset his stomach. Saturday morning, he seemed better."

"There was nothing you could've done." Don squeezed Seth's hand reassuringly. "Jamie was a medical professional. Had he thought it was something serious, he'd have gone to the emergency room."

Katie wondered if she should tell Seth about Gabrielle Pearson and Calexia Industries. No, it was better to wait until she knew more. At this point, telling Seth about her would only raise questions for which she didn't have answers.

Seth's cell phone rang, and he fished it from the pocket of his jeans. "Seth Landers…. Of course, hello." His face blanched. "Wh-what? Are you sure? B-but…how…how can that be?" His eyes searched the concerned faces of Katie and Don. "Thank you for letting me know. Yes…of course."

As he ended the call and placed the phone down on the table, he let out a shuddering breath. "Jamie was poisoned."

*a*s Katie drove back to Victoria Square, she was glad Suzanne hadn't awakened when Seth got the call from the medical examiner's office. It would have been too much for her to bear. Katie knew Seth would help the poor woman deal with the news as soon as he could come to terms with it himself. The poor man had looked shell-shocked, but kept a stoic countenance. After much discussion, Don had convinced him to go lie down, and Katie had headed back toward Victoria Square with the desperate hope that Gabrielle Pearson could provide some answers.

After parking her car in the small lot behind Tealicious, Katie walked to Wood U to tell Ray about Jamie and what she'd learned. Ray was laughing as she entered the shop. Katie looked toward the source of his amusement and saw an attractive woman in her mid- to late-forties grinning at him. The woman wore a charcoal gray pantsuit, black block-heeled pumps, and an emerald green blouse that brought out the color in her eyes.

"I'll come back later," Katie said.

"Wait," Ray said. "Katie Bonner, this is Detective Carol Rigby. Carol, Katie."

"Nice to meet you, Katie. You're actually the person I came to Victoria Square to see." Detective Rigby jerked her head toward the door. "Is there someplace private we could talk?"

"Of course." Katie turned to leave.

Before following her, Detective Rigby said, "Good seeing you, Ray. Be sure and call me so we can have that drink and catch up properly."

"I'll certainly do that."

Ray sounded a lot happier about going out with Carol Rigby than Katie would have liked. He didn't seem like a man who was merely being polite but like one who was looking forward to making good on his promise.

Well, so what? Katie reasoned with herself as she led the detective across the Square to Tealicious. *This woman might be an excellent match for Ray.* She glanced back. No wedding ring on the lady detective's hand. And if the woman could make Ray happy, shouldn't she wish them both all the best? *After all, just because I'm not ready for another relationship, I shouldn't begrudge Ray some happiness. He's been terribly lonely since his wife died. Still....*

And, really, why was she marrying off the guy to a woman he'd probably worked with for years.

You're losing it, girl. Losing it!

"I'm curious about where Jamie Siefert was prior to his death," Detective Rigby said. "This *is* the tea shop where he'd been dining, isn't it?"

"It is." Katie unlocked the door. "In fact, he collapsed just about where you're standing."

"How tragic. And you knew the young man?"

"Not well. I'm better acquainted with his partner, Seth Landers." Katie led the detective over to the table in the back of the shop. "This is the table where he sat, although it has, of course, been cleaned."

"Been cleaned." Detective Rigby frowned and took out her

smartphone. She opened what appeared to be a note-taking app. "Did he vomit here?"

"No! He never vomited," Katie said, appalled. "Each table is cleaned immediately after the patrons dining there leave to make it ready for our next guests. We pride ourselves on our fastidiousness."

The woman nodded. "Naturally."

Was there sarcasm in the detective's tone? Katie couldn't tell and thought she was probably being too defensive. Still, she didn't feel comfortable sharing too much information with the detective. She decided to answer Carol Rigby's questions as simply as possible and offer up no additional information.

"I understand Mr. Seifert was dining with a companion." Detective Rigby leveled her gaze at Katie.

"Yes. He was having lunch with a woman. Our efforts to locate her to determine how Jamie was feeling or acting while he was with her have proven futile so far. We aren't even certain of her identity."

"Well, who do you *think* she was?"

"Brad—our chef—and I went through the receipts for the time Jamie was here, and we believe he was dining with someone from Calexia Industries," Katie said.

Detective Rigby tapped the keys on her smartphone to record the name of the company. "Have you spoken with anyone from the company?"

"No." Although Katie's conscience tugged at her, she didn't offer up the contact information she had obtained for Calexia Industries nor the name *Gabrielle Pearson*. Let the detective discover the lead the same way she had. Besides, if the elusive Ms. Pearson had anything to say that might incriminate Tealicious in the slightest, Katie wanted to know about it before anyone else.

"And your chef—Brad—?"

"Andrews," Katie supplied.

The detective typed away on her keypad. "Yes. Is Chef Andrews here? I'd like to speak to him."

"He's off today. Tealicious and Artisans Alley are both typically closed on Mondays." She gave a hollow little laugh. "It's the only day of the week I get any peace."

"Right. May I have his phone number please?"

"Of course." Katie looked at the contacts screen on her phone and gave the detective Brad's number.

After typing it into her phone, Detective Rigby swiped up to look at something she'd apparently written earlier. "I understand you were at a card game with Mr. Seifert the night before his death."

"I was. We were at Sassy Sally's—the Square's bed and breakfast—with the proprietors Nick Farrell and Don Parsons. And, of course, Seth was there."

"Right. How were Mr. Landers and Mr. Seifert behaving toward each other?" the detective asked. "Any apparent tensions between them?"

Katie's ire flared, even though she knew the detective was only doing her job. "No. As a matter of fact, they were discussing vacations, and Seth said anywhere with Jamie would be heaven."

Detective Rigby arched a brow. "Uh-huh. And that didn't seem a little too over the top to you? A bit too lovey-dovey?"

Katie barked out a brief laugh. "Careful, Detective Rigby, or I'm liable to think you're as cynical as I am. But, no—knowing Seth, I believe he meant what he was saying."

The lady cop smiled. "So you're a cynic, eh?"

Shrugging, Katie said, "I recently ended a long-term relationship."

"Sorry to hear that. But back to business. How did Mr. Seifert seem on Friday night? Was he distracted? Upset about anything? Nervous?"

"No. He seemed fine." Katie paused. "At least from an

emotional standpoint. Physically, he wasn't up to par. He appeared to have had an upset stomach."

"What made you think so?" Carol looked up from her phone. "Did you see him popping antacids?"

"He kept going to the bathroom."

"I see." Carol typed something into her phone.

Feeling it was taking the detective too long to type in "multiple trips to the bathroom," Katie asked, "What are you thinking?"

Carol gave her a tight smile and returned the phone to her suit pocket. "I don't want to speculate."

"But you are," Katie said. "You're thinking maybe his stomach was upset because he was troubled about something, aren't you?"

Inclining her head slightly, Carol said, "Some people make multiple trips to the bathroom during a party to take drugs. Did Mr. Seifert appear to be impaired at any point during the evening?"

"No, not at all." Again, Katie felt outraged on Jamie's behalf, even though she understood that Carol Rigby didn't know him and that she had to get to the truth. "I genuinely felt he had a queasy stomach—that's all."

"Then why didn't he seek medical attention?" Detective Rigby asked.

"I assume Jamie thought he was having a bad reaction to something he'd eaten or that he had a stomach virus and that it would soon work its way out of his system," Katie said. "When I saw him at Tealicious on Saturday, I thought he must be feeling better."

Carol lifted her chin. "Up until the point when he collapsed right outside your door?"

Katie sighed. "Yeah."

"Thank you for your time, Ms. Bonner. I'll be in touch if I need any further information from you."

After the detective left, Katie climbed the interior stairs to her apartment and sank onto the love seat. She desperately hoped the detective didn't get in touch with Seth today. He didn't need to deal with her questions on top of the gamut of emotions he was already experiencing.

Mason wound around her ankles, obviously thrilled to have her home in the middle of the day. She picked up the cat and kissed the top of his head.

"You're the sweetest guy in the whole world," she said.

He meowed as though to say he knew.

A knock sounded at the apartment's exterior door.

Katie hoped Detective Rigby hadn't returned with more questions. She took a deep breath, stood, and crossed to the door. When she opened it to Ray, she let out her breath in relief.

"Nice to see you, too," he said, stepping inside the apartment. "We weren't able to talk when you came to Wood U earlier, so I came to see what you wanted to tell me." He looked around the open area. "Is Margo here yet?"

"No. Isn't one woman batting her eyelashes at you enough for one day?" she asked archly.

Ray blinked. "What do you mean by that?"

"I mean, you looked awfully chummy with Detective Carol Rigby."

Ray laughed. "Carol isn't an eyelash batter. She's a strong, capable, intelligent woman. Like you. But I'm guessing Carol isn't the reason you came to talk with me."

"No." Katie plunked down on the love seat. "I came to tell you that while I was visiting Seth, he got a phone call from the medical examiner's office—Jamie was poisoned."

Sitting beside her, Ray asked, "Did the toxicologist give Seth the name of the poison?"

"Abrin." She wrinkled her brow. "Am I saying that right? It's something I've never heard of before."

"You're saying it right, and it's one of the most toxic substances found in nature," Ray said, his expression grim. "It's also known as rosary peas. It can stay in a person's system for up to three days."

"Do you mean someone ground them up and hid them in his food or something?"

"That, or he chewed them." Ray shook his head. "Either way, Jamie was poisoned. I can't believe he'd knowingly ingest them."

"Where does this stuff grow?"

"I'm pretty sure it's found in Florida."

Katie's brow wrinkled. "Then how could Jamie have possibly eaten it?"

Ray merely shrugged.

"I didn't tell Carol Rigby about the phone call," Katie admitted. "I guessed she either already knew Jamie's cause of death or that she'd find out on her own soon enough. I didn't mention Gabrielle Pearson, either. Did you?"

"No. Carol and I were too busy catching up to discuss investigations—past or present," he said matter-of-factly.

Katie stiffened. "Well, I'd appreciate your not mentioning Gabrielle to Carol when you take her out for that drink, either. I'd prefer to speak with Ms. Pearson before your lovely detective does, if that's possible."

"And why's that?" Ray asked pointedly.

"Because...because...." But she really had no reason based on logic for such a request.

Katie stood and moved to the window. "I imagine you'd better get back to work."

Ray strode toward her. "Why? Is there a throng at the door of Wood U? Or am I being dismissed?"

"I merely don't want you to lose any business on my account."

"Is that so?" He put his hands on his hips. "Twice today your green-eyed monster has reared its ugly head at me."

She scoffed. "You're calling me jealous?"

"Yes, I am." He moved closer. "What is it you want, Katie?"

"I...I don't know what you're talking about."

"Liar." He placed one hand on her neck and ran his thumb along her jawline. "Tell me. Do you want me to kiss you?"

Her mouth had gone dry, and she felt her eyes drift closed. "N-no."

"Open your eyes and tell me that."

Instead, she opened her eyes and moved into his embrace. They kissed hungrily, but Katie eventually pulled away.

"I can't," she whispered.

"You know I'll wait for you if that's what you want." His voice was low and husky.

It took every ounce of Katie's willpower for her not to move back into his arms. "That wouldn't be fair."

"Are you saying there's no future for us beyond friendship?" he asked.

"Not right now." She looked down at the floor. "I want you to be happy—I truly do. But at this point in my life, I'm not in a position to build a life with someone else. I need to be on my own for a while."

"Ah." He gave a mirthless chuckle. "The old 'it's not you, it's me' routine."

"It really *is* me," Katie said. "You shouldn't wait around for a relationship that might never happen."

Ray gently lifted her chin, kissed her forehead, and left her alone.

CHAPTER 9

It had taken more time than Katie wanted before her heart stopped pounding and she could think coherently once again. Confusion was not a pleasant condition to suffer. Upon meeting Ray Davenport, she'd found him to be an unreasonable *old* man who seemed incapable of any state other than suspicion. He'd seen her efforts to get to the truth of a situation as a nuisance. But after she'd saved his life, his attitude had softened.

Were the emotions he felt for her based on gratitude alone? And why—how—could she be attracted to a man so much older than herself? Was she looking for the security of a father figure? Her own father had died when she was only six. Her husband, Chad, hadn't evoked any such attachment, but she considered Seth to be the big brother—male protector—she hadn't had for most of her life.

What was her problem when it came to men? Her best friends —except for Rose and her two college friends Tori Cannon and Kathy Grant, whom she seldom saw—were all men. And most of them were gay.

And then there was Ray.

Thinking of him made her feel confused and unhappy.

Being with him ... now that was another thing.

Katie sat on her love seat, with a cat nestled on each side of her, for more than an hour pondering the complex feelings assaulting her before she trundled down the steps and unlocked the front door to Tealicious. She gave the dining room a final check before she hauled out the food for the meeting. Everything was nicely arranged for her partners. She placed the refreshments on tables she'd pushed together in the back with plates, napkins, and silverware. On one of the tables, an assortment of teas on hotplates stood beside cups and saucers.

Unfolding the brief agenda she'd prepared, she wondered momentarily why she found herself in charge once again. Was volunteering to head up everything something she did because she craved control? Did she have a desire to feel useful or powerful? Or was she simply a lifelong people-pleaser who didn't know how to say no?

The thought bothered her on way too many levels.

Her reverie was interrupted by the opening of the door. "Hello—" Her face fell at the sight of the interloper. "Nona."

"Am I the first one here?" Nona strode over to an empty table and dropped her large black purse on it with a thud. "Is Seth Landers going to be here?"

"No," Katie said. Hadn't Nona bothered to read the note Katie had sent? "But I'll address that when everyone else arrives. Feel free to help yourself to some sandwiches and pastries."

Nona scowled toward the tables laden with refreshments and then at Katie. "Are you sure it's safe? This place has been closed since that young man died after eating here. I hope you're not making us your guinea pigs."

Katie ground her teeth to control her temper. "Tealicious was closed on Sunday out of respect for Jamie, and today is our normal day off. Tomorrow, we'll be back to business as usual."

"Will you? I can't help but wonder if anyone will want to eat at an establishment where someone died right after eating there." She cast a disdainful look around the dining room. "I hate to admit it, but I'm hesitant to partake myself."

"Suit yourself, but there's plenty of food if you change your mind." Katie scoped out the entrance, hoping someone else would arrive and rescue her from Nona.

"Who are you looking for?" Nona asked. "Is it Andy? Is *he* supposed to be here? Are you two still on good terms since the breakup?" Without waiting for answers to her questions, Nona forged ahead. "I'm surprised that either you or he would be interested in buying that old abandoned warehouse with it being the place where his other girlfriend died and all. By the way, what do you think of Andy's new assistant manager?"

"I didn't know Andy had hired a new assistant manager," Katie answered truthfully.

"Oh, yes. She looks rather like a tart if you ask me, but then that *does* seem to be his type."

Katie's fingernails bit into her palms. *If she doesn't shut up, I'm going to scream.*

Nona nodded toward the door. "Well, you can decide for yourself—here they come."

And just when Katie thought it couldn't get any worse than being alone with Nona, she grasped the pendant Moonbeam had given her for strength. The woman had certainly been right—Katie really did need any kind of healing and protection she could get that evening.

Eyeing the woman on Andy's arm, Katie had to make the grudging admission to herself that Nona had also been right. Angelo's new "assistant manager" looked as though she'd been sent over from central casting for the role of trashy girlfriend. She wore a strapless black mini dress that barely covered her naughty bits, and her hair trailed down in fire-engine red coils. Katie tried to keep her face impassive as she wondered whether the woman was wearing a wig.

Oh, good grief. Is he actually bringing her over here?

Thankfully, Sue Sweeney, Ann and Jordan Tanner, and Gilda Ringwald-Stratton came in right behind Andy and his new assistant manager. Katie went over to greet them and spare herself the awkward introduction. By the gleam in Andy's eye, she could tell that he'd looked forward to it.

After saying hello to the group, Katie announced, "Everyone, please fill your plates while I go ahead and get this meeting started." She knew her clenched muscles and queasy stomach wouldn't allow her to eat anything anyway.

Not willing to let his new friend's presence be ignored—as if —Andy addressed the group. "I hope no one minds my bringing Whitney. We're going to dinner right after the meeting."

No one said anything, but Whitney tittered.

Katie broke the uncomfortable silence by saying, "In light of our attorney Seth's personal tragedy, he couldn't be here tonight. However, we have a few days before we reconvene with our final decision. We'll see if Seth is back to work by then, and if not, we'll discuss other alternatives. Seth told me on Friday evening that a developer from Rochester was looking at the warehouse and that we'd better act soon if we want to offer a competing bid."

"The place is going to require quite a bit of work to get it up to par," Gilda said. "We need to take that into consideration when we formulate our offer."

"True, but it's in a prime location," Jordan said. "Its value will only increase, especially after our renovations."

Katie and the other members continued to discuss both the pros and the cons of buying the warehouse. Except, that is, for Andy. He was too busy whispering and giggling with Whitney to even know what the rest of the group was talking about. *Why did he even come?* Katie wondered. But, then again, she knew. He'd come to throw Whitney in her face. Like Katie even cared.

After the partners decided on an acceptable offer for the

property, and calculated the amount of money necessary from each partner, Katie suggested they take a few days to consider whether they—individually—wanted to commit to buying the property.

"If we're not interested in this property, will we retain our status in the partnership?" Sue asked. "Or will the other partners buy us out? This is a bigger investment than the one required for the building that now houses The Flower Child."

"I'll ask Seth—or the attorney we ultimately choose to work with—about that and send out an email with the answer," Katie said. "Everyone, please email me with any other questions or concerns, and I'll try to get answers for you."

Before she could finish dismissing everyone, the entrance door burst open and Margo Bonner strolled in. Always the epitome of elegance, she wore a black peplum suit with a black-and-white gingham belt and trim, black patent peep-toe pumps, carrying a smart Chanel bag. Her silvery hair was wound into a French twist and secured with pearl-headed bobby pins.

Encompassing the room with her smile, she said, "Please don't let me interrupt. Katie, darling, nice to see you." She stepped forward to give her former daughter-in-law an air kiss. "And even better to see those goodies over there on the counter. My flight was delayed, and I'm famished. Will you all excuse me?"

"Actually, that's all I had to say," Katie announced to the group at large. "Feel free to stay as long as you'd like and to have some more goodies—" She said this, although no one had really indulged in the food.

As Margo filled her plate, sampling a morsel or two as she did, she exclaimed about how delicious everything was. "Katie, did you make all this yourself, or did Brad help you?"

"It was all me, Margo." Katie joined her former mother-in-law at the counter and got herself a plate. Now that the meeting was over and the shock at seeing Andy parade his possible new conquest had subsided, she realized she was hungry, too.

"Then you've outdone yourself." Margo turned to take in the group. "Wouldn't you all agree?"

"Oh, yes," Nona said. "I was just about to try a cookie myself."

Margo winked. "You should have two, dear. With your lovely figure, you can afford it."

And, just like that, Nona began filling her plate. As did the rest of the group. Except, of course, for Andy and Whitney because they were out the door and on their way to dinner.

Small talk dominated the next half hour, with Margo catching up on the news surrounding Victoria Square, but finally, the others dispersed, leaving only Katie and Margo sitting at a table by the window overlooking the parking lot to enjoy their tea.

"What in the world has been going on around here?" Margo asked. "The last time I was here on Victoria Square, you had two men falling at your feet. Tonight, they're both with other women."

Katie followed Margo's gaze across the street where she saw Ray and Carol Rigby walking toward Ray's car parked in the lot. Even though that's what Katie had wanted—for Ray to be happy —it hurt more to see the two of them together than it had for her to see Andy and Whitney fawning all over each other.

"Whatever did you do?" Margo asked.

Shrugging, Katie wondered how to answer. Given Margo's judgmental tone, she didn't feel inclined to tell the woman anything. Margo knew that Andy had cheated with Erikka Wiley, so she was presumably asking Katie what she'd done to run off Ray.

Katie's cell phone vibrated in her pocket—she'd turned the sound off during the meeting. She fished out the phone and looked at the screen. The call was coming from an unknown number, but the digits were vaguely familiar to her.

"Excuse me," she said to Margo. Accepting the call, she said, "Hello, Katie Bonner."

"Ms. Bonner, my name is Gabrielle Pearson. I got your message."

"Ms. Pearson, I'm so glad you returned my call. I'm the proprietor of Tealicious, the tea shop where you dined on Saturday with Jamie Siefert."

"Yes, I know." Ms. Pearson's voice was clipped, and Katie was unable to gauge the woman's tone.

"I'd like to speak with you about Jamie," Katie said. "How did he seem while he was with you?"

"He was slightly ill at ease, I thought. But then, lots of men are. You see, I'm a wedding planner."

CHAPTER 10

*T*uesday morning, Katie poured herself a cup of coffee from Artisans Alley vendors' lounge before returning to her office. Before she could get settled, someone knocked on her door. Hoping it was Gabrielle Pearson, she called, "Come in!"

Instead, it was Rose. She came into the office, her face wreathed in distress, and closed the door behind her. "How are you, you poor little thing? I want you to know I'm here for you."

Poor little thing? "What do you mean?" Katie asked.

"I heard about Andy bringing his new girlfriend to last night's meeting." Rose settled in the chair beside Katie's desk and sighed dramatically. "*Everyone* is talking about it."

Katie wondered how *everyone* could be talking about it when not *everyone* was there. "Who says he *has* a new girlfriend? She was introduced as his new assistant manager."

"And I'm the Queen of the May," Rose muttered sarcastically.

Katie continued. "I'm fine. In fact, I'm getting ready to meet the woman who had lunch with Jamie on Saturday."

Raising a hand to her chest, Rose gasped. "You found the mystery woman?"

Katie nodded. "And she's not such a mystery after all...unless you count being a wedding planner as mysterious." Katie did to an extent since Jamie and Seth hadn't—as far as she knew—been planning their nuptials.

"A wedding planner?" Rose echoed, her eyes widening. "I'm intrigued. Could you please get the woman's contact information for me before she leaves?"

Katie raised an eyebrow. "Do you have something you'd like to tell me, Rose?"

The old lady smiled. "Not yet. But it doesn't hurt to be prepared."

"True." Katie chose her words carefully. "But please don't rush into anything. You've only known Walter for a few weeks."

"Oh, I know, dear. But, at our ages, it doesn't pay to dawdle." Rose winked. "Besides, I didn't say I wanted to hire this woman. I'd merely like more information about the work she does."

Uh-huh.

"I'll see if I can get her business card."

"Excellent," Rose said got up and gave a wave of her hand as she left the office.

Katie shook her head and resumed working until once again there came a knock at the door. Rose had returned, but this time she had a tall, striking brunette with her.

Katie rose from behind her desk. "Ms. Pearson?"

"Please call me Gabrielle."

"Could I get the two of you some coffee?" Rose asked.

"None for me, thanks," Gabrielle said.

"I'm fine, too, but thank you, Rose. Would you please pull the door closed on your way out?" Katie gestured toward the chair beside her desk. "Gabrielle, thank you for agreeing to meet with me."

"You're welcome. I'm on a tight schedule, but I hoped you could put me in touch with Mr. Landers." Gabrielle pulled a slip of paper from her barrel purse. "I'd like to return this to him."

Katie examined the five-figure check Gabrielle handed her, apparently a retainer from Jamie that had been marked VOID.

"I was so terribly sorry to hear about Jamie's death," Gabrielle continued. "I didn't even realize what had happened until I saw the article in yesterday's newspaper."

Blanching, Katie asked, "There was an article in the paper? What did it say?"

"It had a photo of Jamie lying on the sidewalk—taken from someone's phone, I imagine—with a crowd gathered around him. The headline read *Is Tealicious Toxic?* and the article went on to say that local medical examiner Jamie Siefert collapsed immediately after eating at Tealicious and died shortly thereafter."

Panicked, Katie grabbed a peppermint from the jar on her desk, unwrapped it, popped it into her mouth, and immediately bit it in two, the crunch sending a surge of endorphins through her.

"That's gotta be murder on your teeth," Gabrielle said, taken aback.

"I know, but Victoria Square will be the death of me long before I have to worry about breaking my teeth." Katie blew out a breath. "Would you like a peppermint?"

Gabrielle shook her head violently. "No, thank you."

Katie took a moment to calm herself. "Would you mind telling me what you and Jamie talked about during your lunch at Tealicious?" Katie asked.

"Not at all. Jamie said he'd recently won a boatload of money in a poker game and that he wanted to surprise his partner with a proposal."

"A poker game?" Katie asked, startled. She hadn't thought Jamie to be that good a player.

Garbrielle nooded and gave a small, sad smile. "He must've been confident of getting a *yes* because he wanted to go ahead and plan the entire wedding as a surprise for Mr. Landers." She sighed. "I thought it was terribly romantic."

It was. Katie had no idea Jamie had been such a dreamer. But she didn't have the luxury of dwelling on that at the moment. "Did Jamie appear to be in any discomfort while you were having lunch?"

Gabrielle shrugged. "I don't know. He only picked at his food, but I chalked that up to his excitement about his plans. Afterward, I left through the back door because I'd been unable to find a parking spot in front of the building. That's why I didn't know what had happened to Jamie until I saw the news story."

"You say Jamie told you he'd won some money in a poker game," Katie said and wondered why neither he nor Seth had mentioned it on Friday night.

"That's right."

"Did he happen to say where he'd been playing?" Katie asked. "I hadn't heard that he'd taken a trip to any of the state casinos recently."

"He didn't say, and I didn't ask," Gabrielle said. "It wasn't my business. I intended to plan his fairy-tale wedding. I'm sorry for your and for Mr. Landers's loss. If you could give me his address, I'd like to send him a note of sympathy along with that voided check."

"I can certainly give you his address for the sympathy card, but I'll be seeing him later today and would be glad to give him the check."

"Thanks. I appreciate your help." Gabrielle waited for Katie to print out Seth's address, then she stood. "Again, I'm sorry for the loss of your friend and the fact that the tragedy occurred at one of your businesses."

"Thanks." Katie barely registered Gabrielle's words because she was thinking, *I have to get my hands on that newspaper.* Then she remembered her promise to Rose. "Do you have a business card? A friend of mine might like to consult you."

Gabrielle smiled and dug into her purse once again, handing Katie five cards. She was obviously optimistic but judging by the voided check, Katie had a feeling Gabrielle's prices would be well out of Rose's reach.

As soon as Gabrielle left her office, Katie reached for her cell phone. She intended to call Margo, but her former mother-in-law must have been having a psychic moment because she called Katie as soon as she picked up the phone.

"I was just going to call you," Katie said, in lieu of a typical greeting. "We have a problem."

"You didn't have to send up *that* alarm," Margo said. "I'm standing in the middle of an empty tea shop."

"No wonder. I need to find a copy of yesterday's paper." She told Margo about the article Gabrielle had mentioned. "I seldom read the newspaper anymore. I get all my news online."

"I'll check with Don and Nick to see if they have an extra copy at Sassy Sally's," Margo said. "Get over here as quickly as you can."

"On my way." Katie ended the call, put her computer to sleep, grabbed her purse, and headed out the door.

She encountered Vance in the vendors' lounge. "Good morning, Katie. I need to speak with you about the second-floor repairs. It's—"

"I'm sorry," she interrupted. "Something's come up and I'm on my way out the door. I trust you to use your best judgment to handle it."

"But this is important," he said, a bit of a whine creeping into his voice.

"Again, I trust you." Katie could see the frustration in Vance's weathered face, but she didn't have time to deal with the floor just then. She could only handle one crisis at a time. "That's why I hired you as my assistant manager." After giving him what she hoped was a reassuring pat on the shoulder, she hurried out the back door and crossed the Square's big parking lot.

Stepping across the threshold into the Tealicious dining room, Katie could see that it was indeed empty. Brad, Margo, and two waitresses stood in the middle of the room looking disgusted, angry, and helpless, respectively.

Before Katie could address the group, Nick burst through the door holding a newspaper aloft.

"Here it is," he announced. "I didn't see this yesterday, or I'd have called and given you all a heads-up."

Nick spread the paper out onto one of the tables, and they all gathered around to read it. The writer of the article hinted that whatever Jamie had ingested at Tealicious had to have caused his demise.

"This is outrageous!" Katie ran both hands through her hair and began to pace. "I'm going to demand they print a retraction!"

Margo straightened and held up a hand. "Not so fast. The article is carefully worded to avoid actually stating that something Jamie ate at Tealicious killed him. Demanding a retraction at this point would only make us look scared or guilty. We need to do two things: find out what really *did* kill Jamie and show the world we've got nothing to hide."

"How do we do that when our patrons are afraid to return?" Brad asked, frustration leaving his brow furrowed.

"With free food." Margo strode to the counter and poured herself a cup of tea from a pretty pansy-patterned bone china pot. "We'll host an open house on Friday. I know it's short notice, but we need to act quickly. I'll write a press release and send it to all the local media." Cup in hand, she turned to Brad. "Can you come up with a couple of new dishes, cakes, or pastries to showcase?"

"Of course," Brad eagerly agreed, warming to the idea. "How about we stage this open house with a fall theme—treats for the grownups as well as for children?"

"I can work with that. That's a marvelous idea," Margo said. She sipped her tea. "Katie, Brad and I can handle the open house. Can you poke around and find out what actually killed Jamie?"

"I'll do my best," Katie said, feeling inadequate to the task.

"It sounds like you've got all bases covered," Nick said. "I need to get back to Sassy Sally's. But please let me know if there's anything I can do to help. Jamie was one of our own. We need to figure out what happened to him." He waved and headed out the door.

"Wait!" Katie called and followed him.

"What's up?" Nick asked.

She explained about her conversation with Gabrielle Pearson.

"What did you—a professional player—think of Jamie as a card player?"

Nick shrugged. "Mediocre at best."

"Then how did he win so big—and where?"

"There are clubs in Rochester—more than one. And there are always private games, as well."

"How would we find out where Jamie played?"

Nick shrugged. "Ask around—but discreetly. Look, I've gotta go."

"Okay. See you later," Katie said and they parted ways.

Although Katie desperately wished she had some idea of how to approach the problem of seeking the truth as to what had happened to Seth's partner, the main thing all of them could do at this point was not to lose hope. However, just then she wasn't feeling all that hopeful.

AN HOUR LATER, upon arriving at Seth's house, Katie was surprised to find him there alone. He was freshly showered and shaved and was wearing jeans and a somber black sweater. She hugged him hello.

"Where's Suzanne?" she asked, looking around the quiet kitchen.

"Her sister arrived from Illinois last night and took her back home." He offered a wan smile slightly. "It was good to have her here, but it's nice not to feel obligated to look after someone else."

"I totally understand." Katie nodded toward the couch. "May we sit?"

"Yes." He drew out the word, letting Katie know he was wondering what was going on.

"I have some news about Jamie," she said, sinking into the cushions of the leather couch. "I found the woman he had lunch with on Saturday."

Although he'd sat beside her, it seemed as though Seth was practically hovering. "Who is she?"

"Her name is Gabrielle Pearson, and she's a wedding planner."

"A wh-what?" he asked, looking confused.

"You heard right. Jamie planned to surprise you with a proposal and a planned wedding."

His eyes filling, Seth dropped his head into his hands. "He knew I'd hate all the planning involved in a wedding but that I'd be thrilled with the end result."

Katie put her arm around his shoulders. "I know."

It took a few long moments before Seth composed himself, but then Katie gave him Jamie's voided check. "Ms. Pearson wanted me to return this to you."

Seth regarded the check with open-mouthed surprise. "This is only the retainer? How much was this going to cost him?"

"Apparently, Jamie wasn't worried about the money," Katie said. "Gabrielle told me Jamie won big in a poker game and was going to use his winnings for your surprise."

"He won big in a poker game? *What* poker game?" Seth asked, looking bewildered.

"I asked the same thing. Gabrielle didn't know." They shared a long look. "Are you thinking what I'm thinking?"

"I am," he said, his mouth tightening. "We have to find out where Jamie won that money, how much he won, and whether or not one of his opponents is responsible for his death."

CHAPTER 11

*S*eth and Katie began their quest at the bank. After sitting down with a bank officer, Seth checked the balance on his and Jamie's shared accounts but—as he expected—there was no unusual activity—no large deposit. After all, the check Gabrielle had returned had a different account number.

"When did Jamie open a new account?" he asked.

The woman studied her implacably manicured hands. "I'm unable to tell you anything about accounts on which you are not a signatory."

Seth leaned across the desk. "Jamie has died—" he began.

"I'm terribly sorry for your loss. However, even if you are the beneficiary on all of Mr. Seifert's accounts, you'll need to provide a death certificate before we can release any information or any monies to you."

"I don't want the money," Seth said. "I just want to know—"

"I feel for you," the woman said holding up a hand. "I really do. But my hands are tied—not only by this bank but by federal regulations. Bring me a note of authorization and Mr. Seifert's death certificate, and I may be able to help you further."

When they left the bank, Seth was clearly frustrated but not angry. He understood the bank officer's position. She was right—it was against the law for her to disclose anything to him without going through the proper channels. He'd known that going in, but he'd taken the chance he might gain some new information.

"What now?" Katie asked.

"Let's try Jamie's office. Maybe we can find something in his desk or on his calendar to give us an indication of where he might've been playing poker."

At the medical examiner's office, Seth parked in Jamie's designated spot. Eyes filled with tears, he looked over at Katie. "Please wake me up from this nightmare."

She lunged forward to hug him. "I wish I could. More than anything, I wish I could."

It took a moment or two for Seth to pull himself back together. Then he straightened, ran a hand through his hair, put on his sunglasses, and got out of the car.

When they walked into the office, it was apparent everyone there knew Seth and thought highly of him. He received lots of hugs and many tears were shed as Seth tried to lead the way to Jamie's office.

"Would it be all right if we went into Jamie's office?" he asked the head medical examiner, Bill Elliot. "I'd like to get his planner —see if there's…you know…anything I need to do or—"

"Of course. Phyllis," the thin, balding man called out. "Let Seth and his friend into Jamie's office, please!" He turned back to Seth. "It's been incredibly hard for the staff to handle losing one of our own," he said echoing what Nick had said. "As soon as we get the final lab results back, we'll let you know what we've found. In the meantime, if there's anything we can do to help you or Jamie's family, just let us know." His voice broke. "I can't tell you how much I'm gonna miss that guy."

Seth hugged the man for the second time. "He was fond of you, too, Dr. Elliot."

Elliot nodded and stepped back.

A woman in a white lab coat arrived, presumably Phyllis, and unlocked the door. She reached in and turned on the overhead light before turning to Seth. "I'm so sorry about Jamie. He was well-loved in this office."

"Thanks," Seth managed, his voice breaking.

Phyllis nodded and she and Elliot left them alone to enter the office.

Katie stood at Seth's side looking into the tidy space. She wished they'd had more time to get to know each other, and that Jamie had been able to surprise Seth with his proposal and wedding. Oh, how she wished that the two of them could have grown old together.

Seth stepped inside and paused to look at the desktop. He picked up the page-a-day calendar turned to the day before Jamie's death, which held nothing but a meeting notice and lab times scheduled. It seemed surreal. Jamie had expected to show up for work the following Monday to continue his life and his work.

Seth leafed through the calendar but set it back down and was drawn to a framed photo of him and Jamie taken on a hike in the Catskills, which was proudly displayed on the desk.

Katie noted the books that lined wood shelves—grim tomes on anatomy and other ghastly subjects that had no doubt fascinated their owner.

Noticing a sticky note at the side of the computer monitor, Katie stepped closer. "Seth, look at this."

The note had an address, phone number, and the notation *Buy-in $500.*

"Bingo." Seth captured the personal photographs, the planner, and placed the sticky note inside the book. "I think we have what we need. If not, we can always come back. These people loved Jamie and want to know the truth about what happened to him almost as much as I do, and they won't expect us to clear out his office on our first visit."

Katie hoped he was right.

As they drove back to Seth's house, he used his car's Bluetooth to call the number on the sticky note.

A gravelly voice answered, "Yeah?"

"I want to play in the next game," Seth said, his tone level.

"Which one?"

Seth glanced at Katie. "The one with the five-hundred-dollar buy-in."

"Name?" Gravel Voice asked.

"Ferrell." Seth inquired as to whether this game would be played at the address written on the sticky note.

Gravel Voice told him no and gave him a new address, which Katie wrote on the sticky note under the address Jamie had written down.

"I'd like to bring my wife as well," Seth said.

"She pays, she plays," Gravel Voice said. "See you tomorrow night at eight."

Katie waited for Seth to enlighten her. She could understand him not giving his name *Landers*—he didn't know how well these people had known Jamie, but she didn't know why he wanted to take his *wife*. "If you're pretending to be Nick, shouldn't you be taking the real Nick or Don along with you to this game?"

"I'm not going," Seth said. "I can't walk in there and be objective enough not to tip my hand. Besides, if any of these people knew Jamie well, they might've been to his office and seen the photograph of me. If one of them is his murderer, recognizing me will only put him or her on guard."

"That's true. So, you're going to ask Nick to go in your place?"

"He's a better poker player than me. And I want you to go with him. You've done more than your fair share of investigating over the past couple of years. I want you there to see what you can learn. Besides, you play a pretty mean hand and can hold your own."

Katie ignored the compliment. "Hmmm…I wonder how to go

about discovering what these card sharks might know about Jamie and/or his death," she mused.

"The first thing you need to do is establish which, if any, of them were at the game where Jamie won the money he told Gabrielle Pearson about." He instructed the Bluetooth to call Nick at Sassy Sally's.

"Hi, Seth," Nick answered seconds later.

"Hey, Nick. I'm in the car with Katie and I wonder if you might be able to help us out with something."

"Sure," Nick said. "Anything."

"I need you to participate in a poker game tomorrow night at eight."

"Ah, you found out where Jamie played and won big?"

"Yeah. Can you do it?"

Katie heard Nick sigh.

"Is that a problem?" Seth asked.

"Well, yeah. Don and I are hosting a wine tasting for a bunch of brides-to-be tomorrow night. I can help out any other night though."

"No," Seth said tersely. "It has to be tomorrow." He explained the situation to Nick.

"We could disguise you," Nick said. "I have a friend at Geva Theater who could make you unrecognizable to your own mother."

"I'll give that some thought and get back with you," Seth said.

"I could ask Don if he'd mind doing this tasting alone." There was hesitation in Nick's voice.

"I'd never ask you to do that. You'd be dishonoring a commitment to both your partner and your business." Seth gave a weary sigh. "We'll think of something. Thanks anyway."

After Seth had ended the call, Katie said, "What about Ray? He knows how to play poker, and he was a detective, so he'll know the proper questions to ask."

"I don't know. Who's going to believe the two of you are married given your age difference?"

"Maybe that'll make the other poker players think Ray is a high roller." Katie nudged him with her elbow. "He'd have to have tons of cash to score a babe like me, right?"

Seth managed a grin as he conceded her point. "All right. Dial him up."

Seconds later, Ray answered. "Wood U."

"Hi, Ray. It's Katie."

"Where are you calling from?" he asked. "Your number came up *Unknown Caller.*"

"Seth Landers and I are driving in his car, and we have a favor to ask. Do you have plans for tomorrow night?"

"Yeah, but it's nothing I can't reschedule. What do you need?"

Seth explained the situation and told Ray he'd reserved a space for Mr. Ferrell and his wife. "There's a five-hundred-dollar buy-in for each of you, and of course, I'll front that."

"My plans are with Carol Rigby," Ray said. "She could accompany me and pretend to be my wife."

"Fine," Katie said starchily. "People at the event would be more likely to believe her as your wife."

"It isn't fine," Seth countered. "I want Katie there. I trust her. Besides, I don't want Detective Rigby or anyone else connected with Jamie's investigation to know what we're doing."

"That's a valid point," Ray conceded. "The lead detective on a case shouldn't be involved in a fishing expedition. It could lead to a claim of entrapment or result in evidence being excluded from the case." He cleared his throat. "Ms. Bonner, at what time tomorrow evening should I pick up my wife?"

Katie chose not to answer that question just yet. "Are you sure you can pull off an undercover operation? You're bound to be rusty since your retirement."

"I'm as sharp as ever," Ray grated. "In fact, Carol's trying to convince me to come out of retirement and rejoin the Sheriff's Office."

Well, bully for her. "I'll be ready at seven. Don't be late," Katie said.

"Might I suggest that on the drive to the game, the two of you come up with a cover story you can both agree on and remember?" Seth asked. "This game could be crucial in helping me find out who killed Jamie."

"Don't worry. I'll come up with something plausible."

"What will you tell Carol when you cancel your date?" Katie asked.

"That I need to help a friend."

Which friend? Seth...or Katie?

WHEN KATIE RETURNED to Artisans Alley, she searched the building for Vance to see if the issue with the floor had been resolved. She found him in the second-floor tenants' bathroom, changing a light bulb.

"Hey, Vance."

"Katie," he said in acknowledgment, all warmth drained from his tone.

Great. He's angry. "I'm sorry I left you in the lurch this morning, but something important came up that I had to address. Did you find what you needed?"

"I wanted your opinion about which stain I should use on the new flooring," he said. "Margo popped in soon after you'd left, so I asked for her advice."

"Good. She's always ready to put her two cents in for the better."

"Yes, and she has excellent taste. When I explained the situation, she suggested we shore up the entire upstairs floor, sand it, and re-stain it for continuity."

Katie's jaw slackened as dollar signs danced in her mind's eye —and the time involved. "That would be wonderful if we could afford to pull it off, but an undertaking like that would cost much more than I was prepared to pay."

"Well, I already went ahead and ordered the additional materials. I got a terrific deal on them and they're non-returnable." He spread his hands. "You told me to use my own judgment."

Katie swallowed. "Yes. I did." She couldn't really blame Vance. She *had* told him to figure it out for himself. But then, why had Margo wafted in and made suggestions she had to have known Katie couldn't afford? Furthermore, Vance should've known they wouldn't be able to shore up the entire second floor. And what about the disruption? Were they going to have to empty all the booths and close down the business for a couple of weeks?

Lesson learned, she guessed. Next time, she'd take a moment to hear Vance out. "We need to sit down and discuss the logistics."

"If you can spare the time," Vance said tartly.

Katie was in no mood to deal with the problem just then. "We'll set up a meeting for later this afternoon. How is four o'clock?"

"Fine."

But it wasn't fine.

At that moment, Katie wasn't sure if things between them would ever be fine again.

CHAPTER 12

*A*fter her conversation with Vance, Katie was so rattled she needed to work off her upset and decided to do a couple of laps power walking around the Square. She was startled when someone fell into step beside her. She stopped dead in her tracks when she saw it was Andy.

"What are you doing?" she asked, annoyed.

"Walking." He'd also stopped. "Or, at least, I *was*."

She shook her head. "You never walk. Your concept of exercise is only what takes place in a gym."

"Look, I wanted to talk with you. Come on." He resumed walking, waiting until she joined him before continuing. "I considered coming to your apartment, but I didn't want either of us to have to contend with wagging tongues and rampant speculation."

"You don't think our walking the Square together will cause any gossip?" Katie asked.

"Not as much as my coming to your apartment would."

She had to admit that was true. "What did you want to say?"

"I wanted you to know I'm sorry about Jamie," he said. "How's Seth holding up?"

"He was a basket case for the first few days, but he appears to be doing better now that we have a lead." *Oops. Didn't mean for that to slip out.*

His steps faltered for a moment. "A lead? What kind of lead?"

"Jamie could've been poisoned at a poker game," she said.

"Let me guess—you and Seth have found which poker game Jamie played at, and you plan to investigate."

She glanced over to see his expression settle into the disapproving frown she'd seen so often when they were dating. "Everything will be fine. We're simply going to play a little poker and find out if any of the other players knew Jamie."

"I know that what you do is no longer any of my business, but it still concerns me when you put yourself in harm's way for other people."

"I'm not only doing this snooping for Seth," Katie said. "Traffic at Tealicious has come to a complete standstill."

"Business will pick back up, Sunshine. Give it a little time."

"I don't have a little time! Not if McKinlay Mill residents believe our food is responsible for a man's death."

"The story will die down," Andy said. "Any minute now, something new will happen to eclipse the rumor of Jamie's death."

She stopped and turned toward him with her hands on her hips. "Like what? A murdered body being found in an abandoned warehouse? Oh, wait, that happened already, and I'm the one who found the body. Should anyone forget that fact, the local newspaper will be happy to provide a refresher."

Andy rested his hands lightly on her shoulders. "I'm sorry. You've found yourself in one horrible situation after another these past few weeks. Is there anything I can do to help?"

Unable to bear his touch, she stepped back causing his hands to fall from her shoulders. "No, and don't give me this 'I care about you' crap when you blatantly telegraphed to everyone at the partnership meeting that Whitney was your new girlfriend."

"That's not true," Andy protested.

"Well, that's the impression you gave. Everybody on the Square is talking about it."

Andy glared at her but didn't refute the accusation.

"Now, I really need to finish my walk," Katie declared.

Andy shrugged. "Fine. But if you need anything—or even just a friendly face—give me a buzz."

Not a chance, buster, she felt like saying. Instead, she turned away and continued walking.

AFTER HER POWER WALK, Katie stopped at Tealicious to meet with Margo and Brad before going to Artisans Alley.

"There you are," Margo said. "Brad and I have been waiting for you." Her eyes raked over Katie. "We don't mind giving you another few minutes, though, if you need to finish getting ready."

Katie took in her former mother-in-law's perfectly creased black slacks, leopard-print blouse, and coral blazer. Then she held her arms akimbo to show Margo she was fine with the jeans and oversize sweatshirt she'd chosen for the day. "I'm good."

Margo frowned. "Right." She placed a briefcase on one of the tables and opened it. "I've made a few fliers for the open house. We can choose one to copy and distribute, or we can opt for more than one."

All the fliers were beautifully designed, so Katie suggested they use them all. "That way people won't think they're seeing the same flier over and over and will hopefully read more than one. They do say you have to see a message seven times before it sinks in."

"Excellent," Margo said. "We should make copies to put at the cash desks at Artisans Alley, and we should also enlist the help of other Victoria Square merchants—Ray, Andy, Nona." She waved her hand dismissively. "I'll take care of that."

"Good luck," Katie said, "but I doubt any of the other merchants will go out of their way to drum up business for Tealicious."

"Oh, they will." Margo tapped the table. "I'll remind them that if customers stop patronizing Tealicious, it won't be long before they'll take all their business to some other quaint town and everyone will be hurting."

Brad smiled, amused. "Ms. Bonner, did you kill that leopard and make it into a blouse yourself?"

Grinning, she said, "Never. I'd never harm an innocent animal. These merchants, on the other hand…. And please, darling, call me Margo."

Just like that, Margo had Brad eating out of the palm of her hand. She had a way with people—Katie had to admit that. At least, the people she wanted to charm. Katie had never been one of those people.

"Here are my ideas for a fall-themed tea," Brad said. "First, a red-velvet cake, with white buttercream icing."

"What else?" Margo asked, sounding enthused.

"What about pumpkin cupcakes?" Katie suggested.

"And pumpkin martinis?" Brad asked.

"No liquor license," Katie reminded Brad.

"I could make a cider Bundt cake," he said.

"That sounds good," Margo said. "Maybe you could make a cider-based punch to go with it."

"I once catered a Halloween party where we bought a giant pumpkin, cut it in half, and slid a punch bowl into it," Brad said. "Voila! It looked terrific. If we're doing this in the evening, we might want to include some savory appetizers, as well."

"Why don't I go on Pinterest to get some more ideas?" Margo volunteered.

"Good idea," Katie agreed. "Hopefully, we can follow up on a successful open house after the arrest of Jamie's killer."

"Do you have any news?" Brad asked.

Katie explained how she and Ray were going undercover at a poker game in an attempt to learn more about Jamie's activities before his death.

"Do you think that's wise?" Brad asked. "What if you're recognized as the proprietress of the tea shop where Jamie was potentially poisoned?"

She hadn't given that a thought. "I'll simply have to disguise myself."

"Oh, darling, you're always so frumpy," Margo said. "But I can play up your finer features and make you unrecognizable."

"Gee, thanks," Katie deadpanned.

Margo either didn't notice or chose not to acknowledge Katie's sarcasm. "No problem. Come to Sassy Sally's this evening and be ready to be transformed."

Realizing one disguise was as good as another, Katie reluctantly agreed.

WITH THEIR PLANS MADE, Katie returned to Artisans Alley. She paused in the vendors' lounge to pour herself a cup of coffee when Rose came in.

"Hey, there." She smiled at the older woman. "Could you come by my office for a minute?"

"Sure," Rose said. "Let me get a cup, and I'll be right there."

When they were both ensconced in her office with their coffee, Katie explained to Rose what happened with Vance the day before. "I know I should've taken time to hear him out about the floor, but I still think he should've gotten my permission to make such a costly move."

"Well, you *did* tell him you trusted him and to use his best judgment," Rose said.

From the way she answered, Katie realized Vance had already

spoken with Rose about the incident and that Rose was in agreement with him.

"Rose, do the Artisans Alley vendors think they've been slighted with this floor issue?"

"No. Everyone understands *that*." Rose pursed her lips.

"What is it everyone *doesn't* understand?" Katie asked.

"Since you're asking, more than a few vendors here feel that since Tealicious opened, Artisans Alley has become rather like one of Cinderella's ugly stepsisters—she's still at the ball, but no one is dancing with her. A little while ago, you brought in fliers announcing the Tealicious open house and expect us to happily hand them out and invite everyone to come." She leaned forward. "Well, what about an event or party for Artisans Alley?"

Katie bristled. "Need I remind you of the Harvest Festival—and the vendor appreciation party—that took place just weeks ago!" She raked her hands through her hair. "And, since the newspaper publicized Jamie's dying after eating there, Tealicious's business is suffering. I've got almost as big a financial stake in it as I do here."

"Oh, *I* understand all that," Rose said. "It's the others who are feeling resentful and overlooked. And they feel it'll be even worse if your partnership buys the abandoned warehouse."

Katie sighed. What in the world did Rose and the rest of the Artisans Alley vendors want from her? "Thanks for letting me know. Right now, I'm dealing with all I can handle, but I'll try to address their feelings. And soon." But she knew from past experience that despite her best efforts, she wasn't going to please everyone.

At that moment, she wasn't sure she cared. And she had what she expected to be an unpleasant meeting with Vance coming up.

It was going to be a long afternoon.

CHAPTER 13

*V*ance arrived promptly for his meeting with Katie. His demeanor was as stiff as his starched shirt collar. He walked into the office and perched on the edge of the chair beside her desk.

Katie tried to sound cheerful, but her greeting came out sounding forced nonetheless. "Thanks for coming. I spoke with Rose a little while ago. She says some of the vendors feel that I've let Artisans Alley fall by the wayside since purchasing Tealicious. Do you agree?"

Vance leaned back in the chair, looking down his nose at her. "To a great extent, I do. Yesterday morning, you couldn't spare me ten minutes to discuss the floor situation. Instead, you instructed me to use my best judgment—which I did. And then you were annoyed by my decision."

"I'm still upset about my friend Jamie's collapse outside Tealicious, his death, and how it's affecting his partner, Seth, who is one of my dearest friends."

"I guess I can see that," Vance grudgingly agreed.

"I'm dismayed because you've committed me to a lot of

money for a cosmetic fix to the floor. It feels like we're prepping for surgery when a simple bandage would suffice."

"I merely wanted to stain the floor and needed your opinion on the aesthetic since it is *your* establishment," Vance said, his expression hardening. "When Margo arrived, I consulted her, thinking she would know your preferences better than me. She pointed out that no matter what we used, the new stain wouldn't match the old and would look garish."

"While I'm aware of that concern, what we're looking at now is a far more extensive undertaking for a space that's, in many cases, unfinished." Katie sighed. "I'm already giving all the upstairs vendors affected by the job a free month's rent for their inconvenience. Now, in order to stain that section of floor, we're going to have to close Artisans Alley and displace them for at least a day or more."

"No, we won't. The upstairs vendors can move items to the lobby and the vendors' lounge and set up there while their portion of the floor is being stained. Ray and I are working on it after hours anyway."

"Really? I'm surprised he has the time now that he's squiring around Carol, the detective." Katie was sorry she'd said the words as soon as they came out of her mouth.

"Is that what this is about?" Vance asked. "Are you jealous of this woman? Everyone knows Ray is crazy about you. If you want him, all you have to do is let him know."

"My objections have nothing to do with Ray and his love life," she said, hoping it was true. "My main focus is Artisans Alley."

He arched a brow. "Oh, really?"

"Yes!" she said feeling exasperated. "Look, maybe I should see if the contractor who worked on the apartment over Tealicious, John Healy, can come in and take care of this. He's a professional—"

Vance shot to his feet. "So now you don't even trust me to repair the floor?"

Katie waved her hands as though to erase her last words. "I do trust you, Vance. Please sit back down so we can work this out."

He snorted a breath and sat, scowling. "Why are you making mountains out of molehills here? This problem is not insurmountable, and all I did was follow your instructions."

"You want mountains?" Katie asked. "I'll give you mountains. There has been virtually no business at Tealicious since Saturday. Granted, the shop was closed Sunday and Monday; but after the newspaper article ran on Monday intimating that something Jamie ate at Tealicious on Saturday led to his demise, no one wants to dine there."

"Are you sure Jamie's death *wasn't* caused by something he ingested at Tealicious?"

Rankled by his question, Katie tried not to show it. "I'm positive. Jamie was intentionally poisoned." Taking a page from Margo's playbook, she added, "Furthermore, if Victoria Square shoppers believe one shop is tainted, it could reflect poorly on the rest. And, of course, once shoppers learn I run Artisans Alley as well as Tealicious, all our vendors could suffer. I'm desperately trying to prevent that."

Vance frowned. "I hadn't considered that."

"Please do. It wouldn't hurt if the vendors thought about the long-term ramifications of this mess, too."

"Do you want me to come right out and tell them?" he asked.

"No. But it wouldn't hurt to try to encourage some *esprit de corps*."

Vance rose once again. "Okay. I'll try and rally the troops."

"Thank you."

Now she just had to hope he'd truly gotten the message—and could also relay it to the sixty-plus Artisans Alley vendors.

～

MOONBEAM CALLED close to closing time with a tempting offer. "Hey, Katie, I'm making homemade tomato bisque with the last of my garden bounty. Would you like to join me at The Flower Child for an early light dinner?"

"I'd love to," Katie said. After the day she'd had—and the evening yet to come—she was thrilled to have an excuse to get away from the problems of the day. Vance would be working on the floor. He could close down for the day.

As she stepped out of her office, Sue Sweeney entered the vendors' lounge. It wasn't that often that the Square's confectioner visited Artisans Alley.

"Hi, Katie," Sue said brightly. "Have you got a minute?"

"I was just heading out." Remembering how much brushing off Vance had cost her, she said, "But, of course, I have *a* minute."

Sue leaned her butt against the counter near the coffee maker. "I've been thinking and it seems like we should have another meeting soon to discuss the warehouse the partnership is considering buying. Exactly what should we do with it? Would we want to rent it out, as we did with the shop currently leased to The Flower Child?" she asked. "Or would we want to use it as a venue to sell some of our own products? Obviously, we don't need another sweet shop here on the Square, but my niece sells screen-printed T-shirts and—"

"Oh, Sue, whether we buy the warehouse or not, please have her reach out to me," Katie said. "I'm sure I could find her a space at Artisans Alley."

"Well, that's the thing. She'd need more than just a booth. She needs a production area as well as a shipping station. If I owned a stake in the building, she wouldn't have to pay rent. Right?"

Of course, it isn't right! Katie wanted to scream, but instead, she chose her words carefully. "That's not the case, Sue. Anyone renting space in the building would have to pay for the privilege. If no one paid rent, then how could we pay our bills?"

Sue sniffed. "That seems rather restrictive."

"It isn't restrictive," Katie said. "It's business." Katie looked pointedly at the clock. "I have another appointment. I really have to go. Maybe we can discuss this later—at a partnership meeting, as you suggested. I'll prepare an email either later tonight or tomorrow to schedule it."

Sue looked less than pleased and without another word, left the vendors' lounge in what could only be described as a huff. Katie locked her office for the night and left the building.

When Katie walked into The Flower Child, her senses were nearly overwhelmed by the scents of sandalwood and eucalyptus. Moonbeam met her at the entrance, put a CLOSED sign on the door, and asked Katie to follow her out back.

The shop's tiny kitchen was quaint, with an apartment-sized stove, a cozy teal-painted cabinet filled with food staples, and an assortment of mismatched dishes. A bistro table sat in the center of the room and had been set with mint-green and lemon-yellow plates, pink cloth napkins, and vintage blue aluminum tumblers. Moonbeam was nothing if not colorful. A small white platter decorated with a green scallop was heaped with oyster crackers. A white enamel pot with a cheerful red stripe under the lip sat on one of the burners with a ladle peeking out of it.

Moonbeam spooned generous portions of the bisque into heavy white bowls. "Have a seat and tell me what you'd like to drink."

"I'm fine with water," Katie said, sitting at the table.

Placing the bowls atop their plates, Moonbeam retrieved a pitcher from the refrigerator. She filled their tumblers before sitting down. "I sense from your deep red aura that you're troubled today."

Katie gave a hollow laugh. "I am. Would you like to know *all* the reasons why, or would you prefer I stick to the top ten?"

"How about the top three," Moonbeam suggested. "Hopefully, I can offer you a possible solution for at least one of them."

Katie heaved a sigh. "Well, the Rochester paper ran a story

trashing Tealicious," Katie said and sipped her water. It was cold and refreshing. She took another drink.

"I saw that," Moonbeam said. "I immediately dismissed the idea of Jamie being poisoned at Tealicious. Not another person who ate there got sick that day. Certainly, other people will realize that."

"Certainly, they won't. Traffic at the shop has come to a screeching halt."

"I'm sorry to hear that, but I'm guessing you have a plan in place to remedy that," Moonbeam said.

"Yes. We're planning an open house on Friday and inviting the public to give us a second chance."

"That soon? Is there anything I can do to help?"

Katie smiled. "You're wonderful to offer, but I think Brad and Margo have it under control."

"Margo?" Moonbeam asked.

"She's my former mother-in-law." Katie gave her head a slight shake. "You'll meet her soon enough. And probably love her. Everyone does," she said with chagrin.

Moonbeam's lips twisted into a wry grin. "I'm guessing not *everyone*."

"Oh, I love Margo. It's just—" Katie shrugged and decided a change of subject was warranted. "So, tell me what's going on with you."

Moonbeam's expression morphed from all-knowing to wide-eyed innocence. "I wonder if there's any way I could become a partner in the Victoria Square merchants group that buys real estate. I was talking with Ann Tanner about the abandoned ware-house the partnership is interested in buying, and I'd like to be a part of that."

"I'll speak to the others and if they agree, ask Seth what it would take to add you as a partner." Katie sighed. "Given my troubles with Tealicious and the cost to replace so much of the second floor at Artisans Alley, I might have to sit this transaction out."

"That would be a shame. I understand that it was because of you that the Square has undergone a real renaissance."

"My magic touch seems to have deserted me of late," Katie admitted.

Moonbeam nodded sympathetically. "I hope things turn around for you soon."

Yeah. So did Katie.

~

THE WOMEN FINISHED their soup and chatted for a pleasant hour before Katie bypassed Artisans Alley and returned to her apartment over the tea shop. Once there, she called Seth. Although she hated to bring up the matter of the abandoned warehouse so soon after the tragedy he'd suffered, she asked him how difficult it would be to add Moonbeam to the partnership.

"It won't be a problem. Text me her number, and I'll give her a call tomorrow explaining the legalities," he said. "Once she hears them, she might change her mind." He changed the subject. "Are you ready for tonight?"

"I must admit, I'm more than a little nervous about the whole thing. I can handle playing poker, but Margo wants me to come to Sassy Sally's before I leave for the game so she can transform me. She says I always look frumpy and that a glamorous transformation would ensure no one at the club would recognize me."

Seth actually laughed. The sound was music to Katie's ears. It gave her hope that he'd survive this heartbreak after all.

"This I've got to see," he said. "I'll meet you at Sassy Sally's in an hour."

CHAPTER 14

*a*fter feeding her cats their evening meal, Katie took a deep breath and addressed them. "Wish me luck."

As expected, they ignored her, never lifting their kitty faces from their food bowls.

As Katie crossed the expanse of asphalt, heading to Sassy Sally's, she texted Ray: *Would it be all right if I meet up with you at Wood U?*

He replied: *I'm going home to get spiffed up, but I don't have a problem meeting you at the shop. Afraid you can't control yourself in your apartment alone with me, my dear wife?*

Katie scowled and declined to reply, slipping her phone back into her jeans pocket.

Once arriving at Sassy Sally's, Nick ushered her upstairs to Margo's room where her former mother-in-law awaited. The room was filled with a stack of dresses and enough cosmetics to transform an entire theater group, making Katie feel like she was backstage at an amateur production of *Moulin Rouge*.

"We'd better get to work quickly," Margo told Nick gravely. "This might be more of a challenge than I'd anticipated."

"Wait a second—" Katie began righteously.

"Nick and I hit the mall and did a little shopping on your behalf," Margo continued as though she hadn't heard Katie.

"You shouldn't have." Katie leveled her gaze at Margo. "Artisans Alley's new flooring has already cost me more than I can afford." *Thanks to you.*

"No worries." Margo gave her a smug smile. "The tags are intact. I'll return what we don't use. I had to estimate your size. I know you're larger than I am, so it was utter guesswork on our part."

Katie glowered past Margo to Nick, who shrugged innocently.

"I think my judgment was accurate," he said.

There was a tap on the door, and then Don and Seth entered the room. Seth's lips were firmly pressed together as though he were trying to keep from smiling, while Don appeared all too eager to escape.

"Look who I found wandering around," Don said.

"Come to see the show?" Katie asked.

"I wouldn't have missed it." He winked. "I can hardly wait to see the finished product."

She didn't appreciate the idea of being a product, but Seth's presence was the reminder Katie needed to keep from stalking out of that room. He needed her to go to this poker game, try not to be recognized as the proprietor of Tealicious, and glean as much information as she could about Jamie's experience at the game in which he'd won so much cash.

Nick grabbed a folded sheet from the bed, tossing it into the air so that it billowed over the full-length mirror. "I want you to be surprised by the transformation."

It took Herculean strength for Katie not to roll her eyes. *Swell.*

Margo made Katie model each of the dresses they'd chosen, finally squeezing her into a tight scarlet sequined cocktail dress with a plunging neckline.

Katie looked down at her chest, appalled at how much

cleavage was exposed. "Shouldn't I have some sort of double-sided tape or something to hold me in?" she asked doubtfully.

"Don't be such a prude," Margo said. "Of course not."

"She's right," Nick agreed. "Men often bring seductively dressed women to these events to throw the others off their game. Of course, Don and I are immune," he said and laughed as he handed her a pair of strappy nude stiletto heels.

Margo came up with a matching silk bolero jacket and sighed. "It's a pity it's already October. That dress was made for summer."

While Katie donned the tiny coat, her mind recoiled at the very notion of being tortured by the stylish shoes—such as they were—for the rest of the evening.

"Go ahead and put them on," Nick instructed. "I'll help you get up once we've finished your hair and makeup."

Katie could've sworn Seth smothered a laugh. He really was enjoying watching his pseudo sister's discomfort and Margo making a painted doll out of her.

Katie had no idea what Nick and Margo were up to next. While Nick worked on her makeup, Margo fussed with her hair. She sat still, afraid that one would gouge her in the eye with a mascara wand or that the other would burn her scalp with a curling iron. She'd been in precarious situations before, but this one was on par as one of the worst. As the two stylists worked, Katie wondered if actors and actresses in their make-up chairs felt as she did—like a piece of meat to be ogled.

As a final touch before allowing Katie to see herself, Margo handed her a pair of drop faux-diamond earrings. She stood back and surveyed her work after Katie had put them on. Looking at Nick, she asked, "Done? Or do we need the triple-strand diamond cuff?"

Nick stroked his chin and assessed their creation. "Let's leave off the cuff. Seth, what do you think?"

Nodding, Seth said, "The cuff would be overkill."

"Then we're ready." With the skill of a magician, Nick whipped off the sheet from the full-length mirror and cried, "Voila!"

Katie stood, turned, and as she saw her reflection, her jaw dropped. Her hair—typically pulled back off her face and worn in a ponytail—fell around her shoulders in voluminous waves. Her skin was radiant, and the smoky eye makeup she wore was dramatic without being overdone. Her lips were lined and tinted in a nude shade, but they seemed fuller somehow.

"Wow," she managed to say after a few seconds. "I don't believe anyone will recognize me. I barely recognize myself."

"You're absolutely stunning," Seth said. "Thank you for doing this for me." He reached into his suit coat's inside pocket, withdrew an envelope, and handed it to her. "Here's the buy-in money."

Margo intercepted the envelope and placed it inside a small silver clutch. "There, you're all set."

"One last thing," Nick said. "Fast-play when you have a really strong hand. It'll help you build the pot and make the others think you've been there before."

"Will do," Katie said.

"Take my arm and hold onto the railing as we go down the stairs," Seth said. "I'll drive you over to Wood U."

Margo, Nick, and Don all waved good-bye as Katie hobbled to Seth's Mercedes, not at all confident she could pull off this charade.

When they arrived at Wood U, the shop was dark and there was no sign of Ray. Seth suggested they get out of the car and walk a bit so Katie could get more comfortable in the four-inch heels.

"Stay there," he said. "I'll come around and get you."

Feeling like a stuffed tube of manicotti, Katie waited until Seth opened the passenger side door of his Mercedes and helped her onto the pavement. They walked across the tarmac and slowly began walking in the direction of Artisans Alley.

The couple was almost to Gilda's Gourmet Baskets when Andy's new assistant manager, Whitney pulled up, cut the engine, and got out of her car. Mouth gaping, she studied Katie's outfit for a long moment before she ran to Angelo's as fast as her platform boots would allow.

Katie looked at Seth. "Good grief. What are the odds that—"

"Don't worry about that tart. Keep walking. We'll turn around and go back once we've reached The Perfect Grape. We don't want anyone to think we're running from them, do we?"

"No," she said firmly.

"Continue holding your head high," Seth advised.

But then Andy burst through Angelo's door, and he jogged to meet up with Seth and Katie, while Whitney trailed in his wake.

"What—? Why—? Who—?" he stammered.

Katie couldn't help but enjoy seeing Andy so flabbergasted he could barely speak. She smiled. "Yes?"

"Whitney said she thought it was you on the sidewalk, but I told her no way would you be dressed like *that*!"

Whitney caught up to him and was still catching her breath. "Honey," she managed to say, "if you'd dressed like that for your man, he might still *be* your man."

Biting back the snarky retort that had sprung to her lips, Katie said, "Sorry, but I have an important event to get to."

A car pulled up beside them. Katie recognized it to be Ray's SUV, but Seth was between her and the vehicle.

Ray rolled down his window. "Seth, would you please escort *my wife* to my vehicle?"

Andy glared at Ray. "What the hell are *you* doing here? And what do you mean, your *wife*?"

Ray shifted the car into park and got out. "I wasn't talking to you. And you—" He broke off, seeing Katie for the first time. His jaw went slack, and he gulped. "Um—"

She smiled. "Hello, *hubby*."

Andy looked as though he was about to explode. "What are you two talking about?"

Katie shrugged. "Ray is escorting me to an event tonight, and some people just might have gotten the impression he's my husband."

"You mean, the poker game," Andy accused. "I thought you were going with Seth."

"I can't attend," Seth said, with a questioning glance at Katie. "Ray graciously agreed to take my place."

"But—" Andy ran his hand through his hair. "I should be the one to go. I happen to be a much better poker player than Ray Davenport."

His words gave Katie the opening she'd been hoping for. "Sorry, Andy, but I don't need you. In fact, I don't *need* anyone to accompany me to this poker game, But Ray has graciously agreed to escort me." She looked pointedly at Whitney. "And I thought my telling you I planned to play poker this evening was in confidence."

"You should've known better than that," Ray muttered.

"We need to get going," Katie told Ray. "We don't want to be late. I'm feeling particularly lucky tonight."

Ray raised an eyebrow and grinned. "So am I."

CHAPTER 15

The not-really-married couple rode in uncomfortable silence for nearly five minutes before Katie broke the quiet. "So, what's our story?"

"I saw you on the street, you took my breath away, and I asked you to marry me. The rest is history," he said. "How's that?"

She hid a smile. "That might be a bit hard for our audience to believe. Our first hurdle is that you're supposed to be Nick Ferrell. How will we keep anyone who might've played poker with Nick from questioning your fake identity?"

"I've been thinking about that." He braked at a traffic light. "I'm a retired banker from Connecticut. What a coincidence that someone living in the area has the same name."

"Why Connecticut?" Katie asked.

"Why not?" The light changed, and he pulled forward. "Do you have a problem with Connecticut? If so, we can be former residents of New Jersey."

"No. I prefer Connecticut. I don't think I can do that Joizy accent." She flicked her wrist. "Keep going."

"As I said, I'm a retired banker. You're an insurance adjuster. With your past experience, I thought you could make that work."

She was flattered that he remembered that prior to taking over Artisans Alley, she'd worked in an insurance office. "How did we meet?"

"My daughter from my first marriage had a fender bender. You handled her claim."

"I'm impressed," she said. "You're good at this."

"I spent a few years working vice before I became a detective," he said modestly.

"Do you miss it?"

"Vice or police work in general?" he asked.

"Both."

Lifting one shoulder, he said, "I do sometimes. I'd be lying if I told you I hadn't been looking forward to this game tonight."

Feeling contrite, Katie said, "I'm sorry I said you might be rusty. I was only razzing you because—"

"Because you don't like my going out with Carol." He spoke matter-of-factly, but Katie still bristled.

"That's not true."

Ray raised his brows at her. "Really." It was a statement rather than a question.

"Okay, maybe—*maybe*—that's part of it," she admitted. "I don't think Carol seems right for you. For one thing, she's trying to talk you into going back into law enforcement—a dangerous occupation—and giving up your shop."

"She isn't trying to get me to do anything," he said. "She's merely offering encouragement. The other night you were practically throwing me at her. What happened?"

"Nothing. I just—" Katie sighed. "I just think you might want to play the field a little more before you decide to see Carol exclusively."

"That's a good point. I hear there's a new assistant manager at Angelo's."

She uttered a cry of indignation. "Don't make me take off this shoe and stab you with it!"

He laughed. "Married ten minutes, and you're already nagging me mercilessly."

"Keep it up, *Nick*." It occurred to her that she didn't know her cover name. "Wait? Who am I—other than Mrs. Nick Ferrell, I mean?"

"Let's go with Kelly, if that suits you. It's still close to Katie, so if you start to write your name for any reason and jot down that *K*, you won't panic."

"You really are good at this," she said.

He winked. "You ain't seen nothin' yet."

Ray deftly drove them through the streets of Rochester to the East End, pulling into a lot beside a tidy, squat brick building where the poker game was being held. Ray parked the car and then came around to help Katie from the passenger seat. She noticed that he put on his new persona the way another man might wear a hat. He got out of the car as Ray Davenport. He opened her door as retired Connecticut banker Nick Ferrell.

Taking her hand and placing it in the crook of his arm, he said, "If I haven't said so already tonight, you look stunning, darling. Do you have our buy-in?"

Having never gone undercover before, she took her cue from him. "Right here, sweetheart." She patted the silver clutch.

"Excellent. Let's go win some money." He led her to the door, knocked once, and then greeted the large man who answered. "Ferrell. First time here. Do we give you the buy-in, or do we pay inside?"

The man jerked his head toward the interior of the room. "Pay at the desk and get your chips."

There was a reception desk set up just inside the door. An elegant woman dressed in a white sheath, her blonde hair done up in a chignon, stood beside a large podium, as though she'd been waiting to greet them. Katie looked beyond her, taking in the plush interior with its wood-paneled walls and its rich carpet of reds and greens, the dark colors no doubt chosen to camouflage spilled drinks. A bar of dark cherry wood stood in one corner, and Katie wondered if the drinks were complimentary or incredibly expensive.

"Welcome to Alexander's," she greeted them. "And you are?"

"Nick Ferrell. And this is my wife, Kelly."

"Nice to meet you," Katie said, although the blonde hadn't introduced herself.

The woman consulted a ledger. "And the buy-in?"

Katie removed the envelope of cash from her purse and handed it over.

The blonde smiled. "We always set couples up at different tables. Not that *you* would, but some couples have devised ways to undermine the other players. Mr. Ferrell, you'll be at table one; and Mrs. Ferrell, you're at table three."

"Thank you." Ray nodded toward the two stacks of chips. "Let me step over here and give my wife a kiss for luck, and then we'll take our seats."

"All right." The woman smiled broadly as Ray led Katie a few feet away.

Putting his hands on her waist, he drew her close.

We're putting on a show, Katie reminded herself as Ray's mouth covered hers. *A show...that's all...*

"If you need to talk to me," he whispered, "rub your nose with your left index finger, and then excuse yourself to go to the bathroom. I'll use the same signal. Got it?"

"Yes."

He lifted his head and said loudly enough that the receptionist could hear, "I'm serious. Don't bankrupt us."

"I won't," she said and giggled theatrically. "I promise."

"All right." He gave her a quick peck on the lips. "Keep your head about you."

They went to the receptionist, got their chips, and took them to their tables. Since the games hadn't started yet, Katie took a seat at the designated round table that could accommodate up to eight players. Like the paneling and bar, it was made of cherry with a green baize in the center. Before each player were rounded slots for chips and brass beverage holders.

Katie nodded to the man and woman already at her table. "Hi, I'm Kelly. Go easy on me. Unlike my husband, I'm still an amateur."

"Gina," the woman said, extending a manicured hand with long red nails. "I'm actually better than my husband at this, but don't tell *him* I said that. He's at table two."

"My husband is at table one," Katie said.

"I'm here solo," the man said. "Albert Whitlock's the name. If either of you gals gets in trouble, I'll try to give you a hand."

Katie and Gina shared a look of restrained disdain. Gina had already said she was good. Besides, how was Albert going to help either of them if they *got in trouble*? What had he even meant by that?

Glancing toward the door where she'd first entered, Katie drew in her breath as Phyllis—Dr. Elliott's assistant—breezed in. Would she recognize Katie? Had she ever worked with Ray?

"Is anything wrong?" Albert asked.

Katie looked in Ray's direction and rubbed her nose with her left index finger. "Uh, no. But I think I should run to the little girl's room before we start to play. Do you know where it is?"

"To your right," Gina said. "We'll watch your chips. And don't worry, you've got plenty of time before the game starts."

Katie brandished a wobbly smile, grabbed her silver clutch, and hurried to the alcove that housed the restrooms. Seconds later, Ray joined her.

"I didn't think we'd be conferring so soon," he whispered.

"We have a problem. Phyllis from the medical examiner's office is here!" Katie hissed.

"Which one is she?" he asked.

"You don't know her?"

He shook his head. "I heard there's been some turnover since I retired. I'm not sure I'd be acquainted with any of the office's current support staff."

"So, she won't recognize you," Katie said.

"No. Why? Will she recognize you?"

"Maybe. I was there yesterday with Seth. That's how I knew her."

He glanced into the room. "What's she wearing?"

"A green silk blouse and black pants."

"All right. She's sitting at my table." He looked at Katie. "That's good. I'll see if I can get her talking about Jamie. Kiss me before you go back. Then when you get back to your table, freshen up your lipstick. That explains us meeting up like this if anyone noticed. We're newlyweds—married April fourth."

"You're really milking this," Katie grated.

"It's for a good cause, right?"

"Yes, it is."

They shared yet another kiss, and Katie was flushed when she went back to the table. As Ray had instructed, she got out her lipstick and compact and reapplied her lipstick.

"I'd know that flush anywhere," Gina said, with a husky laugh. "I believe somebody's getting lucky tonight whether she wins at cards or not."

Blushing, Katie said, "We're still newlyweds—married April 4." She slowed her breathing. "It feels like we're still on our honeymoon."

"How did you meet?" Albert asked.

"I'm an insurance adjuster, and we met when his daughter—now my stepdaughter, although she's not thrilled about that—had a fender-bender."

"Stepkids." Gina rolled her eyes. "Don't get me started."

"How many do you have?" Katie asked.

"Four. Not *all* of them are brats, but the two that are cause as much trouble as they possibly can."

A younger man approached their table with his chips. "Hello. I'm Connor Davis. I'm told this is my table."

"I'm glad of it," Albert said. "Not that I'm anything less than delighted with our female companions, but it's good to have another gentleman at the table."

Katie glanced over at Ray's table. He was already conversing with Phyllis from the medical examiner's office, but he winked at Katie. She was glad he was keeping an eye on her. She was beginning to wonder what she'd gotten herself into.

CHAPTER 16

*A*n older woman, much more casually dressed than Katie took her place at the table. "Hi, everyone, I'm Hazel. Who are you?" They all introduced themselves with Gina giving Katie a sidelong glance. Clearly, she thought Hazel should have spiffed up.

The last player to join them was a guy Katie immediately pegged as a yuppie, judging by his gray three-piece suit with a matching tie. "I'm Greg," he said and didn't bother with any of the niceties, instead signaling for the waitress.

As she took Greg's order for a screwdriver, a distinguished-looking gentleman with silver hair and dressed in a black tux took his place at the dealer's seat. The newcomer patiently waited for the other players to place their drink orders and for the waitress to leave before sitting down.

"Good evening and welcome," he said. "Tonight, we'll be playing five-card stud."

"Five-card stud?" Gina asked. "Nobody plays that game anymore."

"I assure you we do, madam," the dealer said. "We change our weekly game to provide our players more of a challenge. Five-card stud is the original form of the game." He went on to explain the rules of the game for those who were unfamiliar.

"I've only ever played Texas Hold 'Em," Gina grumbled.

"Do you wish to continue with the game?" the dealer asked.

She nodded and looked around to see where the waitress was with her vodka tonic.

Katie wondered which game Jamie might've been playing and with whom. If the game was changed weekly, he wouldn't have been playing five-card stud the previous week. She pondered how to broach the subject of Jamie Siefert and his death.

"We'll begin the game now." The dealer broke open a new deck of cards and shuffled them twice, then distributed the cards around the table. Each player received one face-up card and one face-down card.

The first hand was a yawn. Katie waited as the cards were dealt and, seeing there was no hope of winning, was the first to drop out. The opening ante had only cost her a hundred bucks. Just another four hundred to lose.

Game two wasn't much more interesting, but it was the men who folded, leaving Katie and Gina to toss twenty-dollar chips into the pot until at last Katie called, with more than three hundred in chips before them.

Gina laid her final card on the table. The ace of spades.

Katie had a deuce.

It was the fourth game when Katie's luck changed.

The dealer shuffled and cut the cards, dealing one to each player. Katie's face-up card was the eight of clubs. She peeked at her face-down card and saw that it was the ace of clubs.

In the second round, she got the face-up queen of hearts. Round three brought her the ace of spades.

A pair of aces—which was great. None of the other players appeared to have anything that would beat her...at least, not yet.

Her last card was dealt face down. It was the eight of spades. She increased her bid accordingly, feeling confident no one at the table could beat two pair, aces high. Gina and Connor folded, but Albert, Greg, and Hazel hung in there until the end.

When the players flipped all their cards face up, the dealer pronounced Katie the winner "with the Dead Man's Hand."

"The what?" she asked.

"The Dead Man's Hand," he said. "Haven't you heard of it?" He explained the legend that Wild Bill Hickok was holding two pair —aces and eights—clubs and spades when he was murdered. "There has been a lot of speculation as to the identity of the fifth card, but nothing definitive." He smiled. "So, young lady, either you're very lucky...or you're doomed."

Everyone laughed, but Katie had a bad feeling in the pit of her stomach. What were the odds of her drawing that hand? Did the dealer cheat somehow to give her that hand to issue her a warning? Maybe he'd been the dealer for Jamie the week before and knew Katie was the owner of Tealicious. Anything was possible.

Or maybe she was just paranoid.

As the dealer shuffled the cards for the next hand, Katie asked, "Did any of you hear about the guy who died on Victoria Square last week? My husband knew him, and that's how we found out about this game. Apparently, he played here last week."

"Jamie Seifert," Gina said. "Yeah, I heard about his death on TV. The health department should shut that tea shop down."

Katie took a sip of her white wine to tamp down her annoyance before she spoke. "I heard he was poisoned, but it would have had to have been a very fast-acting poison for him to have ingested it at the tea shop. Plus, none of the other patrons got sick."

"Are you some sort of detective or something?" Albert asked.

Katie froze. "Uh, no, but a friend and I lunched at that tea shop one day last week, and I've been feeling antsy ever since," she said.

"I can imagine," Gina said.

"I remember Jamie," Connor said. "He won a bundle last week."

Katie's eyes widened and her gut tightened, hoping she hadn't just given herself away.

"Fat lot of good winning did him," Greg said. "The poor guy's luck definitely ran out."

~

THREE NERVE-WRACKING HOURS LATER, the evening came to an end. Katie carried an ungodly amount of chips in a canvas bag provided by the dealer to the receptionist to cash them in.

The cool blonde gave her a warm smile. "It appears Lady Luck was with you this evening, Mrs. Ferrell."

"She certainly was," Katie said, trying to keep her expression bland. She'd won just over twenty-one *thousand* dollars. Though she was over the moon, there was no way she wanted to draw additional attention to herself. Even considering the amount the governor would take for the tax payment, she'd have enough to pay Seth back for the buy-in, fix the floor at Artisans Alley, and buy into the warehouse. She still didn't have any idea who might've killed Jamie, but she'd met several people who had played poker with him and probably more than once. She looked forward to comparing notes with Ray.

Then it occurred to her: Where *was* Ray?

Turning back to the ballroom, she zeroed in on his table. He sat slumped in his chair with a half-empty glass of neat bourbon in his right hand, and it was obviously not his first drink of the evening. He faced Phyllis, as though enraptured by her every word. Either that or he was in a stupor.

Unwilling to risk Phyllis recognizing her, Katie headed for the ladies' room to "freshen up," a term which in this instance meant "wait for Phyllis to leave."

Gina entered as Katie sat in front of an antique vanity reapplying her lipstick. "Hey, congrats tonight."

"And to you, too," Katie said. "You didn't do too badly yourself."

Opening her purse, she smiled at Katie in the mirror. "Up five grand. I'd say we did much better than our husbands."

Katie groaned. "How much is Ray—" Quickly correcting her mistake, she added "—my ray of sunshine down?"

Gina smirked. "I don't know, but he's soused to the gills. Will he be angry that you won and he didn't?"

"He shouldn't be." She frowned. "Will your husband be angry with you?"

"Oh, yeah, but I'll buy him dinner at his favorite restaurant tomorrow night and he'll get over it." Gina opened her purse and withdrew a business card, handing it to Katie. "I enjoyed chatting with you tonight. Give me a call sometime, and we'll have lunch."

"Will do." Katie dropped the card into her clutch. "I'd better get out there and get Nick before he makes a bigger fool of himself than he already has."

Laughing again, Gina said, "Ugh, sounds like the honeymoon is over."

"At least for tonight," Katie agreed. "I hate it when he drinks."

"I hate it when Tony drinks, too. *And* when he loses." She applied her lipstick. "When he drinks and wins, he's fine. When he drinks and loses, he's a total jerk. He throws around blame and acts like he wants to kill somebody."

Katie raised an eyebrow. Were Gina's words an indictment?

She forced a smile. "Hope to see you again soon," Katie said and left the room. Once outside, she was relieved to see that Phyllis had gone. Ray was staggering around, probably looking for her.

Spotting her, he headed her way, arms outstretched. "Wifey! Come give us a kiss."

"I'm not giving you anything but a ride home." Furious with him, she held out her hand. "Keys, please."

He dug in his pocket and produced the keys. "You're bootiful when you're angry."

"Let's go." She took his arm and propelled him past the amused staff and out into the parking lot.

"C'mon." He leaned closer, his bourbon breath turning her stomach. "You know you wanna give me a little kiss."

Unlocking the SUV, she said, "Get in the car. Now!"

"Why are you so mad?" He snickered. "Oh, well. We gonna have make-up sex?"

"I'm going to *kill* you if you don't get into the car right this minute," she said angrily.

Still chuckling, he swayed over to the passenger side of the SUV and hauled himself into the vehicle. Katie got into the driver's side, adjusted the seat, put on her seat belt, and made Ray do likewise.

"Yes, Mother," he said.

She kicked off her shoes in order to drive, tossing them onto the passenger side floor. She started the engine and pulled out of the parking lot.

"Issa coast clear?" Ray asked. "How you think we did, Katie? Kelly? Katie Kelly? Kelly Katie? Wifey? Love of my lifey?" He cackled.

It took all of Katie's willpower not to stop the car and strangle him on the spot. "Don't talk to me."

"Ever?" He grabbed her right hand and kissed it. "I *have* to talk to you. You're my best friend."

"Don't touch me while I'm driving. Do you want to get us killed?"

"I'd never hurt you, Katie," Ray simpered.

"Why did you drink so much?" she demanded. "We were at that game to get information on who might've killed Jamie."

"I know." He paused. "So, I can talk to you now?"

"If you speak to me sensibly, you can. Do you think you can do that?"

"Maybe. No promises."

Katie let out an exasperated breath. "How did you do poker-wise?"

"I lost." He blew out a hundred-proof breath. "Including Seth's buy-in money, I lost two thousand dollars. Oh my God—how am I gonna pay Sophie's tuition in January?"

She braked at a traffic light. "I'll give it back to you," she grated.

"You will?" he asked, sounding hopeful. He unbuckled his seat belt and slid close enough to kiss her cheek. "You're the best wife ever."

"Get back in your seat and buckle that seat belt. Now!"

"Yes, dear."

Katie's hands tightened on the wheel, wishing she could fly the car across the county, instead of having to drive for at least another twenty minutes. How could Ray have been so undisciplined? Had he been so irresponsible while working vice? What if he'd blown his cover—their covers?

An annoying sound reverberated through the car. Ray was snoring.

Katie turned onto the expressway ramp, grateful there'd be no more conversation during the rest of the journey.

By the time they arrived at Ray's house, her fury had dissipated, and she was merely super annoyed. She put the SUV in park, yanked the keys from the ignition, and wondered which one opened the front door. All the lights in the house were off, making her feel sure Ray's daughters were asleep, or else she'd toot the horn to get some help.

Still barefoot, she got out of the vehicle, went to the front door, and tried various keys until one worked. Leaving the door ajar, she went back to the SUV, opened the passenger door, and woke Ray.

Blinking and smacking his lips, he said, "Oh, hey, wife."

"Hey, yourself. Let's get you inside."

He waggled his eyebrows. "Yep. Let's get inside so you can have your way with me, little minx. You were all over me tonight."

"Don't start with me," she warned and supported him as they went inside, and then she closed the door behind them and flicked on a light. "What little—" She searched for the proper word. "—affection we showed each other this evening was just that—*show*."

"Oh, no it wasn't." He turned and pulled her into his arms. "You wanted me. Bad. I could tell."

She tried to push him away, but he was stronger than he looked. "Go to bed, and sleep it off, Ray."

"Come to bed with me," he whispered. "After all, you're my wife." He nuzzled her neck.

"*What?!*"

The shriek came from the stairwell.

"Now look what you've done," Katie hissed, this time escaping his embrace.

"I'm proud to call you my wife," he said. "Daughters! Come meet your new stepmother!"

Dressed in a faded, oversized T-shirt featuring Pikachu, Sasha had already stormed into the living room, and Sadie, likewise attired, wasn't far behind. "You're *married?*" she shrieked.

"No, we're not," Katie said.

"Yep." Ray grinned stupidly and spread his arms. "Come give your stepmom a big welcome-to-the family hug."

"How *could* you?" Sadie demanded, before bursting into tears and running back up the stairs.

"We aren't married," Katie said calmly. "Your dad has had a little too much to drink. Now, would you please help—?"

"Why are you dressed like a hooker?" Sasha demanded, her

mouth trembling and tears welling in her eyes. "Where have you been? And where are your *shoes?*"

Katie felt like crying as well. "Please. It's a long story. Help me get your dad's shoes off and get him to his bed so he can sleep it off. He'll explain everything tomorrow morning."

"I hate you!" Sasha screamed and fled the room.

With a sigh, Katie looked at Ray and nodded toward the couch. "Lie down."

At last, he decided to cooperate. He sank onto the cushions and flopped over. Katie removed his shoes and covered him with the afghan that had been on the back of the couch. She looked down at him and saw that he was pursing his lips for a kiss.

Fat chance of that happening!

Knowing he was going to feel like crap the next day—and that was even before his daughters started yelling at him—she turned away in disgust.

Somehow, she managed to leave the house without slamming the front door.

CHAPTER 17

*T*ealicious had never looked so inviting. The walls positively sparkled, and all the furniture, mirrors, and picture frames seemed to have been gilded. It was the night of the open house, and Katie was surrounded by luminaries. George and Amal Clooney were congratulating her on the shop when her phone rang. She didn't have her phone with her. Was it George's phone? Or Amal's? It kept ringing. And ringing. And ringing. Until, at last, George and Amal faded, and Katie realized she'd been dreaming and that the ringing phone was from the real world.

She ran her hand down her face as she rolled over and groped for her phone. Her alarm hadn't even gone off yet. She neglected to look at the caller ID but thought there had better be an emergency. "Hello."

"You've got our dad's car, and we need a ride to school," Sasha Davenport said icily.

"What? Oh, sure," Katie said. "I'll be there right away." She ended the call and looked at the clock, wondering why the girl would call so early. *Where is their school? Pennsylvania?*

After taking a quick shower and feeding the cats, Katie drove to the Davenport home in her own car. Beeping the horn in the driveway, she was surprised when Ray came outside with his daughters.

He obviously hadn't been out of the shower for long because what hair he had left on his balding pate was dripping water onto his shirt collar. He hadn't shaved, and his eyes were bloodshot. Taking a pair of sunglasses from his shirt pocket, he put them on before opening the passenger door.

Eyes downcast, Sasha and Sadie climbed into the back seat of Katie's car as their father slumped onto the passenger seat.

"One of you girls tell Katie how to get to your school," he said before turning to their chauffeur. "Thanks for doing this."

"No problem," Katie grated and backed out of the driveway. Sadie told her to turn right at the end of the street.

It was completely quiet in the car during the drive to school except for Sadie's terse directions. Katie guessed Ray had instructed his daughters to be civil to her since she was doing them a favor. She could understand their anger. They'd lost their mother only two years before and the wound was still raw. That their father would tease them with the idea he'd married a woman they despised was just plain mean. She hadn't thought of Ray as mean for quite some time.

Joining the other vehicles in the drop-off line felt weird to her, but Katie didn't voice her discomfort. Ray glowered when the girls slammed their doors upon getting out of the car without even a token expression of gratitude, but he didn't say anything.

Driving away from the school, Katie asked, "How are you feeling?"

He groaned. "Exactly the way I deserve to feel. Could we please go back to silence until around lunchtime?"

Without another word, Katie opened her purse and handed him an envelope containing his keys and the money she'd promised him. He didn't even open it.

Katie shifted the car back into drive and headed for Victoria

Square. Upon their arrival at Tealicious's parking lot, they got out of the vehicle and went their separate ways without a word. So much for their blissful married life.

Katie entered the building and headed to the kitchen to speak with Brad, noticing a couple of take-out orders already tacked above the pick-up window. Although not as many as usual, Brad was optimistic.

"See?" he whispered to her. "It's turning around."

She nodded. "Slowly but surely. Hopefully, tomorrow's open house will be the trick we need to truly right the ship."

"I think so. Come taste the mini quiches I'm testing. I'll serve your favorites."

The savory aroma made her realize how hungry she was. She sampled a prosciutto-and-Swiss quiche. "That's wonderful."

"Thanks. How'd the game go last night?"

"I won, and pretty big," she said. "But I wasn't very successful as far as the investigation into Jamie's death goes."

"I'll make some tea and you can tell me all about it."

Just as the kettle boiled, Nick arrived.

"Hey, there! How'd it go last night?" he asked.

"I was just getting ready to tell Brad all about it."

"Why don't we discuss it in the dining room where we'll be more comfortable," Brad suggested as Katie took over making the tea and he put an assortment of quiches on a large tray and added plates, cups, and napkins.

Once seated, Katie opened the conversation by telling Nick about her winning hands the previous evening.

He laughed. "Thank goodness! Any wife of *Nick Ferrell* had better do the name proud. And speaking of *Nick*, how did Ray fare?"

"He lost. And he got falling-down drunk," she groused before thanking Brad for the cup of tea he placed in front of her. "I'm so angry with Ray I can barely stand it. I gave him back what he lost out of my winnings. But the game and whether either of us won or lost wasn't the purpose of our attending the event. We were there to gather evidence about Jamie's evening there last week and to try to determine who might've poisoned him."

"And how did *that* go?" Nick asked.

"I did my best, but I still feel as though I failed. And I can only assume Ray's investigation sank to the bottom of a glass of bourbon as he's yet to tell me what he came up with—if anything."

"Don't be so hasty in writing off the evening as far as the investigation went," Brad said. "Tell us what you observed."

"My big winner of the night was something the dealer referred to as the Dead Man's Hand," she said.

"You got black aces and eights?" Nick asked. "No way!"

"Yes, way. And after the dealer told us all the story of the hand being held by Wild Bill Hickok as he was gunned down, he said I was either lucky or doomed." She sipped her tea. "I couldn't help but wonder if he might've recognized me and dealt me the cards on purpose."

"You believe he cheated to give you the cards as a warning?" Brad asked.

She nodded. "But if he was controlling the hands every time, why would he let me win?"

"Perhaps he wasn't controlling the hands every time," Nick said. "Some dealers set a newcomer up to win in order to build his or her confidence. If you lose right away, you're more likely to hedge your bets and quit once your buy-in is spent."

"Still, he gave her the Dead Man's Hand." Brad plucked a spinach quiche from the platter. "That—if intentional—had to have meant *something*."

"True." Nick appeared to mull the situation over as he finished off his tea and refilled the cup. "I wish I'd gone last night. I think I could've gotten a better read on the room than you or Ray."

"You had a prior obligation and it was last minute," Katie reminded him. "Besides, I think I did okay. There was a woman at my table named Gina. She seemed nice and even gave me her card and suggested we have lunch sometime. But in the ladies' room after the game, she asked me if my husband would get angry because I won and he didn't."

"How did she know Ray lost?" Nick asked. "Did they speak?"

"I don't think so. She probably inferred the information by observing the amount of bourbon he consumed. She said she thought we'd both done better than our husbands." Katie rubbed her forehead. "Anyway, I told her I doubted he'd be upset and asked if her husband would be angry with her. She said he would but that she'd take him to his favorite restaurant, and he'd get over it. But if he'd get ticked off at his wife for beating him, how much angrier would he be at a stranger who won money directly from him?"

"True," Brad said, "but Jamie was poisoned. Do you really think some guy would carry poison around in his pocket to get revenge on anyone who'd beat him at a game of cards?"

Nick spread his hands. "Some might. Still, poison is a stretch. You'd think the guy would carry a knife or a gun or something else with the intention of threatening, not actually killing."

"What was Gina's last name?" Brad asked.

"I don't know, but her husband's name was Tony. I left her card in the silver clutch upstairs. Do you want me to get it?"

"Nah, you have a lot to do today. I was simply curious." Brad polished off another mini spinach quiche.

"But take her up on that lunch date," Nick said, "and soon. She might be more talkative about Jamie and the night he won all that cash."

"Okay." Katie sighed.

"Something wrong?" Nick asked.

"Well…we ran into one of Jamie's co-workers."

"What?" Nick wailed.

"Or, at least, Ray did. I don't think she recognized me dressed as hooker Barbie—"

"Hey!" Nick protested. "That's an insult to Margo and me for dolling you up."

"That's apparently the impression I gave Ray's daughters," she deadpanned.

Brad winced.

"But at least we now know where Jamie learned about the game," she remarked.

"Or did *she* learn about it from him?" Brad asked.

Katie shrugged. "Ray might know. And if his hangover ever abates, he might just tell us."

KATIE ALMOST DID AN ABOUT-FACE when she saw Andy waiting for her in Artisans Alley's vendors' lounge. She could tell he was waiting for her because he sat alone at the vintage Formica-and-chrome table drinking a cup of coffee.

"What are you doing here?" she asked, trying not to sound too bitchy.

"I left about a dozen messages on your phone last night." He stood and walked closer. "Didn't you get them?"

"No. I turned my phone off at the game, and I didn't check my messages when I got home." She wasn't about to invite him into her office to talk. If she did, everyone—including even Andy—would think it was a sign they were getting back together. But anyone coming into the lounge would be privy to their conversation. So be it.

"Why'd you call? What was so important?"

"You, Sunshine," he said. "I wanted to make sure you were all right."

"I was fine. I attended a poker game, not five-finger filet or Russian roulette."

His jaw tightened. "You went to a poker game where one of

the players ended up dead less than a week later. I feel justified in being concerned."

"Well, as you can see, I'm in tip-top shape. Thanks for checking in on me." She gave him a smug smile. "As a matter of fact, I got lucky."

His eyes grew wide with anger. "Did Davenport—?"

Katie knew Andy was no longer talking about cards. Before she could come up with a clever retort, Ray walked into the vendors' lounge carrying the shoes she'd worn the night before.

Holding them up by their skinny straps, he asked, "Missing something?"

"Yes." Katie took the shoes. "I might need those later—I think there's a light bulb out in the ladies' room."

"Ha, ha," Ray said. "Got a minute to talk?"

"Sure." She turned to Andy. "Thanks again for your concern."

"But—"

She left him standing in the vendors' lounge as she and Ray entered her office.

And closed the door.

Katie put the strappy stilettos into her bottom desk drawer. "Thanks for returning these. I have no idea how much I owe Margo for them."

"Eh, they're not my size. Plus, I don't know what I'd wear them with even if they were."

"I thought you weren't up to talking until lunchtime."

"The aspirin kicked in sooner than I'd expected it to." He sighed and looked embarrassed—and rightly so. "I want to apologize for acting like a sore-headed bear this morning."

"I'm guessing you'd already been harshly interrogated, tried, and sentenced by the time I saw you."

He nodded. "I'd have been executed, too, if they didn't need me as a taxi service and to pay all their bills."

"They don't need me," Katie said flatly. "Should I sleep with one eye open?"

"It probably wouldn't hurt." He ran a hand over his scruffy cheek. "Thank you for the money. I *will* pay you back."

"Not necessary. I won that money, so I'm not out anything." When she spoke again, her voice had an edge to it. "Besides, we were there to investigate Jamie's death. You shouldn't have to suffer a loss for doing Seth a favor."

"Despite what you probably think, I *did* investigate," Ray said.

"Do you remember how any of your investigative conversations went last night?"

"I remember every conversation I had last night." He gave her a hard stare. "I wasn't *that* drunk."

She snorted. "Oh, yes, you were. I had to practically carry you into your house."

He leaned forward. "Where you then settled me onto my couch and covered me with an afghan before you left."

"I would have done that for a homeless person on the street." She crossed her arms over her chest. "So, did you learn anything at the poker club?"

"Phyllis was a good source of information," he said. "I didn't even have to draw her out. When we went around the table introducing ourselves, she told us her name, where she worked, and that she'd lost a dear friend this week. And she added, 'Well, all of you probably knew him, too. He was a regular here.'"

"A regular? If he was, Seth didn't seem to know about it. Did the other players at your table acknowledge knowing Jamie?"

"Two of them did—Helen Ackerman and Clint Billings. Billings said he played at Jamie's table last week and couldn't believe what a stroke of luck the guy had."

Katie took a peppermint from the jar on her desk. She offered Ray one, but he declined. "Did it appear that this Billings thought Jamie was cheating or something?"

"No. Billings sounded more incredulous than suspicious. Helen hadn't been at Jamie's table last week, but she remembered him as being handsome and nice. She thought he might be a good match for her daughter." He inclined his head. "I didn't tell her he wouldn't have been interested."

"And what else did Phyllis say?" Katie asked.

"Naturally, being a retired banker from Connecticut and playing my first game at that event, I knew nothing about Jamie Seifert." He placed a hand on his chest. "Why, no, I didn't read about his death in the local newspaper. What in the world happened to the young man?"

Katie rolled her eyes at Ray's affected gestures and speech. "Please, just give me the gist of what she said."

"Very well. I'll strip away all the drama. Clearly, you don't live with teenage girls. Phyllis told me Jamie was a talented young medical examiner's assistant working under Dr. William Elliott. When I asked if she and Jamie had been friends, she said everyone at the office loved him. And then she amended that with an *almost.*"

"I'm guessing you jumped all over that *almost.*"

Grinning, he said, "You know I did. I ever-so-innocently asked if her office had one of *those people* who didn't like anyone. She said, 'Oh, no. The person who didn't like Jamie was Tom, and he was kind to everyone else.' She believed Tom was angry with Jamie because he got the job when Tom had recommended his friend for the position."

"Who's Tom? Is he someone who works at the M.E.'s office?"

Ray shrugged. "Apparently. I've never heard of him, but again, they have a lot of turnover."

"Still, that doesn't make sense." She frowned. "Not having your friend get a job should make you angry at the hiring manager rather than the person hired for the position. Maybe there's more to this Tom situation than Phyllis either revealed or realized. I'll ask Seth about it." She glanced at the clock. "He's probably apoplectic about now."

"Why?"

"I turned off my phone and haven't checked my messages, which was why Andy was here checking up on me."

"Is that what he was doing?" Ray asked with some suspicion.

"So he said."

"Let me know what you find out. By the way, how much did you win last night?"

"Over twenty grand," she said.

Ray actually did a double-take. "Wow. You *are* a good poker player."

"I'm good at a lot of things, Ray," she said matter-of-factly.

"Yeah, I noticed. I—I'd better get back to Wood U." He reached for the door handle but didn't turn it. Instead, he pivoted. "I'm, uh, sorry I was such a lecherous jerk last night."

Katie studied his contrite expression. "You ought to be," she said sternly. "What were you thinking, Ray? That you were back in the saddle? Who was that cocky idiot who nearly blew our covers? Not the man I've come to respect and admire."

"I'm sorry I disappointed you, Katie. I promise it will never happen again."

"No, it won't. I think we need to put an end to this co-dependent relationship we've had for the past few months. I was wrong to throw you at Carol and then become jealous of your budding relationship with her." She sighed. "You belong with someone like her—someone closer to your age and who you have more in common with. One thing, though, based on your performance last night, I don't think you should return to law enforcement— at least, not in vice. You might've been a terrific undercover officer in your day, but you aren't anymore."

"Tell me how you *really* feel, Katie."

Her gaze didn't waver. "I just did."

Ray swallowed hard, nodded, and slunk from her office, closing the door behind him.

CHAPTER 18

atie stared at her blank computer monitor. She hadn't had enough sleep or nearly enough coffee that day, but she needed to call Seth and let him know what had happened. Unfortunately, her plan to call Seth was thwarted by the arrival of Maddie Lyndel. The voluptuous redhead had always been as sweet as the day was long; but since she was an upstairs vendor, Katie dreaded to hear what the woman had to say today.

"Good morning." Maddie smiled sweetly and perched on the chair beside Katie's desk. "I heard about your friend Seth's partner. I'm so very sorry...and that he died in front of Tealicious, too. How awful for you."

"Thanks, Maddie." Katie took a deep breath. "Is everything okay?"

"Oh, sure. I just wanted to ask you where I should set up. Vance told us all to set up in either the lobby or the vendors' lounge, but I don't want to be in anyone's way."

Beneath her desk, Katie clenched her fists. "Vance should have worked up placement assignments before he asked everyone to move. I'll take care of this right away."

"Okay. Thanks, Katie." Maddie stood but didn't move toward the door. "I hope I didn't speak out of line."

"You certainly didn't." She managed a smile at the soap-maker. "I'll make sure you have a primo spot."

After Maddie left, Katie texted Vance, asking him to come to her office immediately. She wasn't sure she could speak civilly to him just yet.

His answer was brief. *Coming.*

Katie moved from her desk chair to stand beside her file cabinet, determined not to let him tower over her for the upcoming conversation.

As he approached her office, Katie could tell he sported an attitude, and she wasn't going to allow him to own the discussion.

"I'm pretty busy, Katie," he said in lieu of a greeting. "What do you need?"

"I need you to tell every upstairs vendor not to move their inventory until they have their floor assignments, and then I want to see you in my office."

"I have the situation under control, and—"

"No, you don't," she interrupted.

"Fine."

"Why didn't you develop vendor assignments before telling our upstairs vendors they were being moved for a few days?" she asked.

"I figured if they chose their own spots, they'd be more amenable to moving." He lifted his chin as though to say, *so there.*

"What you didn't stop to consider is the fact that if they choose their own spots, they'll likely want the *same* spots and fight over them like a bunch of spoiled brats," she said.

"I don't care to think of our vendors as juveniles. They're mature enough to make reasonable decisions."

"Oh, really?" She anchored her hands to her hips. "Which ones are getting the prime spots in the lobby and who's going to be buried in the no-traffic vendors' lounge?"

"I-I... Who knows? But I'm sure they'll come to an agreement."

"It's going to be Maddie Lyndel," Katie said. "I don't care where you put everyone else, but she gets prime real estate in the lobby."

"T-then it'll look l-like we're p-playing favorites!" he sputtered.

"We are, in Maddie's case."

"And what if that causes hard feelings?"

Katie leveled an icy glare at him. "Vance, these vendors are getting free rent while we're renovating. They're going to set up where you tell them to set up; and if they aren't happy with their assigned spaces, they can pack up and go home. Prepare the assignment sheet and have it to me tomorrow so the vendors can move after Artisans Alley closes and be ready for the weekend."

The muscle working in his jaw told her Vance was grinding his teeth, but he didn't say anything. He merely turned and stormed out of her office, leaving the door open.

She ventured into the vendors' lounge to get more coffee. Her head was beginning to ache. She'd hoped making Vance her assistant manager would give her fewer problems to deal with. So far, it had only led to more.

It took two cups of coffee to soothe Katie's ragged nerves. She felt like the proverbial bad guy first after her verbal exchange with Ray, and then with Vance—but in the latter's case, she was the boss. If she was a man, Vance probably would have accepted her orders without comment. That she was a woman with firm opinions made her a bitch. Well, so be it. Bottom line, it was she not he, who was responsible for Artisans Alley.

At last, Katie felt capable of making her call to Seth.

"I've been on pins and needles all morning," he told her. "How'd it go?"

"Nothing earth-shattering happened, but I'd rather tell you about the evening in person."

"I'm at my office right now. Why don't I meet you at Tealicious for lunch?"

"That would be great," Katie said. "I'll call Nick to see if he and Don would like to join us."

"All right. See you shortly."

After ending the call with Seth, Katie called Nick and asked if he and Don were free.

"I am, but Don is busy in the office today," Nick said.

"Let's go ahead and meet at Tealicious. That will give us just over half an hour to talk before Seth gets there."

"Uh-oh." Nick sounded wary. "What's up?"

"That's what I've been wondering for almost a week," Katie said. "You dropped a bombshell at the poker game last Friday night but haven't mentioned it since."

"Oh…that," he said contritely. "Okay, I'll meet you in a few minutes."

Not many customers had arrived for lunch or tea, so Katie snagged her favorite table which overlooked Victoria Square's parking lot. She chose the seat facing west, though. For some reason, she didn't feel like taking in Ray's Wood U gift shop. She ordered a pot of tea and asked for three settings. Nick arrived minutes later, looking rather anxious.

Katie poured him some tea from the pot on the table. "Okay, spill."

He sat, picked up the teacup, and inhaled the aroma of the liquid inside it. "I want to be a dad so badly. I want to do for some kid what my parents never did for me."

Katie knew that Nick's parents had more or less disowned him when he outed himself as a young man. It was his Aunt Sally who'd taken him in and loved him unconditionally. Not that any child they fostered or adopted would be gay. Nick had a big heart. It was no wonder he wanted to share that kind of love with a child who needed security.

"Don doesn't think it would be feasible to raise a child in a B&B," Nick continued. "You saw how quickly he shut me down when I started to tell you and Seth we were considering becoming foster parents."

"Well, you wouldn't *have* to raise the child at Sassy Sally's," she said. "You could get a small house or condo nearby."

"I suggested that. I even told Don that if we moved out, we could renovate the mansion to turn our living quarters into additional rooms." He spread his hands. "More rooms equal more profit."

"But he doesn't want to leave," Katie said and sipped her tea.

"No, he doesn't. He says *I'm* the workaholic, but lately, I have a terrible time getting him to leave Sassy Sally's for anything short of a medical emergency." He shook his head. "I adore running the B&B—you know I do—but I don't want that to be the only important thing in our lives. I don't want it to *be* our lives."

Katie could understand that. Her businesses had filled the void left by her late husband. But, unlike Nick, she wasn't sure she wanted anything more. She enjoyed her independence and freedom.

"I told Don maybe we could foster at first," Nick continued. "And then if it doesn't work out, the boy or girl will be able to find another family. But if we foster the child and fall in love with him or her—and vice versa—we could adopt. I know Don loves kids as much as I do. I don't know why he's so reluctant to take the chance."

"You have to admit, adopting a child is a life-changing decision. And it's forever. I'm guessing Don is scared. I certainly would be."

"But scary can be exhilarating. I was scared when we bought

Sassy Sally's but look what a rousing success that turned out to be."

Katie squeezed his hand. "I'm here for you, no matter what you decide. I'd make a terrific auntie, you know."

He smiled. "Yeah, you would."

Seth's car pulled up outside and they watched as he exited the vehicle and entered the tea room.

"Hey, guys," he said as he took the seat beside Katie. "So?"

"First, I'd like to return this to you," Katie said and returned his buy-in money. It only took a few minutes to provide her friends with an overview of the evening's events.

"You won more than twenty grand?" Seth asked with awe.

Nick exhaled on his fingernails and brushed them against his shirt. "It was playing with Don and me that made her a poker wunderkind," he said with no modesty at all.

"What are you going to do with that windfall?"

"Pay for expensive repairs to the Alley," she said, pouring Seth's tea. "And contribute to the cost of the warehouse behind Victoria Square."

Seth winced. "Oh yeah—I need to get right on that contract. Tell us more."

Katie didn't want them to know Ray got drunk "on the job," so she bypassed that part of the story and instead told them about Ray's conversation with Phyllis.

"Who's Tom?" she asked, topping up her cup.

Shrugging, Seth answered, "Just some guy at the medical examiner's office. I think he works in data entry. Why?"

"Phyllis said Tom was the only guy at the M.E.'s office who didn't like Jamie. Were you aware of any problems between the two of them?" Katie asked.

"No, Jamie never mentioned anything, but I'll look through his things again to see if Jamie ever made any note of bad behavior on Tom's part." He added a packet of sweetener to his tea. "If Tom was harassing Jamie, Jamie would have logged it in case he needed to file a report with human resources."

"I thought everyone at the office got along well with Jamie," Nick said. "What was this guy's problem?"

"According to Phyllis, Jamie got the job Tom wanted for a friend of his." Katie frowned. "Which doesn't make sense to me. Why be angry and resentful toward Jamie rather than the hiring manager?"

"Did Phyllis find out about the poker game from Jamie?" Nick asked.

"I suppose so," Katie said. "Or maybe he found out about it from her. She spoke as though he was a regular." She hazarded a glance at Seth, who was looking into his teacup as though it held the answers he sought.

"How did I not know what he was doing?" he asked. "I don't even know how long or how often Jamie had been playing poker with these people. I was busy with my practice, he was busy at work…."

"He wasn't trying to shut you out," Nick said. "I know he wasn't. He hid the poker games from you because he wanted to make this grand gesture to show you how much he loved you."

"Yeah." Seth shrugged. "I guess so." Seth glanced down at the cup of tea he hadn't touched. "Look, I'm sorry, but I've lost my appetite. I'm going to head back to my office. I'll see you both later."

Nick sighed as he watched Seth leave the tea shop. "I wish there was something I could do to help him feel better."

"Me, too."

He stood. "I'd better get back to Sassy Sally's."

"You're abandoning me to a lonely lunch?" Katie asked.

"Go upstairs and spend the time with your cats. I'm sure they wouldn't complain."

No, they wouldn't.

Katie stood and hugged her friend. "I'm sure everything will work out with Don and the fostering. Let me know if there's any way I can help."

"Thanks. See you tomorrow at Jamie's funeral?"

"Of course," she said.

Tomorrow was going to be a huge day. Jamie's funeral in the morning and the open house in the evening. Katie wasn't sure she was ready for it. And she still had the rest of the day to get through.

*a*s always, Nick had been right. Mason and Della were
thrilled with a daytime visit from their cat mom, and
even more so when she shared a little of the tuna from her sandwich with them. They were both settling down for their afternoon nap when Katie headed out the door and off to Artisans
Alley. She was just about to tackle some book work when Margo
dropped in.

"I hope I'm not disturbing you."

"I always have time for you, Margo," Katie said, putting her
computer to sleep. "What's up?"

Margo sighed. "I know you're probably sick of me asking, but
can we go upstairs and visit Chad's Pad? I just feel so close to him
when I'm there."

Of course, they could. Chad had been Margo's only child.
Much as she missed her late husband, Katie couldn't fathom the
depths of Margo's loss.

Katie rose from her chair and grabbed her keys. "Let's go." She
led her former mother-in-law up to the second floor, ignoring
the dirty looks some of the vendors gave her as they packed up

their merchandise in order to temporarily move downstairs. She unlocked the door, and she and Margo went inside.

Katie sank onto the narrow cot still covered with a Hudson Bay blanket as Margo flipped through the stacked, framed paintings and canvases, lovingly drinking in her late son's work.

"Nick told me you cleaned up at the poker table last night," Margo said. "Good on you."

"I hope I made enough to fix the floor, chip in to buy into the warehouse the merchant partnership is considering, and pay for the open house tomorrow evening."

Margo shook her head. "As a partner in Tealicious, I'll take care of the open house. I have as much to lose as you do if the tea shop goes under."

"That's very generous of you. Thank you," Katie said. "Is there anything you need for me to do?"

"Just show up and pray." She took a seat on the cot beside Katie. "I left flyers with all the vendors on the Square."

"Even Nona Fiske?"

Margo smiled. "Even Nona. She'll be there with bells on. They might be really small bells with broken clackers, but she'll be there."

They shared a laugh.

After a moment, Katie said, "I'd like to have had the contractor who renovated Tealicious fix the floor if he isn't backlogged and if Vance and I hadn't already fought so many battles over it."

"Vance and Ray will get it done. Just be patient." The older woman folded her hands in her lap. "As for Vance, it's vital your employees know they're valued and heard, but they must never forget that *you* are their employer." She stood. "Thank you for letting me visit, but now we should both get back to work."

"Yes, we should."

Placing a hand on Katie's shoulder, Margo said, "I'm proud of the businesswoman you've become. Chad would be as well."

Thinking back on her last conversation with Vance, Katie wasn't so sure.

Determined to have a productive remainder of the day, Katie returned to her office. She composed an email to the merchant partnership, including Moonbeam, instructing the partners to let Seth know if they were still interested in buying the abandoned warehouse. She reminded them that time was of the essence if they wanted to make an offer before another buyer swooped in and obtained the property.

Remembering Sue Sweeney's hope that her niece could have a rent-free place to operate her business if the partnership bought the warehouse, she included a reminder that their buying the building would entail turning it into a profitable enterprise for all the partners. She requested their ideas and suggestions, and she copied Seth on the email before sending it.

Katie dropped her head into her hands, wondering for the hundredth—thousandth?—time how she always managed to get in over her head. She ran Artisans Alley. She was president of the Merchants Association. After making Artisans Alley a successful venture, she opened Tealicious with Margo. The tea shop was barely up and running when she encouraged a group of Victoria Square merchants to form a partnership and buy the vacant building that currently housed The Flower Child. And now the partnership had designs on another property—with Katie leading the charge.

She couldn't help but wonder if she hadn't just become not only a workaholic, but a megalomaniac. While work wasn't the *only* thing of value in her life, it often took precedent over everything else. She considered her failed—disastrous—relationship with Andy and how only hours ago she'd quashed any thoughts of a relationship with Ray. Would she ever meet anyone with whom she'd want to share her life? Did she even want to? Maybe her businesses, her friends, and her cats were enough.

Either way, she had too much to think about to get lost in

daydreams. No fairy godmother was going to come to turn the tea shop into the bustling establishment it once was. But if this Cinderella was willing to roll up her sleeves and work—and she certainly was—then perhaps the following evening would be the beginning of the reboot Tealicious so desperately needed.

She pushed away from her desk, deciding to go on home and choose her outfits for Jamie's funeral the next day and the open house tomorrow that night. She packed up her things, locked the office door, and left through the back exit.

Walking across the Square toward her apartment, she became vaguely aware of a car slowing near her. She assumed the driver was searching for a parking spot until he shouted at her.

"Kelly! Kelly Ferrell!"

Turning in surprise, she recognized the driver. "Connor!" He'd been seated at her table at the poker tournament. If memory served, he didn't do too badly. But now he was *here*...where she wasn't Kelly Ferrell, but Katie Bonner. "Uh, uh...what brings you to Victoria Square?"

Her mind raced. She couldn't go home now. Nor could she visit any of the other stores. Her ruse would be exposed. Her only option was to walk to Sassy Sally's and hope Connor wasn't planning to go to Wood U.

"—Gilda's Gift Baskets," he was saying. "I have a friend in the hospital who adores Gilda's arrangements."

"I'm sorry to hear your friend is ill," Katie said.

"Thanks. Luckily, she's expected to make a full recovery. What about you?"

Purposefully mistaking his meaning and using humor to deflect, she said, "Oh, I think I've nearly made a full recovery from last night."

Connor laughed. "I mean, what are you doing here?"

"Just browsing at the moment." She smiled. "I come here often. I find it charming."

"It *is* charming. I should come here more often myself."

"You should!" She mentally added *not*.

"I need to park and make a quick dash into Gilda's," he said. "I hate to cut our reunion short, but my friend is expecting me."

"It was good seeing you."

"Likewise. Will you be at Jamie's funeral tomorrow?"

She tried to keep the dread she felt from being obvious. "Uh, yes."

"We'll talk more then." He waved to her before driving on and pulling into a vacant space.

When she was certain Connor wasn't looking, she ducked behind Nona Fiske's quilt shop and furtively made her way to Sassy Sally's. Maybe Nick, Don, and Margo could help her figure out how she was going to make it through Jamie's funeral while juggling two personas.

DESPITE THE COOL WEATHER, Katie was sweating when she got to Sassy Sally's. Don was at the reception desk, but he came around to meet her, immediately picking up on her distress.

"Are you all right?" he asked.

Nodding, she said, "I need a glass of water. Actually, I could go for something a lot stronger."

"Of course. Come on."

Katie followed Don into the kitchen, where he opened the liquor cabinet and pulled out a bottle of Black Velvet whisky. He then filled an old fashion glass with ice, measured a shot and a half of the amber liquid, and filled the glass with ginger ale. Between sips, Katie explained that Connor Davis had just spotted her on the Square.

"And Connor Davis is—?" he prompted.

"One of the men who played poker at my table last night."

"Are you sure he saw you?"

"He pulled up alongside me as I was walking from Artisans Alley to Tealicious and asked what I was doing here. He was headed to Gilda's shop and appeared to be in a hurry. I hope he doesn't enter Wood U and see Ray."

Don blew out a breath. "I hope so, too."

"But the worst is, he's going to Jamie's funeral tomorrow and expects to see me there."

Don groaned. "I knew this entire harebrained scheme was going to come back to bite us."

Nick came into the kitchen. "Which harebrained scheme are we discussing?"

Don filled him in while Katie drained her glass of what Nick often teased her as whiskey pop and tried to will her hands not to tremble.

"We have to tell Seth," Nick said.

"We can't." Katie shook her head. "He'll be upset."

"Why?" Don asked. "He's the one who put you up to the ruse in the first place."

She set down the glass and got up from her stool at the kitchen island. "This is a nightmare. How can I go to the funeral as both Katie Bonner *and* Kelly Ferrell? Plus, I can't have Ray pose as my husband again. Not only would it make tongues wag on the Square, but after this morning, I'm not even sure Ray and I are friends anymore."

"What?" Nick raised a hand to his throat. "What?"

Katie heaved a sigh. "I realized last night that he and I have an unhealthy, codependent relationship that needs to end," she said. "I can't go running to Ray every time I have a problem, and he can't continue thinking we'll ever be in an intimate relationship."

"And you don't think your friendship can survive?" Nick asked.

"I don't know. Maybe we'll get there someday, but it's going to take me a while to get over last night. And last night is precisely why I wouldn't trust him to do any more undercover work, either." She ran her hands through her hair. "The only solution is for me to not attend Jamie's funeral."

"If that's what you're planning to do, you have to call Seth," Nick said. "He'll be so hurt if you miss the funeral with no explanation."

"I agree. But a phone call won't cut it. I have to tell him in person."

Thirty minutes later, Katie was sitting beside Seth on the dark leather couch in his living room.

"You know how much I care about you and how much I cared for Jamie," she said, before launching into the story of how one of the men who'd played poker with her the night before would be coming to the funeral. "And Connor isn't the only one. I'm sure Phyllis will be there, too. Of course, Phyllis probably remembers me as Katie Bonner; and either she didn't recognize me last night or she didn't notice me because we didn't speak."

"I'd have loved having your support at the funeral," Seth said. "But I'm the reason you're in this predicament, and I can't have Jamie's service disrupted by people demanding to know who you are. I'd appreciate your asking Ray to stay away as well."

Katie considered asking Seth if he'd mind calling or texting Ray. Instead, she said, "Of course. I'll explain the situation and ask him not to attend." She'd send a text. That way, they wouldn't have to talk.

"There is *something* you could do that might be beneficial," Seth said.

"Of course. Anything."

"Would you contact the woman who wanted to have lunch sometime—Gina, was it?—and see if she's free tomorrow? It seems like she might have more to tell about the evening when Jamie won all that money."

"I'll do that," Katie said. "If I can't attend the service, I can at least help with the investigation. Maybe later we could visit the cemetery together."

Seth offered her a wan smile and patted her hand. "I'd like that, and I think Jamie would approve, too."

Katie hugged her pseudo big brother. It was the least she could do.

CHAPTER 20

On Friday morning, Katie slunk into Artisans Alley using the back entrance and hoping no one would disturb her. She'd texted Ray the evening before asking him not to attend Jamie's funeral—along with an explanation of why she was making the request. He'd texted back, *can we talk?* She hadn't replied. Instead, she made arrangements to meet Gina Solero for lunch at one of the swanky restaurants near the poker club in Rochester. Knowing she'd leave directly from Artisans Alley to meet Gina, Katie had taken extra time with her hair and makeup before coming into work so she'd look more like her Kelly Ferrell persona.

She managed to get a cup of coffee and hurried into her office without anyone accosting her. But while she waited for her computer to boot up, there came the dreaded tap on her door.

Rolling her eyes, she called, "Come in."

It was Rose. She handed Katie a sheet of paper. "Vance said to give you this. It's the placement arrangement for the vendors. He said to tell you they'd agreed to set everything up in their new spots after the close of business today."

"Why didn't he bring this to me himself?" Katie asked.

"He said he was going to work on the floor." She tilted her head. "Wow, you look extra pretty today. Is that what you're wearing to Jamie's funeral?"

Katie felt self-conscious about her red silk blouse and black slacks. "I'm not going to be able to make it to the funeral." She swallowed convulsively. "Seth needs me to run an errand for him instead."

"That's weird," Rose said. "What kind of errand?"

"It's...um...it's personal." She changed the subject. "Will you and Walter be at the open house at Tealicious tonight?"

"Is that tonight?" Rose adopted a crestfallen expression. "Shucks. Walter got us tickets to his lodge's fall formal."

"Couldn't you swing by beforehand and show us all how beautiful you look?" Katie asked.

"Oh, sweetie, that's all right—you'll see the photos afterward." She jerked her head toward the door. "I'd better get back to the cash desk. Good luck with that mysterious errand."

Katie wished she could explain the entire situation to Rose; but she was half afraid that if she told her friend what she'd been up to, Rose would either want to get involved or would inadvertently strike the match that would set the gossip fires ablaze.

She picked up the placement assignment sheet, made sure Maddie Lyndel got the spot Katie had promised her, and skimmed the rest. There would be grumbling among the vendors, but they'd simply have to deal with their dissatisfaction. No one was thrilled with this floor situation. She crossed her fingers. Hopefully, everything could go back to normal soon.

GINA WAS ALREADY SIPPING a martini by the time Katie arrived at the restaurant. The hostess who'd escorted her to the table asked if she'd like one as well. Katie politely declined, instead asking for sparkling water with a twist of lime.

After hanging her purse on the back of the chair, she sat down on the cushioned seat and smiled at her dining companion. "It's good to see you again."

"Likewise." Gina raised her glass and simpered. "But you're making me drink alone."

"I'm afraid so," Katie said. "I need to have my wits about me when I return to work—I'm afraid no one else will have theirs."

"Lots of idiots in the insurance world, huh?"

That had been the job Katie held in her cover story—insurance adjuster. "I'm afraid they're not restricted to insurance." She gave a rueful laugh.

"True," Gina said. "So, was your husband ticked that you won and he lost?"

"Yes!" Katie saw the opportunity to interject a little honesty into the conversation. "He behaved like such a jerk. I'm still angry with him. And I even gave him back the money he lost out of *my* winnings."

"Oooh." Gina winced. "That probably wasn't a good idea."

"Really? Why not?"

"You rubbed his face in the fact that you won and he lost. Your giving him the money was akin to offering him a condescending pat on the head." Gina shook her head. "Very emasculating."

Katie frowned. "I hadn't considered that. How about you? Was your husband angry after the game on Wednesday night?"

"Not terribly. He didn't lose as much as I'd imagined," she said.

"But he lost more the previous week?" Katie asked, struggling to find a way to bring up Jamie and who might've wanted him dead.

"He did. The only one who really cleaned up at that game was Jamie Seifert."

Happy that the conversation was turning in the direction she wanted it to go, Katie opened her mouth to speak. But before she could do so, their waitress arrived with Katie's water.

As soon as the server walked away, Katie asked, "So, how much did Jamie Seifert win last week?"

"I don't remember the exact amount, but my husband Tony wasn't the only one who went home in a rage that night."

Katie sipped her water. "But why were they so angry? Did they think Jamie cheated or something?"

"Well…" Gina drew out the word. "We're a pretty competitive group. None of us are good losers. But, yeah, there was some suspicion."

Katie leaned forward. "Really? Did he have a partner or count cards or what?"

Gina polished off her martini. "Let's just say the dealer at Jamie's table that night has been banned."

Katie gasped. "So, they *were* cheating?"

"Nothing that could be proven, but the event facilitators thought it would be best if the dealer didn't return."

Katie turned that development over in her mind. She couldn't believe Jamie would cheat. "Who was the dealer?"

"His name was *Robert* or *Roberts*—could've been a last name. Why?" She managed a sly grin. "Are you hoping he can help you win big, too?"

"I've already managed to do that on my own," Katie said, "Although the odds are typically against me."

"They weren't the other night," Gina said.

"Trust me—that was a fluke. So, tell me what the other people who were at our table are like."

Gina signaled the server for another martini and they gave their orders at the same time, with Katie opting for the restaurant's version of the regional dish chicken French, while Gina ordered a small house salad, which wasn't likely to mop up the alcohol she seemed determined to imbibe.

Once the waitress left them, Gina returned to the business at hand. "Who do you want to know about?"

"Let's start with Connor Davis," Katie said. "I saw him

yesterday afternoon on Victoria Square in McKinlay Mill. He said he was shopping for a friend who was in the hospital."

"I wonder who?" Gina's brow probably would've furrowed, but Katie suspected the woman's forehead had been immobilized by Botox. "You must go to McKinlay Mill often. Didn't you say you had lunch at that tea shop there a week or two ago?"

"I live in the area," Katie said vaguely. "Have you ever been there?"

The waitress arrived with Gina's martini and refilled Katie's water glass. "Your food should be out soon, ladies," she said, before sashaying away.

"McKinlay Mill? No, I haven't been there." Gina slid one of the queen olives off the frill pick and popped it into her mouth, chewed, and swallowed. "I'll have to check it out one of these days."

"You should," Katie said. "I believe you'd enjoy it. But tell me more about Connor. I didn't realize he and Jamie Seifert were friends."

"Were they?" Gina asked.

"Apparently. He told me he was attending the man's funeral today." She shrugged one shoulder. "I'd intended to go pay my respects, but work obligations took precedence."

"Connor is nice enough, I guess. Tony thinks he's gay because he works with flowers, but I told my husband he's a Neanderthal." She shook her head. "Tony grew up with some antiquated sexist beliefs passed on from his parents—such as men are doctors, scientists, and firefighters while women are nurses, secretaries, and homemakers. He never quite adjusted to modern thinking."

Katie gave a knowing nod. "We all have our ingrained notions to overcome, I suppose. I was fortunate, though—I was taught that women should be fearless and that we can do anything."

"Lucky you," Gina said darkly. "Unfortunately, I had parents like Tony's and was taught that a woman's place is in the home. I finally pleased my folks by marrying rich, so I have a beautiful home to show off to one and all." She paused and looked off into the distance with what seemed like disappointment. Then Gina shook herself. "Uh, who else do you want to know about?"

Their food arrived, but Gina only picked at her salad. By the time they finished, Katie had discovered that Connor Davis owned a flower shop and dated someone who worked at Rochester's prestigious Lamberton Conservatory. Albert was an attorney. He'd been a brilliant criminal defense attorney at one time, but for some reason, he now mainly drew up wills and trusts. Gina had warned her not to let Hazel's "sweet little old lady" guise fool her. Hazel had been a federal court clerk for years and knew the law better than most attorneys. As for Greg, he was an accountant—Gina didn't know much about him other than that.

Concerned over the amount of alcohol Gina had consumed, Katie offered to drive her home.

Gina waved away Katie's worries. "One of Tony's guys drove me today. I always request a driver when I'm going out to lunch."

"Must be nice," Katie teased. "What does Tony do?"

"He's a serial entrepreneur. He's into all sorts of different ventures."

Katie couldn't help but wonder—in light of Jamie's murder—if all of Tony's businesses were legitimate.

CHAPTER 21

*A*fter finishing her work at Artisans Alley, Katie crossed the Square to Sassy Sally's to check in with Margo to make sure everything was ready for that evening's open house.

When she entered the bed and breakfast, she found Don and Nick standing at the reception desk.

"Hi," she said. "How was Jamie's funeral?"

The men shrugged.

"Sad. But we can talk about that later," Nick said. "How'd your lunch with Gina go?"

"Is Margo around? I don't want to have to keep repeating the story."

"I'm here." Margo swept into the room in pink slacks and a white cashmere sweater. "Nick said you had lunch with Gina from the poker game. How did that go?"

"Why don't we discuss it in the parlor?" Don said. "All the guests are out at the moment, and I could use a glass of Merlot."

"Sounds wonderful." Margo led the way.

Katie lowered herself onto a sumptuous brocade wingback chair near the glowing fireplace and gratefully accepted the glass of wine Don offered her. "Thank you."

"So, tell us about lunch with Gina," Nick said, settling onto the couch and putting his feet up on the matching leather ottoman.

"One thing I can tell you is that Gina enjoys her martinis," Katie said.

"Who doesn't?" Margo grinned as she sat on the identical wingback chair on the other side of the fireplace.

"I also learned that two of the people who sat at my table are in the legal profession." Katie sipped the wine.

Don took his seat beside Nick. "Does that mean you're thinking *Seth* could have been the target? That Jamie was killed as some sort of revenge against Seth?"

"I don't know, but it's an angle that might warrant further consideration." Katie started with Albert Whitlock. "According to Gina, he was once a much sought-after attorney, but now he's only doing wills and trusts."

"How old was Mr. Whitlock?" Margo asked. "Attorneys often reduce their caseload as they age and decide to begin stepping away from the business."

"Whitlock appeared to be in his mid-fifties to early sixties," Katie said.

"Is it possible he was taken down by some sort of scandal?" Nick asked.

"Or what if the evidence presented by the medical examiner's office was responsible for Whitlock losing a high-profile case?" Don suggested. "If something like that destroyed Whitlock's career, then that could be a motive for murdering Jamie."

Nick took a legal pad and pen from a drawer in the table beside him. "I'm going to make a suspect list. Who's the other person in the legal field, Katie? Didn't you say there were two?"

"I did. The other one was an older woman named Hazel. I didn't catch her last name, but that shouldn't be difficult to find online since she was a federal court clerk." Katie took another sip of the delicious wine. She hadn't realized how desperately she needed to decompress this afternoon.

"Once again, a court case could cause a murderer to want to strike out at either Jamie or Seth," Don said.

"I'm adding this Hazel to the list," Nick said. "I'm not getting a *killer* vibe from her, but you never know."

"Who else was at the table?" Margo asked.

"There was Greg, an accountant who seemed rather full of himself," she said. "And Connor—he's the one I told you about yesterday. I wonder if he attended Jamie's funeral like he told me he planned?"

"Without seeing him, I couldn't say." Nick didn't look up from the pad as he continued scribbling notes about the suspects. "Who else have we got?"

"Well, other than me and Gina, the only other person I haven't mentioned is the dealer." Katie took a breath. "Which brings me to something else Gina told me. Some of the players thought Jamie and the dealer at his table that night were somehow cheating."

Nick gaped at her. "What?"

Katie nodded. "They couldn't prove anything, and the club didn't refuse to pay out Jamie's winnings, but the dealer was fired."

"That's outrageous!" Nick threw down his pad and pen. "Jamie would never cheat!"

"But you said yourself that Jamie was only a mediocre player. How does someone like that win so big? Pure luck?" Katie asked.

"That's a good question," Don said softly.

"Oh, come on," Nick cried.

"Remember last Friday night when Jamie said it would be such a rush to win at a big casino? You don't think the game he won at was merely a trial run, do you?" Don asked.

"How can you even joke about such a thing?" Nick said angrily.

"I'm not joking." Don raised his hands defensively. "Jamie wanted to do something wonderfully romantic for the love of his life. But with his student loans and other debts, he simply didn't have the money to make it happen. Unless he made a deal with some card shark...."

"Absolutely not! Jamie. Wouldn't. Cheat," Nick asserted.

"Playing devil's advocate," Margo interjected gently, "maybe he would if he thought the money he was winning was coming from unscrupulous people who had no intention of doing anything good with it. It doesn't sound as though the crème de la crème play at this event."

"Speaking of unscrupulous people," Katie said, "I'm wondering if Gina's husband, Tony Solero, might be one."

At the name *Tony Solero*, Nick lifted his head. He and Don looked at Katie and then shared a glance.

"Is this the same Tony Solero who's reputed to be involved in organized crime?" Don asked.

KATIE CUT short her visit with her friends and hurried back to her apartment and her laptop. As she read the results of her search on Tony, her gut tightened. He'd been indicted on a number of charges, including wire fraud, racketeering, and tax evasion. He'd evaded some charges, but others were still pending.

No wonder Gina drank so heavily.

Katie didn't have time to ponder the significance of what she'd found. It was time to turn her attention to her own problems.

Taking time to dress, she carefully did her makeup and hair before heading down to the tearoom.

Katie had inspected everything in Tealicious's dining room. Every tablecloth was wrinkle-free, with vases filled with colorful chrysanthemums and baby's breath. Brad had set up a buffet table across the back wall which was covered with the most delectable cookies, petit fours, plates of sliced cake, platters filled with appetizers, and the promised pumpkin half filled with cider punch.

Katie straightened her skirt and stood against the counter, her gaze darting between the door and the big window, anxiously waiting.

Margo wore a royal blue tea-length brocade dress and came to stand beside her. "Penny for your thoughts?"

"I'd give you a dollar to take them away," Katie said. "I wonder how much of what I learned from Gina—and my Google search on her husband—to tell Seth."

"Everything. First off, he asked you to go, and he deserves to know everything. Plus, he understands more about what might've been going on in Jamie's life, and Seth knows whether any of the other players at your table could have a grudge against *him*."

"I know you're right—but I dread it. Unless he calls me, I'm waiting until tomorrow to reach out to him." She sighed. "I don't want to dump all this mess on him right after Jamie's funeral."

"That's understandable," Margo said. "And considerate. I imagine the man needs to be alone with his grief tonight."

Brad joined them, looking divinely handsome in a black tux with a pale blue bow tie and cummerbund. "Shouldn't people be showing up by now?"

Margo patted his arm. "They'll be here. Don't worry."

Katie managed a weak smile, but she could feel her optimism waning.

As with the partnership meeting, Nona Fiske was the first to arrive. Ignoring Katie and Brad, she made a beeline for Margo.

"Margo, you add a touch of elegance and class everywhere you go," Nona said sweetly, with a snide sidelong glance at Katie.

"As do you, Nona." Margo took the woman by the elbow. "Let's have some tea."

"My former mother-in-law missed her calling when she didn't go into politics," Katie muttered to Brad.

"Let's hope Nona isn't our only guest," he said.

"She's the first of many," Katie said and cast a worried glance toward the front window and the lack of cars on the Square. However, within minutes of Nona's arrival, people did begin to trickle into the tea shop.

Jordan and Ann Tanner arrived, followed by Sue Sweeney. Other Victoria Square merchants also put in brief appearances, but Ray and Andy were no shows. Katie felt slightly stung by their snubs, but as she'd essentially cut ties with both men, their absence was probably for the best.

Gabrielle Pearson arrived with her teenage daughter in tow. It was a wonderful testament that the woman who dined with Jamie only moments before he collapsed had returned to Tealicious, so she obviously thought the food at the tea shop was safe to eat.

Thanks to Margot's press release, members of the local media showed up and entered the dining room, and one reporter had a camera crew in tow. Thankfully, Margo took over the handling of the press. Katie made sure she was aware that Gabrielle was there, too.

Other than Liz Meyer, Maddie Lyndel, and Gwen Hardy, none of the other Artisans Alley vendors showed up at the open house. The fact that the majority of Katie's vendors—including Vance and Rose—would shun the open house did more than sting like the absence of Ray Davenport and Andy Rust did. Their lack of support downright hurt. Despite Margo's beautiful flyers, the shop wasn't flooded with Artisans Alley shoppers, either. Which brought on a new worry.

What was Katie supposed to do with all that leftover food?

CHAPTER 22

After the not-very successful open house at Tealicious, Katie returned to the apartment above the tea shop, got ready for bed, and contemplated the aftermath. She wouldn't know how the local press would interpret the event until the next day—if they even decided to report it. And the staggering amount of leftovers gave her pause. There was nothing wrong with it, but as the owner, she wanted Tealicious to only serve fresh food, and that was doubly important after the unflattering press of the week before. She decided to sleep on the matter.

The next morning Katie decided to donate the leftover food to a local food pantry. With that in mind, after showering and dressing, Katie went downstairs to Tealicious to find Brad already in the kitchen and in a cheerful mood.

"Why are you so happy?" she asked. "Last night was practically a bust."

"No, it wasn't. Didn't you see the coverage on the local news channel last night?"

She hadn't. "I was pooped and went to bed early. They made us look good?" she asked cautiously.

"The reporter interviewed Margo *and* Gabrielle," he said.

"Margo was fantastic, but Gabrielle was even better. The vibe the story gave off was that if you weren't in attendance, then you wish you were. Plus, the coverage was at the beginning of the evening when all the vendors were there, so it looked as though we had more people than we actually did."

"That's a relief. Did the reporter say anything about Jamie?" she asked.

"The story segued into a reminder that Jamie Seifert had died only a week ago on Victoria Square and that the investigation into his suspicious death is ongoing."

Katie groaned. "Great. We get some nice press that *might* actually begin to turn things around again only to have them throw out the reminder that Jamie died after eating here."

"Actually, that wasn't specified," Brad said. "The newscast said Jamie collapsed on the Square, not outside of—or after eating at —Tealicious."

"That's something, I guess." She picked up one of the boxes Brad had already prepared. "I'll pick up some newspapers after I drop these off at the food pantry."

Brad gathered up the other box, and they went outside to Katie's car. "I'm already seeing an increase in reservations this morning."

"That's a good sign," Katie said, "but I don't want to be overly optimistic."

Shaking his head, he said, "No, I believe we'll have more traffic this afternoon than we have since Jamie's death."

Katie felt some relief, but she wasn't about to let her guard down yet. It seemed every time she did, some other catastrophe occurred.

Next, she called the local food pantry. She'd dealt with its manager before, as had Jordan Tanner, the only other food merchant on the Square. Both establishments often donated their surplus and Katie made an appointment to drop off the previous evening's leftovers.

At the food pantry, she was greeted by a tall, gaunt man with shoulder-length brown hair. He wasn't unkempt, but his clothes hung on him as though he was a scarecrow.

"Good morning," he said as he strode toward Katie's car. "I can help you carry those boxes."

By the look of him, Katie wasn't sure he had the strength to help, but she didn't want to insult him, either. Still, she gave him the lighter of the two boxes. They carried the cartons into the shelter.

Katie's helper opened one of the boxes and peered inside. "Oh, wow. May I have one of these?"

"Sure," she said. "Help yourself."

He popped one of the mini quiches into his mouth and closed his eyes, apparently savoring the flavors. "Thank you. I used to eat food like this at my brother's fancy parties—canapes, quiches, petits fours."

"Don't you attend your brother's parties anymore?" she asked.

"No." He looked longingly back into the box. "We had a parting of the ways."

"Have another," she encouraged him. "I won't tell."

He smiled as he took another quiche from the box. "And now I'll put the box in the refrigerator, I promise. I'm sure everyone we distribute these to will be as grateful for your generosity as I am."

Handing him a business card she'd taken from her wallet, Katie said, "Here. If you're ever in need of some quiche, give me a call and I'll see what I can do."

The man took the card. "It's a pleasure to meet you, Ms. Bonner. My name is Jimmy Solero."

Katie barely hid her shock. *Solero.* Could there be a connection between this man and Gina's husband Tony? She didn't feel comfortable asking.

After stopping at the local grocery store to pick up a few copies of the Rochester newspaper she'd promised Brad, Katie drove back to Tealicious. Rather than entering the tea shop, however, she went upstairs to her apartment. Consumed with discovering information about Jimmy Solero, she gave the cats an affectionate pat before taking a seat at her desk and opening her laptop.

An online search yielded confirmation that Tony and Jimmy were brothers. Jimmy was slightly younger and had worked for Tony's construction company as a project manager. He was convicted of taking a bribe from a subcontractor, was fired from his brother's company, and served a year in prison. And now he worked for the local food pantry—she hadn't needed a news article to tell her that part.

Poor Jimmy. If Tony would destroy his own brother for tainting his company's reputation, what would the man do to Jamie, believing Jamie had cheated him out of a lot of money?

Katie shut down the laptop and scanned the newspapers for coverage of the Tealicious open house. She was happy to see that, as Brad reported, the article was favorable. She clipped it from one of the copies and took it downstairs to share with Brad.

To her surprise, Katie found Margo in the dining room.

"Brad, are you able to take a break and speak with Margo and me for a few minutes?" she asked.

"Sure. I'll let my sous chef know where I am." He went into the kitchen.

"Is everything all right?" Margo asked.

Katie waved her hand. "We got some good press about the open house last night—thanks to you."

"I can see that reflected in the number of reservations we've received this morning," Margo said. "The evening might not have been as successful as we'd hoped, but it made people wonder—or reminded them—of what they were missing."

Brad returned, and the three of them sat at one of the tables.

"What's up?" he asked.

"This morning when I took the leftover food to the homeless shelter, I met Jimmy Solero," Katie said. "I looked him up online and confirmed that he's Tony Solero's brother. He was fired from Tony's company and went to jail for a year for bribery. That knowledge made me wonder what Tony might do to someone who he felt cheated him out of a substantial amount of money at a poker table."

"Could you ask Gina about Jimmy?" Brad asked. "Maybe there's something there you don't know—like maybe Jimmy was a drug addict."

"I wish I *could* speak with Gina about him, but there's no way. I introduced myself to him as Katie Bonner when I delivered food to the shelter from Tealicious. The only way to ask Gina about Jimmy would be to confess my identity."

"Not necessarily," Margo said. "You could say you met Jimmy while doing some volunteer work. I think it would be good to get Gina's take on Tony and Jimmy's relationship."

"Just so you know you aren't the only one trying to find Jamie's murderer," Brad said, "Nick went with Seth to his office this morning to poke through old case files. They're looking for any red flags from Jamie's rulings that might explain who could have had a motive for killing him."

"I know it's possible, but I simply can't comprehend why someone would poison Jamie to get back at Seth," Katie said. "If that was the case, wouldn't the killer reach out to taunt Seth in some way? What would be the point in using Jamie to get revenge on Seth if the killer never let Seth know why he was suffering?"

"Excellent point," Brad murmured.

"Perhaps, but a person who'd poison another wouldn't be the most logical, level-headed person on the planet," Margo said, raising her hands for emphasis. "I believe the lost money might be the better motive, especially if some of the other players truly believed that Jamie had cheated."

Brad leaned back in his chair and steepled his hands. "Those are two of the big motives: passion or gain."

Katie groaned. "Passion? First, we have Jamie painted as a card cheater, and now we're going to consider the possibility he was betraying Seth?"

"Not necessarily," Margo said. "What if it was unrequited love?"

"With obsessive people—the type of person who'd poison a man and leave him to suffer for three days prior to his death—a rebuffed overture could be the very thing to set them off." Brad frowned. "I need to stop watching so many true crime shows. I think they're starting to warp my brain and fill my head with too much disturbing information."

"But who at the poker game could've had a crush on Jamie?" Katie wondered.

Margo leaned forward. "You tell us."

"Gina said her husband thought Connor Davis might be gay—but he based that on the fact he owns a flower shop."

"Hey, plenty of people thought I was gay when I first showed an interest in baking," Brad said.

"And just because Jamie was poisoned the evening of the poker game doesn't mean her was dosed *at* it," Margo pointed out.

She was right.

Katie realized that tracking down Jamie's killer—or even discovering a motive for his murder—might prove to be much harder than she'd anticipated.

THE SUN WAS SHINING as Katie headed back to Artisans Alley, and there was just enough of a chill in the air to make it feel crisp and refreshing. Even though her conversation with Brad and Margo had led to more questions than answers, she thought they'd made some progress—at least, in driving traffic back to the tea shop.

"Hey! Ms. Bonner!"

Katie turned to see who was calling to her from the other side of the street. It was Carol Rigby. The detective exited Wood U and was now crossing the parking lot to intercept Katie.

"Good morning, detective. What can I do for you?" Katie asked.

The detective's gaze was positively chilling. "Stay out of my investigation."

"Excuse me?" Katie asked, taken aback.

Carol rolled her eyes. "Ray told me about the stupid stunt the two of you pulled the other night. Pretending to be a married couple and buying into a poker game? Really! Don't go stepping on my toes again, or you'll regret it."

Katie glowered. "It's Ray you should be threatening—he got stinking drunk and was practically useless that evening," she said. "By the way, are you aware that some of the club's players believe Jamie cheated at the game in order to win? And did you know the dealer at his table that night got fired?"

Carol's eyes widened. She hadn't known.

Katie pressed on. "And, of course, you know about Tony Solero being one of the players who felt he'd been cheated. Several players there are involved in the legal profession and at least one worked for the medical examiner's office."

Carol clenched her fists. "Just keep out of my way."

"Or what?" Katie challenged.

"Or you could be charged with obstruction of justice."

"It seems to me you could be accused of negligence. And how would that look on your résumé?"

"Don't cross me again," Carol grated.

Katie didn't bother to reply. She turned and headed for Artisans Alley, but she felt the heat of Carol's scorching glare on her back the entire distance.

CHAPTER 23

Katie did her best to brush off her unpleasant encounter with Detective Rigby, but as she entered Artisans Alley, her ire at being snubbed by both Rose and Vance the evening before at Tealicious was like a fresh wound. Rose could have made an appearance before going to her new boyfriend's event. And where had Vance been? Had he neglected to come to the open house simply because he was angry with her over the situation with the Alley's floor? If so, that was just plain petty. Especially since he knew there'd be free food—and he had a hearty appetite.

Katie decided to give him the benefit of the doubt—maybe something unexpected had happened. She'd ask. And she wouldn't go empty-handed.

After dumping her purse in her office and locking it again, she went to the vendors' lounge and poured two cups of coffee before heading for the stairs.

She found Vance staining the floor near Maddie Lyndel's booth. "Hi. I brought you a coffee."

Either he was super-focused on his work, or he was ignoring her. At last, he straightened and accepted the cup. "Thanks."

"So, how's it going?" she asked.

"Fine."

Katie was determined not to allow herself to be frustrated by Vance's monosyllabic responses. "And did any of the vendors have trouble getting moved yesterday evening?"

"No."

His childish attitude was beginning to annoy her.

"They seem to be resigned to their assignments. Did anyone complain?" Before Vance could respond, she added, "Let's see if you can answer that last question with a full sentence rather than some sort of grunt I'd expect from a caveman."

Lips tightening, he said, "No one complained—at least, not to me."

"Good." He'd apparently had no trouble getting the vendors moved, so that wasn't his excuse for not attending the open house. "Brad, Margo, and I missed you and Janie last night."

Rather than provide any sort of explanation as to why he and his wife had missed the event, Vance said, "I'd better get back to work."

Okay, if that's the way he wanted to play it, she decided she should probably start coming up with a detailed job description. Sadly, if Vance didn't want to follow her instructions, it was time to find an assistant manager who would.

Without another word, Katie turned and marched back toward her office.

"Oh, Katie!" Rose stopped her at the bottom of the stairs. "Would you like to see how dapper Walter and I looked last night?"

"No, thank you," Katie said, her tone icy. "Had you really wanted me to see you, you'd have stopped by the Tealicious's open house on your way. Now, if you'll excuse me, I need to get back to work." And with that, Katie turned and continued on to her office feeling certain Rose was gaping at her back. She'd never been so brusque with Rose, but at that moment she was afraid she might lose her temper and that would be even worse.

Closing the office door behind her, Katie slumped against it and let out a ragged breath. How had her entire life gotten so out of control? For some reason, her encounters with Vance and Rose made it easier to pretend to be someone else. Maybe she actually wished she could *be* someone else for a few moments.

She collapsed into the chair in front of her desk, picked up her phone, and called Gina Solero. After three rings, Katie was getting ready to end the call when Gina answered.

"Kelly, hi. How are you?"

It was evident from Gina's tone that she wondered why Kelly Ferrell was contacting her so soon after their lunch. Was she afraid her new friend was going to be a nuisance?

"I'm fine, Gina, and I hope you are." She forced out a weak laugh. "I'm sorry to call you out of the blue like this, but I had the oddest thing happen earlier today. I took a donation to my local food pantry and ran into a man named Jimmy Solero. I wondered if he's your in-law."

There was a pause, and Katie could easily imagine Gina pursing her lips, gathering her thoughts, and deciding how to respond.

"Jimmy?" Gina asked. "No. Doesn't ring a bell. I can ask Tony if he knows him if you want me to."

"Oh, no, don't bother. I was just curious if this guy was a relative of Tony's." She offered another feeble laugh. "It was hard to imagine a sophisticate like you—and, I imagine, your husband— with a family member who works at a food pantry."

Gina gave a laugh that sounded every bit as contrived as Katie's.

"Well, I won't keep you," Katie said. "Thanks again for meeting me for lunch yesterday. I thoroughly enjoyed it and hope we can do it again sometime."

"Likewise," Gina said rather coolly—or was it guardedly? "We'll talk soon," she said and ended the call.

Katie put her phone away, feeling the entire episode had left a bad taste in her mouth. From pretending to be as much of a snob as Gina to lying that she'd enjoyed lunch. She was glad the call was over, but she couldn't help but wonder why Gina would deny knowing Jimmy. Was it possible Tony had shut Jimmy out of his life before he married Gina and had neglected to tell her about his younger brother? Or was there more to the story than that?

Either way, Katie doubted she'd ever hear from Gina Solero again—which was fine with her. It was time for Kelly Ferrell to disappear. Unless, of course, Seth should need her to make another appearance.

Realizing she didn't need to be *Kelly Ferrell* to investigate, Katie awakened her computer and conducted a search for a poker dealer named *Roberts*. Her query led her to a forum where local games were discussed. She created an anonymous account and said she was an amateur player who'd recently heard about a dealer with the name of *Roberts* who'd supposedly been fired for cheating.

Not sure whether the man's first or last name is Roberts, she typed, *but I'd like to be aware if I find myself at a table with a dealer who is a suspected cheat.*

Within moments the replies began coming in.

I heard about that, said someone whose username was CRZY4-CARDS. *Happened in Rochester, right? He and some doctor split a fortune.*

A commentator with the handle DOCH weighed in. *The dealer's name is Ted Roberts. He's a good person and an excellent dealer. He was falsely accused. Think about it: if he was going to cheat, wouldn't he do it in Atlantic City or Vegas where he could get a much larger payout?*

I heard he and some guy double-crossed some mobster, LUCKY-

DOG2 posted. *The one dude is dead already—I saw it in the newspaper. Ted Roberts had better sleep with one eye open.*

The rest of the responses either vilified Ted Roberts and speculated about the man's guilt, or they defended the man. Katie deleted her account, not caring what the faceless strangers believed. She had what she needed—the name of the dealer who had worked Jamie's table on the night he was poisoned.

Now how could she find Ted Roberts? She went back to social media and searched for people named *Ted Roberts* in the Rochester area. When that name yielded too many results, she tried *Theodore Roberts*. Still too many.

Frustrated, she called Nick. She remembered Brad saying he was with Seth, but he might have the information she needed off the top of his head.

"Hi," Nick said. "What's up, Katie?"

"Hey, there. Are you still with Seth?"

"No, he just dropped me back at Sassy Sally's. Is anything wrong?"

Katie explained that she'd learned the identity of the dealer at Jamie's table on the night he won—the man some of the players thought helped Jamie win. "His name is Ted Roberts, but I'm having trouble locating him. Any thoughts?"

"Don and I have known Ted for over a year. We met him at a tournament. I can ask him to come here to Sassy Sally's for a drink." He uttered a low growl. "Ted's a good guy, and he'd never cheat. I'm as sure of him as I am of Jamie—maybe more so. I'll give him a call and ring you right back."

FORTY-FIVE MINUTES LATER, Katie was sitting with Nick, Don, and Ted Roberts in Sassy Sally's front parlor having a glass of white wine. Ted had a shock of steel gray hair and piercing blue eyes—looking rather Paul Newman-esque, in Katie's opinion. He also had a built-in B.S. detector.

"Nick, I know you didn't invite me here to shoot the breeze," he said. "Why don't you tell me why I'm here."

"We were friends of Jamie Siefert," Nick admitted.

"And he died shortly after eating at my tea shop," Katie added. "We're trying to find out who killed him and why."

Ted tossed back a swig of his bourbon. "Well, it wasn't me."

"We never thought it was," Don assured him. "Nor do we think you or he are guilty of cheating."

"Ah, you heard about that, too, huh." Ted offered a half-smile. "You people get around."

"I'm sorry you lost your job," Katie said.

"It was one of many," Ted said with a shrug. "But I was—still am—outraged at the accusation."

"Why did some of the players think Jamie cheated?" Nick asked.

"Because he did."

Katie's jaw dropped at Ted's simple statement, and so did Nick's. Don didn't appear to be fazed.

Regaining her voice, Katie asked, "What makes you think so?"

"Someone at the table was feeding him information," Ted said.

"Who?" Nick asked.

"I don't know, but there had to be another player at the table giving him signals. That night, the game was Texas Hold 'Em. I'm pretty sure Siefert and another player were colluding to raise the stakes so that Siefert won substantially more than he would have otherwise."

"But Jamie couldn't have won if he didn't have winning hands," Don said.

"Which is why some of the other players thought I was the one helping him." Ted finished off the bourbon. "If Siefert had a lousy hand, he almost immediately folded. But if he had something—basically anything—he and the other player would orchestrate inflated bidding."

"Ted, you have to know who this other player was," Nick said, refilling Ted's glass.

"I have my suspicions, but I'm not accusing anybody. Having been on the wrong end of a false accusation, I can assure you it stinks." Ted stared down at the caramel-colored liquid in his glass. "I'm sorry for your loss, though. Seifert seemed to be a nice guy. He tipped me five hundred bucks after the game."

"Do you think his partner is the one who poisoned him?" Katie asked.

"Hard to say. I don't know why he would. Seifert didn't strike me as the type who'd welch on a bargain." He shrugged. "And the newspaper said he was poisoned? That doesn't sound like a heat-of-the-moment retaliation to me. It had to be planned."

The question was ... why?

CHAPTER 24

*a*fter Roberts left, Nick, Don, and Katie mulled over what he'd told them about someone helping Jamie cheat.

"Should we tell Seth?" Don asked.

"Tell Seth what?" Seth asked, entering and overhearing Don's question.

Don dropped his eyes to the coffee table, and Katie looked at Nick.

Nick took the initiative to answer the question. "Ted Roberts, the dealer who worked Jamie's table the night he was poisoned, told us he believes someone at the table colluded with Jamie."

"Colluded with him to do what?" Seth asked. "Cheat?"

Katie nodded. "He thinks so. He believes this partner and Jamie upped the ante for Jamie to win so they could split the money."

"Jamie was the most honest man I've ever met—that's one of the things I loved most about him." Seth's expression darkened. "He wouldn't cheat. I won't believe it."

"Maybe he didn't consider it cheating if he simply bettered his odds of winning," Nick said gently. "He seemed desperate to marry you and take you on a romantic vacation. The man wanted to sweep you off your feet."

"He already had," Seth said. "But, yes, Jamie was insecure. He didn't always feel that he contributed enough financially to our household. Sure, he had those student debts looming over him. I offered more than once to pay them off, but he was too proud to let me do it." He blew out a breath. "Had I known how badly he wanted to marry me and have a honeymoon, I'd have made it happen."

"But *he* wanted to do that for *you*," Don said.

"I know." Seth motioned for Don to pour him a glass of wine. "Jamie always felt like he needed to impress me or do something monumental to prove his love. That was so unnecessary. I'd give anything to have him back."

Don handed Seth a glass of wine. Nick got up and hugged his best friend while Katie sat there feeling helpless.

Once Seth had composed himself, Katie asked, "Did you learn anything useful from your files today?"

Shaking his head, Seth said, "Not really. I had a case last year where I successfully defended a frivolous lawsuit filed by Albert Whitlock on behalf of his wealthy client. The failed lawsuit was pretty much the nail in the coffin for Whitlock."

"I remember you mentioning that," Don said. "But Whitlock had suffered more losses than he'd achieved wins over the past two or three years prior to that lawsuit, right?"

"That's true, and he'd been exhibiting diminished prowess in the courtroom as well," Seth said. "But it was after this case that Whitlock began focusing his practice on wills and trusts. Still, Albert Whitlock is admittedly an expert in those areas, and I've even recommended clients to him."

"Recently?" Nick asked.

"Yes." Seth sipped his wine. "I can't imagine he has any animosity toward me. He'd have lost that lawsuit I referenced no matter who defended it."

"Can you recall anything about a Jimmy Solero bribery case?" Katie asked Seth.

"It doesn't ring a bell," he said. "Given the last name, I'm guessing he's related to Tony Solero?"

Katie nodded. "I met Jimmy Solero when I took the leftover food from last night's open house to the food pantry. When I handed him my card, he told me his name."

"Naturally, you went straight to your trusty laptop and played Nancy Drew," Nick teased.

"Of course, I did. I learned that he's Tony's younger brother and that he'd been arrested for bribery relating to one of Tony's construction companies. Anyway, the guy served one year in prison, and now he's working at a food pantry? How could Tony be so cold?"

"I imagine he didn't want to be tainted by Jimmy's criminal record," Don said. "However, I'd lay odds that if he bribed someone in conjunction with his position in his brother's construction company, it was at Tony's behest."

"I had that same thought," Katie said. "So, I decided to have *Kelly Ferrell* call Gina Solero and ask her about Jimmy—you know, to get her take on the brothers' relationship."

"And what did she say?" Nick asked.

"That's just it—she acted as though she didn't even know a Jimmy Solero." Katie spread her hands. "Granted, she could have married Tony after he and Jimmy had parted ways, but wouldn't she still know her husband had a brother?"

"That is strange," Seth said. "She'd almost have to know you'd realize she was either lying or stupid, especially given the ease with which people can look everything up on the Internet these days."

"She even offered to ask Tony if he knew a Jimmy Solero," Katie said. "That was the cherry on the sundae to me. I told her no and pretended I'd thought it hard to imagine a sophisticate like her would have a brother-in-law like Jimmy." She rolled her eyes. "I nearly choked on that, but it wasn't entirely a lie. I can't imagine a nice guy like Jimmy would have *her* as a sister-in-law."

Margo entered the room carrying a couple of pizza boxes. "Will someone please pour me a glass of that white wine? Andy Rust might be a jerk, but he makes delicious pizza."

She placed the boxes on the coffee table while Nick got up to get plates, silverware, and napkins. Don poured her the requested glass of wine.

Katie smiled at Seth, wondering if he was as glad as she was not to have to go home to an empty home just yet. It was great to be here with good food, great friends, and wonderful conversation, but it was only a temporary escape from the isolation that was beginning to feel all too commonplace.

ON SUNDAY MORNING, Katie's alarm rang much too soon. She crawled out of bed, showered, dressed, and fed the cats. Feeling that baking would help her better acclimate to the day, she went downstairs to Tealicious.

"Good morning," she greeted Brad as she grabbed an apron from the hook.

"Hi, there. Glad to see you're up and ready to work."

"I was going to make a batch of scones," she said, "but I'll do anything else you need me to do as well."

"Scones would be fantastic. I have a feeling we're going to feed a lot of people today," he said. "We got terrific coverage in the local papers yesterday, and I can simply imagine everyone waking up this morning and saying, 'You know what? We should go by Tealicious this afternoon.'"

Katie managed a weak laugh. "Well, I hope you're right. I'd much prefer being here today than at Artisans Alley."

"Still having trouble with the floor?" he asked.

She measured flour into a mixing bowl. "It's not just that. I was really hurt that neither Vance nor Rose came to support us at the open house on Friday night. And yesterday, I feel like I was downright rude to Rose."

"That doesn't sound like you, and I know how much you care about Rose." He took out another mixing bowl, adding butter and sugar, and started to cream the mixture.

"I do care about Rose," Katie said. "That's why I feel so rotten. She asked me if I'd like to see photos of her and Walter all dressed up for their lodge event, and I told her no."

"You didn't!" Brad's tone made Katie feel even worse.

"I did," she admitted with shame and added baking soda to her dry mixture.

"Look," Brad said gently, "maybe Rose didn't realize how much you needed her support on Friday. I think you should talk with her."

"What would I say?"

"I'd start by asking to see the photographs." He placed a hand on her shoulder. "Tell her you've been really stressed and that you'd love to see how nice she and Walter looked on Friday night."

"You're such a charmer." She grinned. "Would you like to talk to Rose on my behalf?"

"No." He deftly broke an egg into the bowl with one hand. "One evening isn't worth ruining a friendship over. I'm sure Rose didn't intend to be hurtful."

"I know, but I feel like Rose's new boyfriend has got her behaving irrationally."

"People in love are always irrational," he said.

"I guess that's true."

As Katie finished mixing the ingredients for the scones, she correlated Rose's irrational behavior to Jamie's. How far would Jamie have been willing to go to show his love for Seth? Did he— as Ted Roberts had suggested—work with a partner in order to better his chances of winning? And if so, who could it be?

CHAPTER 25

*A*s soon as she arrived at Artisans Alley, Katie sought Rose out. She wasn't at the cash desk, but Katie found her tidying her booth on the main sales floor.

"Hi, there," Katie said.

"Good morning." Rose's voice was icy, and she didn't look up from her task.

Katie swallowed her pride before speaking. "I want to tell you that I'm so sorry for the way I behaved yesterday afternoon."

At Katie's words, Rose stopped what she was doing and looked up.

"I was so hurt when two of my favorite people didn't come to the Tealicious open house that I had a bit of a meltdown," she continued.

"Two?" Rose inquired

"You and Vance."

Rose said nothing, her expression impassive.

"I was hurt because if Tealicious fails, it adversely affects Artisans Alley. Their financial successes are deeply intertwined."

"I had no idea," Rose said looking thoughtful.

"Plus, I don't have a clue as to how I'm going to mend the rift between me and Vance. It could make or break the future of Artisans Alley."

Rose looked stricken "What are you saying?"

"That I can't keep the Alley alive on my own. If Vance were to leave...."

Rose gaped at her. She had her husband's social security to depend on and owned her own home, but her earnings from sales at the Alley gave her a little mad money to spend.

"Anyway," Katie continued, placing her hand gently on Rose's arm. "I consider you to be a good friend and I'd love to see the photos of you and Walter if you're still inclined to show them to me."

Rose's eyes widened in delight. "Of course, I will!" She pulled out her phone and tapped the gallery icon. "I'm sorry we didn't come to the open house before going to Walter's event. I just didn't realize our stopping by there would mean that much to you."

"Why not?" Katie asked.

Rose lowered her head. "I kind of got the impression you were turning your back on all your old friends."

Katie gasped. "Rose, whatever would give you that idea?"

"We all heard about your argument with Ray, and then you didn't attend Jamie's funeral."

Katie heaved a heavy sigh. "I have a confession to make." She looked around to make sure no one was listening to them before telling Rose about her and Ray's undercover operation at the poker game to get information on who might've wanted to harm Jamie. "Then I was walking to my apartment the day before the funeral and was recognized by one of the people who'd attended the game and had met me as Kelly Ferrell. When he said he'd see me at the funeral, I didn't know what to do. I spoke with Seth, and we decided the best course of action would be for me to resume my fake identity and go to lunch with another of the people I'd met at the game and try to get information from her. Believe me, I felt terrible not being there for Seth."

"The man who said he'd see you at the funeral," Rose said. "Was his name Connor Davis?"

"Yes. How did you know?"

"Connor Davis was the only person at the funeral that no one else seemed to know." Rose stepped out of her booth. "Let's go to the vendors' lounge and get coffee."

Katie fell into step beside Rose.

"Walter was a police officer, you know, so he notices when people don't particularly seem to belong somewhere," Rose continued. "It was apparent Davis wasn't a friend of Seth's, he wasn't a friend of Suzanne Seifert, and he wasn't from the medical examiner's office. So, we wondered how he had known Jamie."

"How did you find out his name?" Katie asked. "Did you go over and introduce yourselves?"

"We didn't have to. Walter recognized him." Rose blushed. "Connor owns the shop in Rochester where Walter buys all my flowers."

"What was Connor's behavior like at the service?"

"He was kind of weepy," Rose said with a sad shake of her head. "He must've known Jamie well."

Interesting.

"I've got to get to work. I'll talk to you later," Katie said.

"I'll be around," Rose said with a smile.

After grabbing a cup of coffee, Katie returned to her office. She closed her door, sat down at her computer, and searched for Connor Davis on social media.

Within minutes she'd learned that Connor's partner, Luther Stapleton, worked at the conservatory in Rochester. So, he was gay. Was he a potential lover spurned after all?

As both her businesses were closed the next day, it would be a good time to browse around the Lamberton Conservatory, spend some time relaxing among the fall foliage, and seek out the man Connor had been dating. Maybe speaking with Luther would give her a better idea of who Connor was as a person.

If Jamie *had* been the type of person who was inclined to cheat at poker, would Connor have volunteered to help him? Maybe Connor wanted to impress his partner with a grand romantic gesture as much as Jamie had.

Seeing Jamie listed as one of Connor's friends on the social media platform, Katie clicked through to Jamie's page—realizing as she did so that she and Jamie had never been friends on social media. Not that there was anything unusual in that. Katie didn't give much attention to her personal page, preferring to keep her private life as confidential as possible while living in such a small town. She mostly updated the Artisans Alley and Tealicious pages.

Jamie's profile page had many photos of him and Seth on Seth's sailboat, *Temporary Relief*, on Seth's deck, in the garden, and selfies at restaurants and other venues. Feeling melancholy, she scrolled through the photos that acted as a timeline for Jamie's relationship with Seth. Katie quickly learned, however, that before Seth had been in his life, Jamie had apparently played the field—nothing serious, no special someone, but casual dates at the beach, on the lake, or at a sports bar. There were several photos of Jamie shirtless and/or striking rather seductive poses. Katie had considered Jamie attractive, but these images looked like modeling photos. Had Jamie modeled while he was in college or grad school?

She wasn't surprised when she stumbled across a photo of Jamie and Connor. Both men were shirtless, but it wasn't a romantic photograph. Like the solo pictures of Jamie, this image was posed as though it had been shot during some sort of modeling campaign. Maybe Jamie and Connor had modeled together. If so, they'd known each other far longer than Katie had thought. Had they trusted each other enough to plot to win the poker game together? Would she lose Seth's friendship if she ran that thought past him? It was something she would have to ponder.

～

KATIE'S PHONE RANG, and she was surprised to see that it was Gina Solero calling.

"Hi, Gina. What's up?"

"I feel like a jerk for being so rude to you yesterday," she said. "I was simply aggravated. I didn't want you to know about my husband's falling out with his brother. I was afraid you'd think our entire family is a dysfunctional mess."

Katie laughed. "I haven't met a family yet that *isn't* a mess—my own included. I thought maybe your family was the exception."

"Hardly." Gina lowered her voice slightly. "How was Jimmy when you saw him? Did he appear to be well?"

"Yes. He looked fine," Katie said. "And he was so friendly."

"I've always had a soft spot for Jimmy, but I wasn't able to sway Tony to bring him back into the fold after their falling out." She sighed. "I'd love to see Jimmy again. Maybe we could go see him tomorrow and then have lunch."

We? Go see Jimmy Solero? Nope. That can't happen.

"I'd love to," Katie said, "but unfortunately I have plans tomorrow. Can I give you a call later in the week when, hopefully, my schedule will ease up?"

"Sure," Gina said. "I'll look forward to talking with you then."

"Great. Bye." Katie hit the end-call icon as Vance appeared at her office door.

"Hey."

"Hey, yourself. What's up?"

Vance looked down at the ugly stained carpet Katie hadn't yet replaced in her seedy office. "I wanted to apologize for the tension that's been between you and me for the past few days," he said contritely. "I realize you have a lot on your mind, and I've been stressing about this floor situation because I want it to proceed as smoothly as possible. After all, it's essentially the first time I've overseen such a big project in my role as assistant manager for Artisans Alley."

Katie nodded, realizing Rose must have spoken to Vance. "It's been a bad week," she admitted. "Right after we talked about the floor, Jamie died, and I stuck you with the whole project. I feel I've heaped too much responsibility on you, and I'm sorry for that."

"Nonsense," Vance said. "I welcome the challenge. I'm...um... I'm also sorry Janie and I weren't able to attend the open house on Friday night. She wasn't feeling well. But I guarantee we'll be in soon."

Vance's wife had multiple sclerosis, so it was entirely possible she hadn't been feeling up to attending the event. But why hadn't he simply told her that yesterday? Either way, the air between them felt clearer.

"Thank you, Vance," she said. "Now, tell me all about the progress you've made and how we can get Artisans Alley back on an even keel."

Vance offered her a shy smile. "Well..." he began.

LATER THAT AFTERNOON, Katie was updating the Tealicious website with the good press the tearoom had received from Rochester's top newspaper when there was a tap on the door.

Ray poked his head into the office. "May I please come in?" he asked sheepishly.

"Sure." Katie sat back in her chair and folded her hands in her lap.

"Do you know where I might find Vance?" he asked, as he

came inside the office and closed the door behind him. "I have a question about the work we're doing on the floor today."

"I'm sorry. I spoke with him earlier, but I haven't seen him in a while." Katie noticed how weary Ray looked, and she gave him a wry smile. "Are the girls still angry with you?"

"A little," he said. "They even called Sophie at school so she could be ticked off at me, too."

"They'll get over it soon enough," Katie said.

"I hope so. Carol and I are taking them to dinner this evening, so that should help."

"Dinner always helps." Her words triggered her promise of a home-cooked meal to Ray. "About that meal I was supposed to make for you—"

"Not necessary," he interrupted.

"How about a gift card so you can take Carol and the girls out again?" she suggested.

"I don't think the ladies in my life would appreciate that." He smiled sadly. "See you, Katie." With that, he turned and left the office.

Katie felt a pang of regret, but she realized his moving on with Carol was probably for the best.

Still, it took several minutes before she could get back to work.

CHAPTER 26

The Alley had closed some ten minutes before, and as Katie was winding things down in her office, she kept ruminating over the question that had formed a rut in her brain. She decided to call Nick.

"Hey, Katie, what's up?"

"I called to ask you if Jamie was ever a model."

He laughed. "Uh-huh, you did a deep dive on Jamie's social media page and found those hot shirtless pics, didn't you?"

"Yes, but it takes a snoop to know one," she said defensively. "Besides, I was trying to figure out how Jamie knew Connor Davis. From the look of one of those photos, I'm guessing they modeled together."

"I'm putting you on speaker, so I can look for myself."

"The photo I'm talking about has—"

"I see it," he interrupted. "Oh, wow. I remember this guy from the funeral because he hovered near the casket for way too long —in my opinion—and he wept as though he was heartbroken. Do you think Connor was an ex-boyfriend?"

"It's likely. Tomorrow, I'm going to the Lambert Conservatory where Connor's current partner works. Hopefully, I can learn more about Connor from him."

"Katie, you can't merely go up to a stranger and ask him about his boyfriend!"

"I know that," she said. "I'll use some finesse. And while I won't wear the flashy clothes or the heavy makeup, I suppose I'll need to be *Kelly* at the conservatory."

"You're not making sense to me, sweetheart," Nick said. "What do you hope to learn from Connor's partner?"

"I think it's likely Jamie and Connor helped each other with the poker game just to impress their partners. Whether former lovers or merely friends, I believe the two had a strong enough bond to trust each other."

Nick huffed. "You're taking it as a fact that Jamie cheated. He could've won fairly, you know."

"Do you believe he did?" Katie asked.

"I want to," he said quietly.

"So do I, but I'm getting cynical as I age. What's that adage, 'trust but verify'?" she asked. "Well, I'm hoping to get some verification tomorrow."

"But is it wise to go poking around as Kelly Ferrell?" he asked.

"It's better to sleuth around as Kelly rather than Katie. If someone gets angry with my putting my nose in their business, they'll have a much harder time tracking an alias."

"Maybe, but you know yourself that a determined person can find you, no matter who you say you are," he said. "Past experiences have taught us that."

"I know," she said. "I'll be careful."

"You'd better, girl. You'd just better."

ON MONDAY MORNING, Katie lay awake in bed for several minutes savoring the warmth and comfort. Neither of the cats had stirred yet, and it was delightful not to hear the racket of the Tealicious staff preparing for the day. This was the one day of the week when nothing was expected of her, and she had the luxury of relaxing under the covers for a few more minutes.

It wasn't long, though, before Mason was sitting on her chest butting his head against her chin.

"Aw, come on," she protested. "Do I *have* to?"

Mason's answer was another gentle chin-butt.

She threw back the covers and went to the kitchen to serve up the cats' breakfast.

While they were eating, she got back into bed to check her email. She, along with the other merchant partners, had received an email from Seth. He'd scheduled a meeting for the next afternoon for the partners to meet at his office and go over the final offer before it was submitted to the warehouse owner. He requested that anyone unable to attend the meeting send him an email authorizing him to serve as their proxy in voting to accept or to reject the offer. The proxy vote would be used only if required to meet a quorum.

The email was professional and concise—Seth at his business best.

She sent back a brief reply confirming that she'd be present at the meeting. If she learned anything at the conservatory today, they could discuss her findings privately either before or after the meeting—but, of course, she didn't mention anything about her excursion in the email.

Katie tried to contact Margo to see if she'd like to tag along on the trip to the conservatory, but her call went straight to voice mail. She declined to leave a message.

Opening her closet, Katie wondered what kind of outfit Kelly Ferrell would wear to a conservatory. She opted for skinny jeans, ankle boots, a lightweight sweater, and a knee-length coat. She added a chunky scarf because, she decided, Kelly would.

~

THE LAMBERTON CONSERVATORY resided in the heart of Highland Park, known for its acres and acres of lilacs that bloom in May, their beauty and intoxicating perfume luring thousands of visitors from around the world every spring. The foliage throughout the park and around the conservatory was at full peak with the trees ablaze in spectacular color, making Katie glad she lived in a part of the country that experienced all four seasons.

While the conservatory itself wasn't as large as Katie had initially thought, she quickly realized she could get so enchanted looking at the orchids, cacti, and other exotic plants, that she might forget the reasons for her visit. She needed to speak with Luther Stapleton, the Director of Public Services, and she thought she'd devised a plausible reason for doing so.

Upon finding his office, she tapped lightly on the door.

"You may enter," he called.

Upon entering the office, she was surprised that Stapleton was quite a bit older than she'd expected. While Connor appeared to be in his early thirties, this man was in his mid- to late-fifties—a chunky man in an expensive suit, his demeanor stiff and formal.

Stapleton arched an eyebrow. "Yes?"

"Hello, Mr. Stapleton. I'm Kelly Ferrell. Would you have a moment to speak to me?"

He gestured for her to enter and sit. "How can I help you?"

"I'd like to get some information about your wedding facilities."

"I see." His eyes flew to her left hand where there was no sign of an engagement ring.

"The information isn't for me," she said, with a breathy laugh. "It's for my friend, Rose. She's met someone and is eager to get married."

"You don't approve?" he asked.

"I'm not sure," Katie said. "I don't know her intended very well, and in fact, Rose hasn't known him for very long."

"Ah, she better be careful that he isn't a gigolo," Mr. Stapleton said.

"I don't think Rose has a significant amount of assets, but thoughts of that nature have crossed my mind as well." Katie attempted to steer the conversation around to Connor. "Are you married, Mr. Stapleton?"

The man shook his head, rather sadly Katie thought. "No."

"Oh." Crap. Now what was she supposed to say?

"At the rate I'm going, I doubt I'll ever be," Stapleton said, his cold persona beginning to thaw.

"I'm with you there," Katie said honestly. "I recently got out of a long-term relationship and then sabotaged any chance of a relationship I could have had with another man."

Stapleton took off his glasses and shook his head. "Where did your friend meet *her* guy? Maybe we should give her methods a try."

"She met him when she called nine-one-one. I don't recommend it."

Katie and Stapleton shared a laugh.

"Want to hear something terrible?" she asked, leaning across the desk. "I have another friend who had a fabulous guy in his life. This guy wanted to marry him and take him away on a romantic honeymoon."

"Let me guess—one of them cheated?" he asked.

"Not the way you might imagine," Katie said. "He cheated at cards to win enough money for the trip. I really want a man someday who'll try to sweep me off my feet like that."

"So. Do. I." Mr. Stapleton sighed. "So, what happened? I'm guessing from your tone that your friend and his guy didn't live happily ever after."

"They didn't. My friend's partner died." She shook her head. "It was all very tragic."

He groaned. "Keep your Romeos—I'd be happy with a man who'd stay faithful and who'd simply be good to me."

"Yeah," Katie said. "Me, too."

Katie made more small talk asking about price packages, catering, flowers, etc., to keep her cover story intact, and Stapleton gave her a couple of brochures, indicating she really needed to speak to a member of their events staff.

"I'll give my friend these leaflets and have her call for more information." Katie rose from her seat. "Thank you for your help."

Stapleton stood. "I'm always happy to sing the conservatory's praises. It was nice meeting you."

"You, too." Katie gave him a smile and left his office.

It was time to do a little snooping at the conservatory. Jamie had been poisoned by rosary peas—something not native to the area. What better place to find such a poison than a structure filled with exotic plants. She asked one of the conservatory's worker bees but he didn't seem to know what she was talking about. Still, she wouldn't be surprised if the conservatory had such a plant among its collection.

As she walked to the parking lot to retrieve her car, Katie knew one thing for certain—if Connor Davis had helped Jamie cheat at poker, it wasn't because he wanted to surprise Luther Stapleton with some grand romantic gesture, which was too bad. It seemed like he deserved it.

CHAPTER 27

*B*ased on what she'd learned from Luther Stapleton, he and Connor had broken up because Connor had been unfaithful. Now "Kelly" was on her way to Connor's flower shop to do more sleuthing.

Katie pulled into a parking space near the front of the quaint stuccoed building with the Spanish tiled roof. The sign over the door proclaimed GERANIUM, accompanied by a painted rendering of said flower. She reapplied her dark lipstick before going into the shop, where she was greeted by a solid white cat.

"Hello," she said, bending to pet the graceful creature who was rubbing against her shin. "Aren't you gorgeous?"

"Hi. May I help you?" Connor asked as he came out from the back of the shop. "Oh, hey. It's nice to see you again."

"It's good to see you, too. What a beautiful shop you have." She looked down at the cat. "And who is this beauty?"

"That's my assistant, Snowflake." He smiled. "She's great with the customers and works for cat food and treats."

"Sounds like quite the bargain."

"She is," he said. "How may I help you today?"

"I want to get some flowers for my mother-in-law. She's visiting us from Connecticut." Katie rolled her eyes with all the drama of a teenaged girl. "I can't believe I'm still trying to win that woman over. She wouldn't even accompany me to the Lamberton Conservatory this morning, and I was only going to try to impress her."

Connor's smile froze, and he inclined his head but said nothing.

Katie decided another push was in order. "I imagine you adore that place."

"Yes, it's lovely," he said.

What was it going to take to bring the man around to discussing the conservatory and, hopefully, Luther Stapleton? "Do you go every chance you get?"

His smiling disappearing altogether, he admitted, "Not as much as I used to. My ex works there."

"Oh, no." Katie raised her hand to her chest. "I'm so sorry. I hope I didn't bring up painful memories."

"Of course not. The conservatory *is* an incredible place that I used to enjoy visiting very much—that is until my boyfriend cheated on me."

"Wait, *what?*" The words escaped before Katie could stop them. "I mean, why would anyone cheat on you? You're handsome, successful, you own your own business—"

Connor's smile reappeared but was more reserved now. "Thank you. I appreciate your kind words."

"Believe me, I went through my fair share of failed relationships before I met Nick," she said. "The right one will come along for you, too."

"I thought he already had." He gave his head a slight shake as though to dislodge the sadness. "But enough about the lovelorn, what are you thinking of getting your mother-in-law?"

"A swift kick—oh, you mean, the flowers." She grinned.

"Those white roses are breathtaking. How about a bouquet with those, some pink lilies, and a little greenery?"

"Coming right up," he said.

As he went in the back to prepare the arrangement, Katie turned her attention to Snowflake again. Caressing the cat's regal head, she wondered which man was lying about his lover being unfaithful—Connor or Luther Stapleton? She also speculated about Connor's statement about thinking the right one already had come along—had he be referring to Luther or Jamie?

THE ENTIRE DRIVE back to McKinlay Mill, Katie wrestled with those questions. Why would either man lie about his lover being unfaithful? Luther had no reason whatsoever. As a stranger, he probably didn't care a fig what she thought. He could've just as easily said, "I cheated on my boyfriend and then realized I'd made a mistake. It was too late, though; he wouldn't take me back."

Connor could have said anything from "we had differences about how to manage our finances" to "I caught him in a lie." He didn't have to say his boyfriend had been unfaithful.

Was one of the men lying? Were *both* of them lying? If so, why?

She drove to Sassy Sally's and took the flowers inside to Margo, who was sitting in the living room.

"Katie, what a wonderful surprise! How thoughtful."

Feeling a bit sheepish, Katie explained how she came to get the flowers for Margo. "I pretended I was getting the flowers for Nick's mean mom, who wouldn't even accompany me to the Lamberton Conservatory today. I really did try to call and ask you to go, by the way, but I didn't leave a message when you didn't answer. I thought you might still be sleeping."

"No. I was up and at 'em early." Margo leaned back against the couch cushions and looked up at the ceiling. "Connor thought he'd already met Mr. Right...and you don't know if he was talking about Luther Stapleton or Jamie Seifert. Hmmm... Is there any chance Connor and Jamie were dating when Jamie met Seth?"

"I don't know." Katie placed the vase of flowers on the coffee table and sat beside Margo. "If Jamie had broken Connor's heart, that would certainly give Connor a motive for his murder; but why would Connor help Jamie cheat at poker so Jamie had enough money to marry Seth?"

"Maybe we have it wrong," Margo said. "Maybe Connor isn't the one who helped Jamie cheat. But, as they saw each other on Wednesday evening, Connor could still conceivably be the killer. Did Jamie go to these weekly games regularly?"

"Apparently he was well known at the poker club," Katie said. "Seth didn't know. He must've been keeping the games secret."

"Then let's say he regularly attended the games. Anyone with a grudge against him could have plotted to murder him at the game." Margo sat up and leaned her elbows on her knees. "Were you served food at this event?"

"No, only drinks."

"Still, the poison could have been administered through a beverage."

"That's true," Katie said, "but I think in the case of this partic-ular poison, solid food might've been a better choice."

"That could be why it took so long to work," Margo observed.

Katie had looked the poison up online. The seeds from it had to have been ground into a powder to not be noticed.

"The poison could've been mixed into a cocktail, I suppose." Katie spoke her thoughts aloud. "And while the symptoms were painful, the poison was slow acting."

"I think we should take another look at the people in the medical examiner's office," Margo said. "Who would know poisons better than the people trained to detect it?"

"That's fair, but if it was someone in the medical examiner's office, wouldn't he or she make sure the police never received the toxicology report?"

Margo spread her hands. "That might have been an impossibility. You know very well that when you're working with other people, you can seldom control what they're going to do."

"That's true," Katie said.

"And didn't you say there was a woman at the poker game from the medical examiner's office?"

"I did. Her name is Phyllis." Katie sighed. "Unfortunately, she sat at Ray's table, and I didn't get the opportunity to speak with her."

"Then go talk with her. Find out what she knows," Margo said.

"But how? She might recognize me as Katie Bonner rather than Kelly Ferrell."

"Then call her, dear. That way you can be whichever persona you choose." She frowned. "I think I'd go with Kelly Ferrell. Tell her she spoke with your husband at the event, make up an excuse to talk with her, and then—"

"What? Ask her if she and Jamie cheated the week before?"

Margo shrugged. "Not in so many words…."

Giving a little groan of frustration, Katie said, "I don't know what to do, Margo. It's looking more and more like Jamie wasn't the man Seth adored, and I don't want to ruin Seth's memories. I merely want to find out who killed the man."

"I understand. It's all right—we'll figure it out." Changing the subject, Margo said, "Oh, by the way, I appreciate your almost invitation to the conservatory, but I couldn't have gone even if I'd answered your call in time."

"Why not?" Katie asked. "Busy morning?"

"Absolutely." Margo beamed. "I met with a Realtor and looked at some properties."

"Properties…you mean, business opportunities?"

"No—residential sites," Margo said. "I've decided to move to McKinlay Mill."

Blown away by Margo's news, Katie sat there, dumbfounded.

"Well, aren't you going to say something?" Margo asked, her gaze penetrating.

Katie's forced laugh was feeble. "Welcome to the neighborhood."

CHAPTER 28

*M*argo blathered on and on about the various properties she'd inspected, but none of them were to her liking. She might just have to widen her net.

Yeah, make it really *wide*, Katie thought. *Two or three counties over ought to do the trick.*

Heavy-hearted, Katie trudged back to her apartment to change clothes before heading to Artisans Alley, trying to process Margo's big announcement. With Margo in McKinlay Mill, Chad's ghost and their shared past would be with Katie all the time—not that it wasn't already, but the specter would loom even larger with Chad's mother living nearby. On the other hand, she could use some help running Tealicious, and Margo *was* a full partner. Why shouldn't she be sharing the workload, as well as the finances?

But at the moment, Artisans Alley was her top priority and with new determination, Katie made a beeline up the stairs to check on the progress being made on the floor. Since it was a workday for Wood U, she wasn't surprised that Ray wasn't giving Vance a helping hand.

"Hi, there." She knelt beside Vance. "Got an extra brush?"

"Sure do." He handed her a paintbrush. "I appreciate the assistance. Together we should be able to get this knocked out today, and the floor should be dry enough by Wednesday evening to allow the vendors to put their booths back where they belong."

"That's terrific," she said, as she dipped her brush into the stain. "Vance, how do you get along with Janie's mom?"

"Eh, pretty good. Why do you ask?"

She told him about Margo's decision to move to McKinlay Mill. "On the one hand, I believe it could be nice to have her here full time."

"But on the other, it's hard for a young widow to live in such close proximity to her late husband's mother," Vance said.

"Exactly. I mean, Margo was great about my relationship with Andy, but I know she'll be comparing everyone I date from here on out to Chad."

"Don't you do that, too?" he asked.

"Yeah, I guess." She sighed. "I don't know. I'm conflicted about so many things in my life right now. I wish Jamie's killer would be caught and brought to justice so Tealicious could get out from under this cloud of suspicion. Business was better on Saturday, but I want to repair the tearoom's reputation once and for all."

"I understand. Rose told me how you and Ray went under-cover at that poker game—that took a lot of guts."

She snorted derisively. "I'm not so sure about that anymore. I wish I'd simply attended the game *by* myself *as* myself. It's too hard following up on leads as Kelly Ferrell when the people I need to question live in such close proximity."

"And you had to miss Jamie's funeral," Vance said. "That had to be tough."

"It was. I felt like I was really letting Seth down."

They worked in companionable silence for a long while, as a myriad of thoughts pinged through Katie's brain like a super-charged pinball game. One thought stuck, however, and Katie realized she needed to call Phyllis before the medical examiner's office closed.

She handed Vance her brush. "I'm sorry, but there's something I need to take care of." She climbed to her feet, feeling the stress from the job on her knees and back. She was twenty years younger than Vance. He might need a bonus for doing all this work.

"Thanks for helping with the floor," he said.

Katie gave a weary laugh. "Well, I'm the building's owner. I've got to be prepared to do what she needs. Besides, it was nice catching up with you. And it'll give me a chance to give that soaker tub of mine a real workout tonight."

He laughed. "That's my plan for tonight as well."

Katie returned to her office, stopping first at the washroom to scrub her stained hands. She closed the door and called Phyllis.

"Hey, Phyllis," she said when the other woman came on the line. "This is Kelly Ferrell. You sat with my husband at the poker table last Wednesday at the club on Alexander Street, and I wanted to call and apologize to you for his rude behavior."

"Oh, he wasn't rude," Phyllis said.

"As drunk as he was when we left the game, I didn't know what he might've said or done," Katie said. "I wish the event organizers had allowed us to sit at the same table, so I could've kept a more watchful eye on him."

"He was fine, apart from having a morbid curiosity about Jamie Seifert."

Broaching that subject was easier than Katie had anticipated. She hadn't dreamed Phyllis would bring it up.

"That was a sad occurrence," Katie agreed. "It certainly rocked the McKinlay Mill community, and it did rouse our interest. Did you know Jamie well?"

"Of course. You *are* aware we worked together at the medical examiner's office, but I'm also the one who introduced Jamie to the poker game. He was talking with me one evening about some reports he needed typed up, and I said they'd have to wait—I needed to get to my poker game."

Katie laughed. "And you offered to take him with you?"

"Well, not right away, but he was so inquisitive that I finally asked if he could get his hands on five hundred dollars within thirty minutes. He said yes, and I said, 'Then come and check it out for yourself.' And he did."

"You two were able to bond over a love of poker," Katie asked.

"Something like that."

Katie found Phyllis's response a bit cagey. She pressed on. "Were you delighted when your protégé won big that evening? I think I'd have asked him for a finder's fee had I been in your position."

"I suppose I should have," Phyllis said and laughed. "But it doesn't matter anymore, does it?"

"No, I guess not." Time to find out what else Phyllis knew about the dead man. "I believe a guy sitting at my table was friends with Jamie—Connor Davis?"

"Yes, they appeared to be really close. Had it not been for Jamie being so head over heels in love with Seth Lawson, I'd have thought Jamie and Connor would have made an excellent match."

"For some reason, I got the impression Jamie and Connor *had* dated in the past," Katie said.

"Oh, I don't think so," Phyllis said. "I don't think Jamie was ever serious about anyone until he got involved with Seth. Before they started dating, Jamie would go out with groups of friends but never any one of them in particular." She paused. "I hope I answered all your questions, but I really need to get back to work now, Katie—I mean, Kelly."

Katie's stomach did a flip-flop and she gulped. Was Phyllis letting her know she wasn't fooled by the ruse—that she knew she'd been talking with Katie Bonner all along? And if Phyllis knew, who else did?

"Th-thanks for your time, Phyllis."

"Anytime, dear."

Katie hung up the phone, feeling sick with despair. She was still sitting at her desk staring into space when two of the Davenport sisters barged into her office. Startled, Katie sat straighter.

"What's wrong with you?" Sasha asked, although not with sincerity. "You look like you've just seen a ghost."

Without giving Katie time to answer, Sadie surged ahead. "Well, whatever it is, it can't be as bad as what's going on with *us*."

"We're looking for our dad," Sasha said rudely. "He's not upstairs with Vance."

"N-no." Katie finally snapped out of her reverie enough to ask, "Isn't he at Wood U?"

"No," Sadie said. "That's the first place we looked, of course."

"He closed the shop?" Katie asked.

"Duh!" Sasha said. "And that's not like him. We need the money." The sisters rolled their eyes at each other as though Katie was dense.

"He's probably with Carol," Katie said. "

"That's *exactly* what we're worried about!" Sasha exclaimed.

"I take it you didn't enjoy dinner last night," Katie stated, remembering Ray telling her that he and Carol were taking the girls out.

"The food was fine—it was the company we could have done without," Sadie growled.

"It was sickening. Dad and Carol kept smiling, like they were keeping some kind of major secret, and making goo-goo eyes at each other," Sasha said.

"And they giggled and whispered and acted like we weren't even there," Sadie said. "They were absolutely gross."

"Have you told your dad how you feel?" Katie asked. "Maybe you should let him know you'd like him and Carol to exercise some restraint—especially out in public."

"That's not the only thing," Sadie said. "She's trying to convince Dad to go back into police work—maybe as a consultant. But that could still be dangerous. We've already lost our mom, and—"

As hard as she tried not to, Katie couldn't help tuning out the girls' voices. The last thing Ray needed to do was return to police work. Their undercover mission had been a total bust. And after her conversation with Phyllis, she was pretty sure they hadn't fooled anyone.

"What do you want from me?" Katie asked bluntly.

The sisters seemed startled by her question, their eyes wide and frightened.

"Well..." Sasha started, but she didn't seem to have an answer.

"You made it abundantly clear that you didn't want me to be a part of your father's life—even as friends. Well, ladies, you got your wish."

"But—but," Sadie started.

Katie rose from her seat. "I suggest you go home and think about what you want for your *own* lives and come to terms with how your father has decided to live *his*."

"Why are you being so mean?" Sasha asked.

"You could ask yourselves the same question. I've lost a friend. You still have your dad, but life often hands us hardships we never envisioned." Like Chad dying, Andy's infidelity, and now Margo's threat to reside in or near McKinlay Mill.

Sasha's eyes filled with tears. She turned to her older sister, whose eyes were also welling.

"I'm sorry, I know you girls are just kids—"

"We are not!" Sadie declared.

"Yeah, you are," Katie asserted, "but you need to learn a lesson, too. Your actions have consequences. Let me tell you from bitter experience that the sooner you learn that, the less grief you'll endure."

"What are you saying?" Sadie asked.

"Be careful what you wish for. You may just get it."

CHAPTER 29

*A*fter the brutal conversation with Sadie and Sasha, Katie felt like ten different kinds of rat. But as far as she was concerned, her connection with the Davenport sisters and their father was severed. Still, the entire encounter left a bitter tang on her tongue.

Once closing time arrived, Katie left Artisans Alley and walked to her apartment, fed Mason and Della, and sank onto the love seat. She felt exhausted, and the idea of a long soak in her tub was as alluring as a siren song. But then her phone rang. She groaned, not prepared to deal with anything or anybody else that day. Still, she glanced at the screen. When she saw it was Nick, she answered the call.

"I need you to go somewhere with me," he whispered.

Katie's hackles rose. "What's wrong?"

"I'll explain when I pick you up. Can you be ready in ten?"

"Yeah, sure," she said, "but—"

"Great, love, thanks! See you soon!"

She wondered why he'd spoken in such a loud, jovial tone then, but he'd ended the call before she could ask. She supposed perhaps someone else—Don? Margo?—had come into the room.

There was definitely something strange brewing at Sassy Sally's, and Katie had a bad feeling about whatever it was. Given the day she'd had, the last thing she needed was to get caught up in more drama, but she'd do whatever Nick needed her to do. After all, he had always been there to help her.

The man was prompt—she had to give him that. Precisely ten minutes after his call, he was tapping on her door.

Opening the door, she said, "Come on in."

"No time." He jerked his head toward the parking lot. "Hurry and grab your purse. Then come get in the car."

As soon as Katie was buckled into the passenger seat of Nick's car, she asked, "Will you please tell me what's going on?"

"We're going to see a woman who wants to plan an event at Sassy Sally's."

She frowned. "Don't they usually come to you? And why would you need me to go along for that? You plan events every day without my assistance."

"Well, there *is* a little more to it than that." He glanced over and gave her a sheepish grin. "This woman fosters children, and I want to pick her brain about the process while I'm there."

"Once again, I don't know how I can be of any help to you."

"I just need you along for moral support." He backed out of the parking space. "Don isn't amenable to the idea of our fostering a child—I've told you that already. If I make the commitment to go through with this for real—which I'm seriously considering—then I'll need your help convincing Don that we need a baby to complete our family."

Katie didn't want to be dragged into the middle of Nick and Don's family drama, but she leaned back against the seat in resignation.

They drove to a large brick home with a fenced backyard. An affable collie greeted them at the gate.

"What a beautiful home," Katie said, thinking this place would make a wonderful bed and breakfast if the owner ever wanted to sell.

A pretty, middle-aged woman came out onto the porch with a blond cherub on her hip. Katie heard Nick's sharp intake of breath. The man was a goner.

Stepping up and onto the porch, Nick held out his arms. The baby reached for Nick as though he'd known him his entire short life. The woman handed over the child, and Nick hugged him close, his face wreathed in emotion. And then the baby threw up down the front of Nick's shirt.

"I'm so sorry," the woman said in horror. "Sebastian has a sensitive tummy. Come on in, and I'll get a damp cloth to get that off your shirt."

They followed the woman into the kitchen where she wet a dishcloth and handed it to Nick before taking the baby.

"I'll change Sebastian, and then I'll be right back." She took the baby out of the room.

Nick tried to hide his revulsion as he wiped yellow goo off his white button-down shirt, but Katie knew him well enough to see it.

"I don't believe we've met." The woman returned with Sebastian in a fresh onesie. She stretched a hand out to Katie. "I'm Clarissa."

Katie shook the woman's hand. "Katie Bonner. It's a pleasure to meet you."

"Are you Nick's sister?" Clarissa asked.

"No, just a good friend."

Nick held the cloth aloft between two fingers. "What should I do with this?"

"I'll take it." Clarissa took the cloth, walked over to the washer and dryer in the corner, and tossed the cloth into the washer. "I do laundry every day." She laughed. "It's a never-ending cycle. I wash the clothes, and he dirties them." Looking at the baby, she asked, "Don't you, sweet boy?"

The baby giggled happily.

Nick smiled. "He's gorgeous."

"Thank you," Clarissa said. "Would either of you like something to drink?"

They both declined.

"Please sit," Clarissa said, gesturing to the kitchen table.

They did.

"Do you have other children?" Katie asked.

"My husband and I have two children who are away at college, and one who's working in the city as a tax attorney, and our three fosters: this little guy and a brother and sister, ages ten and twelve. My husband took them for ice cream, so I could talk with Nick about the surprise holiday package I want to book for my parents."

"Tell us more about Sebastian," Nick said.

"He's such a good baby," Clarissa said, eyeing the baby with pride. "As you've seen, he does have an awfully sensitive stomach. He was a little colicky when he was brought to us, but some simethicone drops cleared that right up. He does sleep through the night, which is wonderful." She rolled her eyes. "Two out of my three children didn't sleep through the night until they were six months old."

"What did you do?" Nick asked.

Clarissa laughed. "I didn't sleep through the night for six months, either. But I did nap during the day some when they did —not always, but sometimes, I simply *had* to. It was exhausting."

"I can only imagine," Katie said. "How did Sebastian come to be with you?"

"Um..." Clarissa cleared her throat and down at Sebastian, as though not wanting to talk about it in front of the child.

Katie was sure Sebastian wouldn't comprehend what she was saying and was too young to remember it even if he could understand. Besides, no matter how tragic his beginnings had been, didn't he have the right to know—eventually?

"Monroe County Foster Care." Clarissa gave a shaky laugh. "Sebastian was left in a cardboard box in front of a fire station in Gates when he was two months old. There was a note inside that said simply, 'Please take care of my baby, Sebastian, and make sure he finds a good home.' That's all we know."

"I'm sure every effort was made to find Sebastian's parents," Katie said.

"Naturally." Clarissa shrugged slightly.

Sebastian wound his tiny fist into her hair and yanked.

"Ow!" Clarissa blinked back the tears that had sprung to her eyes as she gently removed Sebastian's hand from her hair. Then she kissed his chubby fist and pushed her hair away from her face. "I usually keep my hair up for that reason." She handed the baby to Nick. "If you don't mind keeping an eye on him for a moment, I'll run upstairs and put my hair up. Otherwise, he's going to keep pulling it and distracting us. Thanks."

"No problem!" Nick called, as Clarissa hurried from the kitchen. He bounced the baby on his lap.

The bouncing made Sebastian laugh, but warning bells went off in Katie's head.

"Nick, remember the sensitive stomach," she said.

"Oh. Right." Nick smiled at Sebastian. "We don't want to make your tummy upset again, do we?"

Sebastian stilled.

"What is it, sweetheart?" Nick asked him. "Are you all right?"

The baby's face reddened, and he looked determined. And then came the odor.

Nick held Sebastian up and off his lap as the child laughed. "Um...Clarissa! I think Sebastian needs to be changed!"

"Okay," she called. "Bring him up, and you can do it."

As he rose from his chair with a cooing Sebastian in his arms, Nick shot Katie a look of pure dread.

"That'll be fun," Katie said with a smile. She managed to wait until he was out of the kitchen before she buried her head in her hands and laughed.

When Nick, Clarissa, and Sebastian came downstairs, Sebastian was wearing yet another clean onesie and was nestled contentedly against Clarissa's neck. Nick appeared traumatized and more than a little green around the gills. The wet spots on his shirt hadn't dried yet, but new spots had joined the previous ones. Katie didn't know what had happened upstairs, but it had apparently not been pleasant.

"Tell me about your parents," Nick said, sinking onto the kitchen chair he'd occupied before his trip upstairs.

Before Clarissa could answer him, someone entered the room.

When Clarissa broke into a wide smile, Katie thought she was getting ready to meet the woman's husband and the two foster children he'd taken for ice cream. She, too, smiled in anticipation of the meeting as she swiveled in her chair.

Katie's smile froze as she recognized the newcomer.

"Connor, this is Nick Ferrell and Katie Bonner," Clarissa said. "Nick is interested in becoming a foster father. Nick, Katie, this is my brother, Connor."

CHAPTER 30

*N*ick had been uncharacteristically quiet on the drive back to McKinlay Mill. When Katie tried to talk, he cut her off, saying he "just can't right now." When he dropped Katie off at her apartment, she wasted no time before calling Seth. She felt panicky and needed his wise counsel.

"Hey, pseudo sis," he answered, his words slightly slurred.

"Are you all right?" she asked. "Have you been drinking?"

"Just tossing back a couple after a long day at work—is that okay with you, *Mom?*" There was a thread of steel woven into his teasing.

He was right. Given what Seth had been through, he was entitled to "toss back a couple." That didn't keep her from being concerned.

"Have you eaten?" Maybe she could intervene...in the nicest possible way.

"No."

"Neither have I," she said. "How about I bring over Chinese food?"

"Jamie loved Chinese food," Seth said, sounding maudlin.

"I can bring something else," she suggested. *Anything but an*

Angelo's pizza, she thought.

"No, I'd like Chinese food...in honor of Jamie."

"All right. I'll be there soon." Katie wanted to beg him not to have anything more to drink before she got there, but she didn't dare. He was absolutely right—she wasn't his mother.

When she arrived at Seth's house half an hour later and knocked on the door, he called, "Come on in."

Sure enough, the door was unlocked. She walked inside and locked the door behind her. Seth slouched on the couch with a highball glass in his hand.

Pretending everything was hunky-dory, Katie held up the big brown paper bag. "I hope you're hungry."

"Not really." He stood. "But I'll have some since you've gone to all this trouble."

In the kitchen, Katie set the scotch bottle aside and got out plates and silverware before unpacking the Hunan pork, fried rice, and eggrolls. She filled two tall glasses with water, hoping to encourage Seth to lay off the booze. His eyes were bloodshot, and she wondered if his condition was from drinking or weeping—or both.

He sat at the table, avoiding her gaze. "Thank you for this."

Katie felt a pang of guilt. She should've been paying more attention to her friend's emotional state. She'd been in a similar situation and could well imagine how he felt. Instead, she'd called to ask him for his advice on her problems.

In her defense, she hadn't known who else to talk with. Ray would have been the obvious choice to discuss their blown covers—apparently, Phyllis had known all along—but they'd made the mutual decision to step away from each other. She couldn't continue to go running back to consult with him at the first sign of trouble.

They ate in silence for several minutes, with Katie castigating herself for being so selfish when Seth was still in such obvious pain and vowing to be a better friend.

Eventually, Seth put down his fork and asked, "Are you going to tell me what's on your mind?"

She looked up into his beautiful, sincere face, and her eyes filled with tears. "I missed Jamie's funeral for nothing."

"What do you mean?"

"I went to lunch with Gina Solero because we couldn't risk Connor Davis learning who I was and blowing my cover to the poker game attendees. But it was all for nothing. Phyllis from the medical examiner's office knew who I was all along." She explained about her phone call earlier that day.

"It could have been a mistake." His tone belied his words.

"That's not all. Nick and I were at Connor's sister's house this evening. We didn't know she was his sister, of course, until he arrived, and she introduced us."

"Did Connor confront you about your deception?" Seth asked.

"I told his sister we'd met previously, and I asked to speak with him outside," Katie said. "I led Connor to believe that I hadn't wanted to reveal my true identity at the poker game because of the controversy surrounding Tealicious. I went on to say I had pretended to be married because I'd recently gotten out of a long-term relationship and didn't want to encourage any of the poker players who might want to ask me out." She spread her hands. "That makes me sound like I'm vain, but so be it. Better that than to tell the truth—that I'd brought along an ex-cop thinking he might be able to help me discover who'd poisoned Jamie but instead he acted like a frat boy who thought he was on a date."

Seth took a sip of his water. "Do you think Connor bought it?"

"I'm not sure, but I doubt it matters much at this point." She sighed. "If Phyllis knew who I really was all along, then I made a fool of myself all the way around."

Seth gave a feeble laugh. "Katie, you won over twenty grand at that game. I doubt anyone thought you looked foolish. Lucky, more like."

There was that.

"Why were you and Nick at Connor's sister's house?" Seth continued.

"She wants to surprise her parents with a gift package for a stay at Sassy Sally's for the holidays," Katie said. "Nick wanted me to go with him to Clarissa's house because she fosters children— including a gorgeous baby boy—and Nick wanted more information about fostering."

"And how did *that* go?" he asked.

Katie giggled. "He absolutely refused to talk about it with me on the way home."

"Nick? Refused to talk?" Seth asked, sounding incredulous.

Nodding, Katie said, "He quickly learned that caring for a baby isn't all sunshine and teddy bears. The baby threw up on Nick the minute we arrived."

Seth's jaw dropped, and then he started to laugh. "Are you serious?"

"Oh, yes. Then after the baby gave Clarissa's hair a mighty yank, she handed off the boy to Nick again. Shortly thereafter, Nick got to change a particularly stinky, poopy diaper."

Wiping tears from his eyes, Seth said, "I'd have loved to have seen that."

"I'm guessing the clothes he was wearing will go straight into the garbage...or the fireplace," she said, joining in Seth's laughter.

"So, he's over his desire to foster a baby?" Seth asked.

"At least for the time being." As she sipped her water, she had a deliciously wicked thought. "We should tell Don to inform Nick that he's changed his mind and is all-in on adopting a baby."

He shook his head. "You are a cruel, cruel woman."

Was she? Katie pushed a clump of rice around her plate and decided to test that theory. "Did you and Jamie ever talk about having children?"

Seth shook his head sadly. "We never even talked about marriage, that's why it was such a shock to learn he wanted to make such a grand gesture with a proposal and a flashy wedding ceremony." He looked down at his plate. "We did talk about getting a dog—a rescue." He looked thoughtful. "Maybe I should consider it more seriously now." His voice cracked. "I absolutely hate being alone."

Tears sprang to Katie's eyes, and she got up from the table and moved to stand behind Seth, wrapping her arms around him and resting her chin on the top of his head. She didn't know what to say, how to comfort him, so she just hung on. He raised a hand to pat her arm and they clung together for a long moment. Then, finally, Seth cleared his throat. "Do you think I could have another helping of that pork?"

Katie pulled away. "You sure can."

She sat back down and doled out another portion of the meat and vegetables, nestling them beside the rice and half-eaten eggroll on his plate. "So, what kind of dog were you thinking of getting?"

KATIE DROVE the dark streets along McKinlay Mill's main drag and returned to her apartment over Tealicious on Victoria Square. With all she'd endured that day, to say she felt emotionally exhausted was putting it lightly. What she needed was a long soak in a fragrant, hot tub of water. Probably the best perk about her new, but smaller digs was the soaker tub she'd determined would be essential to her mental health.

She ran the bath, poured herself a generous glass of wine, lit a couple of vanilla-scented candles, and sank into her tub while the cats tentatively dipped their paws into the bubbles. Her body was stiff and sore from staining the Alley's second floor, and she decided she would definitely have to include some extra cash in Vance's Christmas bonus this year.

One of the subjects she finally allowed herself to consider was the new situation with her former mother-in-law. Katie hadn't mentioned Margo's move to Seth, although she was certain he was the one Margo would hire for the closing once she found the perfect property. Although she wondered if he and Margo had already discussed the move. Katie hadn't wanted to spoil the evening by bringing up yet another serious topic of discussion after she had Seth laughing about Nick and his eye-opening experience with little Sebastian. It felt good to see the man laugh, especially given the condition she'd found him in when she'd first arrived at his house.

Katie couldn't quite decide how she felt about Margo's impending move. With a jolt, Katie realized she was probably the only "family" Margo had left. The poor woman's parents were gone, her son was gone, and now she was reaching out to the daughter-in-law she'd never fully accepted before her son had died. It was sad really. Like Seth, Katie knew no one wanted to be alone, especially as they grew older.

Other than her friends and the odd cousin across the pond, Katie didn't have family either. Maybe having Margo in McKinlay Mill wouldn't be so bad.

She got out of the tub, wrapped a bath sheet around herself to dry off, donned her flannel pajamas and robe, and retrieved her phone.

"Hello, darling girl," Margo answered. "Is everything all right?"

"Everything's fine," Katie said. "I was just wondering if you'd like me to go with you to look at some of these houses you're considering."

"I'd absolutely love it," Margo said, sounding delighted. "Are you free tomorrow?"

CHAPTER 31

The next morning, after feeding the cats and getting ready for the day, Katie headed downstairs to Tealicious to give Brad a hand with the tea shop's desserts and was surprised to find Margo already there.

"Margo, what are you doing here?" she asked.

"She's *baking*," Brad said, widening his eyes at Katie behind Margo's back. "Isn't that *marvelous?*"

"That's right," Margo said, wiping her hands on the bib apron that covered her pink silk blouse and dark slacks. "I've been a silent partner long enough. I've realized you've been doing all the work, Katie, while I've done nothing more strenuous than open a checkbook and pick up a pen. I'm here to roll up my sleeves and help."

Brad's eyes silently pleaded with Katie to help him out. "I've tried to assure her that isn't necessary."

Katie felt a twinge of pride that Margo apparently wasn't as talented in the kitchen as she was—after all, the woman seemed so accomplished in everything else—but she was also pleased that Margo was trying.

In order to get Margo out of Brad's way, she asked, "Margo,

is there any way Brad could take over for you? Brad, I hate to drag Margo away, but I need to get to Artisans Alley soon and wanted to talk with her about some of the properties she's considering."

"Oh, yes, Brad," Margo said, excitedly, handing him the wooden spoon she'd been using to stir the dough. "You can finish up here, can't you?"

"Yes, I'll manage," he said. Behind Margo's back, he mouthed *thank you* to Katie and then smiled broadly at Margo when she turned.

"Thanks, darling." She patted his cheek. "You're doing a fabulous job with this place. Isn't he, Katie?"

"Absolutely." Katie prepared a pot of tea, as Margo got her laptop bag off a shelf in the kitchen.

By the time Katie joined Margo in the dining room with their tea, Margo had pulled up a browser window with four tabs, each with a property she was considering.

The first screen showcased a beautiful three-bedroom, two-bath ranch house with an airy, open floor plan. Katie especially loved the white country kitchen with its marble counters, subway tiles, and big island perfect for rolling out pastry and making cut-out cookies; but given Brad's reaction to having Margo's help that morning, she realized that particular feature might not be as important to her former mother-in-law as it would be to her. Katie poured their tea and tried to be noncommittal about the property.

The second home was slightly smaller, and it had a home office with a gorgeous view of the lake.

"I love that office," Katie said. "I can easily imagine you ensconced in that room, surrounded by books on the floor-to-ceiling shelves, your reading glasses perched on your nose as you study your laptop screen."

Margo leaned back so she could peer at Katie. "Since when do I *perch* my reading glasses on my nose?"

Laughing, Katie said, "Never. I doubt you even *need* reading glasses, but if you did, you wouldn't be a *percher*."

Margo grinned. "I plead the fifth." She sipped her tea.

The third was a huge Victorian home with turrets and spires.

"That's breathtaking," Katie said, "but it seems to be rather large for just one person...unless, of course, you plan on turning it into a bed and breakfast one of these days."

"Well, you never know." She opened the last tab. "What do you think of this one?"

The fourth home was a mock-Tudor, originally built in the 1920s but completely remodeled just the year before.

"That's beautiful. It could be a showplace." She smiled at Margo. "I can just see you sweeping down that staircase."

"Yes." Margo sighed. "That staircase is a consideration as I get older. But I'm touring the Victorian this afternoon if you'd like to join me."

"I'd love to," Katie said, "but I have a meeting at Seth's office about the warehouse property this afternoon."

"All right. I'll call the realtor and reschedule for tomorrow morning. Does that work for you?"

"It does." Katie wondered why Margo would be so accommodating for her. "But you don't have to change your plans on my account."

"Of course, I do," Margo said. "I know you were responsible for a lot of the furnishings at Sassy Sally's, and I'd love to make my home comfy but as stylish as that. Besides, you know all the local antique shops so well." She added a splash of milk to her tea. "I know you're swamped, Katie, but I'd truly appreciate your input with regard to decorating and making the house a real home. After all, it'll be yours someday."

Katie froze, her teacup halfway to her mouth, her stomach doing a somersault. Although her mouth had gone dry at Margo's words, she put the cup back down on the table. "What do you mean?"

"Who else do I have to leave all my worldly goods to?" Margo asked.

A myriad of emotions flooded through Katie: shock, for one and an unexpected flush of affection for another. "You'd better not be leaving anything to anyone for a *very* long time," she said, her tone light if a little wobbly. "And don't even think of leaving me with an undecorated house. I've had it up to here—" She raised her hand to chin level. "—with renovations lately."

They shared a hearty laugh.

"I won't, dear. Now, shall we look at some other listings?"

KATIE FOUND herself humming a cheerful tune as she walked across the parking lot to Artisans Alley. Despite the nip in the air, which made her pull her coat more tightly about her, it was a beautiful, clear morning, and Katie crossed her fingers that things were finally looking up. Unfortunately, that feeling was not destined to last.

The lights were on in the vendors' lounge, and the aroma of fresh coffee filled the air. Katie had just fished her key from her pocket to unlock her office when she noticed she didn't need it. Someone had already been there and had jimmied the door, its casing splintered.

Not wanting to jump to conclusions but not wanting to be reckless, Katie backed off, retreating to a far corner of the vendors' lounge and called Vance's cell phone.

"Good morning, Katie!" he said. "The vendors are delighted that they'll be able to move back to their usual booths tonight after hours."

"That's great, Vance. Could you come down to the vendors' lounge for a moment please?"

"Sure. Is there anything wrong?"

"I don't know, but I've got a bad feeling," she said.

"I'm on my way," he said and abruptly ended the call.

When Vance arrived in the vendors' lounge, Katie quickly told him what had happened.

"Could it have been someone we know?" she asked. "A handyman, maybe?" She knew it was unlikely, but it didn't hurt to inquire.

"You know better." He puffed out his chest. "I'll go check it out."

"We'll both go," she said. "Two are always better than one—that's why I called you."

Katie went ahead of Vance and flung open the door. The tiny room was dark and appeared to be empty. She flipped on the light and poked her head inside, taking in the tidy desk, the computer, and file cabinets.

"It doesn't look to me like there's anything out of place," Vance said. "What do you think?"

Shaking her head, Katie said, "No. Maybe the intruder got interrupted before he or she did anything more than pry the door open."

"Who do you think would have done such a thing?" Vance scratched his chin. "I suppose some people could think we have a safe or something back here, but there's a note on the wall by the cash desks that plainly states that there's no significant amount of cash is kept on the premises."

Katie looked around her office warily. It unnerved her to think of someone breaking into her office, going through her things.... She quickly went around the desk and began opening drawers. Nothing seemed to be out of place or rifled through, so she was glad about that. Still....

"Do you think I should file a police report?" she asked Vance. "I mean, there hasn't been anything taken or disturbed."

"Nevertheless, someone tried to break into your office and might try again," he said. "I believe it would be good to have this break-in on record in case something else happens either to you or to one of us vendors. And it would be helpful for us to know if there have been other break-ins in the area."

"You're right." Katie stepped back out into the vendors' lounge with Vance. "I want to leave everything the way we found it until I've spoken with the police." She also wanted to clean her office from top to bottom to help eliminate some of the revulsion she felt at the thought of someone possibly going inside, sitting at her desk, and sifting through her personal items.

She poured herself a cup of coffee, took out her phone, and sat at one of the tables. Vance sat across from her as she dialed the Sheriff's Office. And then he, too, got some coffee and waited with her until a uniformed Sheriff's deputy arrived.

The deputy inspected the office door and asked, "Was there anyone strange in the building this morning?"

"Artisans Alley is open to the public," Vance said. "There are always strangers on the premises."

"Have there been any other break-ins reported in the area?" Katie asked.

"Not recently," the officer replied.

Carol Rigby entered the vendors' lounge. "Hello." She nodded to the uniformed deputy. "Murphy."

He returned the gesture. "Detective."

"Why are you here, Carol?" Katie asked evenly. "I wouldn't have thought a break-in worthy of your interest."

"I was having breakfast with Ray over at Wood U and heard the call come over the police scanner." She gave Katie a smug smile. "I thought I'd come and make sure our friends here were okay."

Katie cringed at the woman's simpering tone. "Everyone here is fantastic."

Obviously aware of the tension, Deputy Murphy asked, "Ms. Bonner, you indicated nothing was missing or vandalized in your office—is that correct?"

"Nothing that I can see," she said.

"I'll fill out the report and leave a copy at the front desk." He handed Katie a card. "Let the Sheriff's Office know if you have any further trouble."

"Thank you." Katie tucked the card into her pocket. "I will."

Carol waited until the deputy had gone before she turned back to Katie. "Do you think this break-in could have anything to do with your botched attempts to investigate Jamie Seifert's murder?"

Vance stiffened beside Katie. "You're out of line, lady."

Carol glowered at him. "And I don't believe my conversation with your employer is any of your concern."

"It's all right, Vance," Katie said. "No, Carol, I don't think the break-in is related to Jamie's death." Despite her confident words, she couldn't help but wonder if perhaps it *was*. Could Phyllis, Connor, or even Tony Solero, have tried to get into her office to see what she might've uncovered? If so, the joke was on them.

She hadn't uncovered a damn thing that was worthwhile.

CHAPTER 32

Katie had removed everything from her desk, giving it a thorough cleaning, when Rose stopped by.

The older woman held out her arms to envelop Katie in a hug. "Vance told me what happened. I'm so sorry. He said nothing was taken, but I know how vulnerable someone breaking into your office can make you feel."

Katie pulled back. "Thanks, but I'm fine."

"I know better," Rose said, peering over the top of her glasses with a knowing look. "Walter said he'll send me a link to an online support group that you can log onto any time—day or night—in case you need it."

"That's very thoughtful."

Rose's reaction made Katie realize that the vendors were likely to be on edge over the break-in. Most of them didn't carry insurance on the items in their booths. "I'd better send an email to let the vendors know everything is okay and that the break-in was likely an anomaly, but we'll step up security nevertheless."

"Would you like me to take care of that for you while you're cleaning up in here?" Rose asked.

"Please. Thank you for your help."

Rose smiled. "I'm happy to do it. Well, I'm not glad there was a break-in by any stretch of the imagination, but…you know what I mean."

Katie smiled. "I do." Her phone pinged alerting her that she'd received a text. She fished it out of her pocket, looked at the screen, and saw that it was from Ray.

Hey, need my help with anything?

No.

She deleted it.

"Anything important?" Rose asked.

"Not in the least," Katie said brightly, ignoring the sting of loss she hated to admit and reminded herself that it was for the best that she and Ray had moved on in opposite directions.

Before Rose could leave to send the email for Katie, Vance arrived with the materials needed to repair the office door and frame.

"Rose, did you tell Katie the news?" Vance asked.

"Given everything that has happened here this morning, I completely forgot," Rose said.

"Well, tell me!" Katie exclaimed. "We could all use some good news."

"Walter has invited me to accompany him to his daughter's home in Rhode Island for Thanksgiving." Rose grinned, positively glowing at the thought of her upcoming trip.

"That's wonderful," Katie said with just a tinge of concern. Things with Rose and Walter were moving incredibly fast. They'd only met a few weeks before. "Have you met any of Walter's family yet?"

"Nope. I'll be meeting them all on Thanksgiving." Rose drew in a breath. "I'd better do a lot of power walking before then."

"I don't think that will make a bit of difference," Katie said. "They're going to love you."

Vance set the wood for the door aside, and Rose took the hint.

"Goodness, I'd better go draft that email. I'll let you see it before I send it."

"Thanks, Rose." Katie watched her friend leave before she retreated farther into her office to give Vance room to work.

As happy as Katie was for her friend, she couldn't get the thought of the intruder out of her head. Why would anybody try to get into her office? Had it been someone hoping to find money or other valuables who was interrupted before conducting a search? Or had it been someone looking for her? Or maybe trying to see what they could find out about her? McKinlay Mill was a small community. It wouldn't take a lot of digging to find out where Katie lived or what her daily habits were.

Katie suppressed a shudder as she swabbed her desk with sanitary wipes.

She didn't like feeling so vulnerable.

~

NOT LONG AFTER Katie got everything squared away in her office, Moonbeam dropped in to visit. Even though the room was now spotless, Katie thought she could still feel the presence of whoever had broken the lock on her door. The new lock Vance had installed made her feel safer—but not entirely secure.

Moonbeam placed a pink tulle bag tied with a maroon ribbon on Katie's desk. "I heard what happened and brought you something. "It's a calming tea blend. Now, I realize you have all sorts of specialty teas at Tealicious, but this particular blend is of my own making. I use various plant extracts and oils that'll soothe your soul."

"Thank you." Katie squinted slightly. "So, who told you about the break-in?"

"Janie Ingram. In fact, she's watching the shop for me so I could hop over here for a minute to bring you this. I need to get back soon."

"Are you getting any vibes about who might've broken in?" Katie asked. "Do you think the motive was robbery? Or...something else?"

Moonbeam frowned, her expression thoughtful. "I'm not sure. But I don't think either of us believes it was a robbery attempt, do we?" She stepped toward the door. "I'll see you at Seth's office later this afternoon."

"Yes...and thank you for the tea!"

Once the door had closed behind Moonbeam, Katie opened the pouch and inhaled the tea's aroma. It wasn't at all pleasant, but maybe later she might get up the nerve to try it to see if it would help soothe her ragged nerves.

Katie took another sniff and wrinkled her nose.

Much later.

She took out a pad of paper from her top desk drawer and picked up a pen, intending to do what she called noodling. She intended to list everything she knew about Jamie's death. Maybe that would help clarify her thoughts.

He'd won a boatload of money playing poker just days before his death.

He'd intended to spend that money on a flashy wedding and a destination honeymoon.

He's been poisoned by a rare toxin.

Several people in the Medical Examiner's Office where he worked knew about poisons.

Katie tapped the end of her pen against the yellow legal pad, pondering her conversation with Jamie's colleague, Phyllis. She was the one who'd suggested he play at the same poker club she did.

Something about Phyllis bothered Katie, but she wasn't able to pin down exactly what it was.

There was no doubt about it; she needed to speak with the woman again. And this time, in person.

～

Katie left Artisans Alley early, deciding to drive into the city and pay a visit to Phyllis at her office before going to Seth's law practice for the Victoria Square merchants partnership meeting. As luck would have it, Phyllis was manning the front desk when Katie walked through the door.

"Hello, Katie," Phyllis said, her voice as warm and cozy as a fuzzy blanket. "Congratulations on your success at the poker game—I don't think I had the opportunity to compliment you on your success when we last spoke."

"Thank you." Katie's tone was measured and cautious. She didn't for a moment trust Phyllis.

"As many times as I've played," Phyllis continued, "I've never won anywhere near as much as you did in a single night. But I don't imagine you came here to gloat. What can I do for you?"

"I came by to see you. I feel I owe you an apology and an explanation about that night."

"You don't owe me either one." Phyllis gave her an enigmatic smile. "You've already apologized for your friend getting wasted, and that was unnecessary also. Even if you really *had* been Kelly Ferrell and married to the old coot, you wouldn't have needed to apologize to me for his rude behavior—it was *his* place to do that."

"Yes, of course, it was," Katie said.

"Take it from me—the only person you're responsible for is you. Never apologize or make excuses for anyone else. Again, going back to Davenport, if the two of you were involved and you were that embarrassed by his behavior, then you might want to rethink your relationship—not go around apologizing for him. If you're ashamed to be with someone, don't be with him."

Katie wondered why Phyllis was telling her all this, but she merely said, "That's an excellent point, Phyllis. You speak as though you've been in that position before."

"In my younger days, I was embarrassed by all sorts of people —my parents, my siblings, my cousins." She shrugged. "Not anymore. I realized early on that I'm me, and they're no reflection on me whatsoever. You make your own way in this world, Katie. Don't let anyone steer you in the wrong direction."

"Why didn't you let me know that you weren't fooled by my deception at the poker game?" she asked.

Smirking, Phyllis said, "I guessed you and Ray had your reasons for pretending to be undercover at that game, and I also imagined it had to do with Jamie Seifert's death. I tend to mind my own business, dear. That's something else you might want to consider."

"Excuse me?" Katie asked.

"My mother used to tell me, 'never stick your nose where it doesn't belong, or it could get cut off.' Those are wise words everyone should heed," Phyllis said boldly. "Don't you agree?"

They stared at each other for a moment—Phyllis looking at Katie with a certain amount of satisfaction, and Katie regarding Phyllis with defiance.

Was Phyllis offering a warning or a threat? Either way, Katie wouldn't be cowed by this woman.

"I'd better get back to work," Phyllis said at last. "Thank you for stopping by."

Refusing to accept her dismissal, Katie asked, "Did you and Jamie work together to win during his last night at the poker tables?"

Phyllis chuckled. "Whyever would you think that?"

"Someone helped him win, and it makes sense that it would be you," she said.

"And who told you our beloved, upstanding Jamie was a cheater?" Phyllis asked.

Was Phyllis being sarcastic when she called Jamie *beloved* and *upstanding*? It certainly sounded like it. But why? "That's irrelevant."

"Not to me, it isn't."

Katie leaned toward Phyllis. "Why don't you believe Jamie was an upstanding man?"

"I didn't say that," Phyllis said. "In fact, I said exactly the opposite."

"But you said it sarcastically. Why didn't you like Jamie?"

Phyllis leaned forward and lowered her voice. "I liked Jamie just fine. I simply felt that if he'd been inclined to have a partner helping him win, it *should* have been me." Her tone became absolutely menacing. "*I'm* the one who introduced him to that game. I deserved a share of that money. *Me*, not that simpering little Connor Davis."

"So, it *was* Connor who helped Jamie cheat?" Katie asked.

"It couldn't be proven that Jamie cheated at all. But if he did, it was Connor who helped him pull it off. And that was wrong. Any way you look at it, it was *wrong*." She closed her eyes and took a deep breath. "As I said, I need to get back to work." With that, she turned and strode down the hall and through a door marked EMPLOYEES ONLY.

Yes, what Jamie had done was wrong. But if Phyllis thought so, too, why had she been so willing to do the same?

CHAPTER 33

*K*atie was the last merchant to arrive at the meeting at Seth's office. His secretary quickly ushered her into the conference room. Katie fielded questioning glances from a few of the other merchants—including Andy—as well as Seth. Nona Fiske downright glared at her.

Katie shook her head slightly at Seth and smiled. "How about that traffic?"

Traffic had, in fact, been a breeze. And given how recently her conversation with Phyllis had taken place, she could practically hear the woman in her head admonishing, "You don't owe these people an explanation or an apology." In that regard, Katie supposed Phyllis was right.

Unfortunately, Phyllis factored so heavily into Katie's thoughts that she found it difficult to concentrate on Seth's presentation. When the amount of the proposed offer was raised for a vote, Moonbeam had to nudge Katie to remind her to pay attention.

Finally, the amount was agreed upon, and Seth said he'd take the offer to the owner.

"If the owner is amenable to the terms, I'll present a plan to the bank to ensure the partnership can get financing," Seth said. "I foresee no problems in having this deal go through. Does anyone have any questions?"

No one did.

"Terrific. Unless there's some sort of problem, I'll send you an email to let you know when you need to be here for the closing." His eyes locked onto Katie as the other participants began shuffling out of the room. "Katie, could you stay behind for a moment please?"

"Of course."

Seth led her from the conference room and into his office. He closed the door and took a seat behind his desk. Katie sat on one of the club chairs in front of it.

"I wanted to let you know that while going through some of Jamie's clothes, I found the deposit slip for the money he won at the poker game." He opened the desk's middle drawer and removed a slip of paper, handing it to her.

Katie's eyes widened when she took in the number. "Wow. Everyone said he won big, but that's more than twice what I won. No wonder the other players weren't surprised by my poker prowess."

Seth nodded. "I also heard about the break-in from Rose," he said. "You're bound to be shaken from the experience."

"I am," she admitted. "But the main thing is everyone's fine and nothing seems to have been taken. Whoever did it had to be pretty brazen—he or she had to have broken in *after* Artisans Alley had opened for vendor restock. There was no way someone could've broken into the building earlier without tripping the alarm."

"This person was either audacious enough or could blend in well enough to make others think he or she belonged there if caught trying to get into your office," Seth said.

"That's the thing—since nothing was disturbed or taken, tt

makes me think the intruder was interrupted before completing his or her task."

"A scenario that's entirely possible." Seth leaned back in his chair and steepled his fingers. "It's likely this person will return to finish the job since he or she is obviously not easily intimidated. Promise me you'll be extra vigilant."

"I will," Katie said.

"I mean it," he said. "I can't lose someone else I love."

WALKING OUT TO HER CAR, Katie decided that if even *some* of the stories she'd heard about him were true, then Tony Solero might be the very type of person to walk into a crowded public place and attempt to break into a private office. But who could she ask who might tell her the truth? Perhaps his brother, Jimmy?

She drove to the food pantry and arrived just as Jimmy was locking the door for the day.

Rolling down her window, she said, "Mr. Solero, hi."

Jimmy turned, bent at the waist to get a better look inside her car, and then walked forward. "Oh, hey, Ms. Bonner. Sorry, but we're closed."

"That's all right. I really wanted to speak with you. May I buy you dinner at that diner across the road?"

"Um, yeah, okay. I'll meet you there."

Katie pulled across the road and parked in front of the restaurant. She locked her car, went inside, and snagged a table by the window. If Jimmy decided to bail on her, she could see him leaving the food pantry. He probably believed she was crazy for wanting to talk with him out of the blue like this. But, instead of going in the other direction, he drove to the diner. Katie took that as a good sign.

He slid into the booth across from her. "This is a surprise."

"I know," she said. "I'm sorry for being so direct, but I need your advice."

Raising his brows, he asked, "You need advice from me? This ought to be good."

Before Katie could respond, the waitress came over and asked for their drink order. Both asked for sodas, and the waitress hurried off to get them.

"I didn't mention it the first time I met you because I wasn't sure who you were," Katie said, "but I'm acquainted with your sister-in-law, Gina."

His face was an inscrutable mask. "All right."

The waitress returned with their drinks. "Have you made up your minds, or do you need another minute?"

"Give us another minute," Jimmy said. "I'm not sure I'll be staying."

"Okay." With a worried glance at Katie, the waitress walked away.

"I'll get straight to the point," Katie said. "When I met Gina, I was pretending to be someone else."

Jimmy froze. "You're a cop?"

"No," she answered quickly. "But if you read the newspapers, then you know that a man died outside my tea shop on Victoria Square not long ago. With that incident so fresh in people's minds, I didn't want to go into a poker game filled with strangers and have them all judge me based on that single episode."

"That, I understand." He took a sip of his cola.

She sighed. "I wanted to be someone other than Katie Bonner, so I registered at the poker game under a false name. They didn't seem to care as long as I had the buy-in money."

"Makes sense."

The waitress, apparently sensing that things were amicable between Katie and Jimmy now, returned to their table. "Have you made up your minds about what you'd like to eat?"

"Sure," Katie said. "I'd like the chef salad please."

"And bring me a burger and fries," Jimmy said. "Thanks."

"Thank *you*," the waitress said. "I'll get your food out to you as quickly as I can."

"Did you win?" Jimmy asked Katie after the waitress had left.

"What?" she asked.

"At the poker game—did you win?"

"I did," she said. "No way near as much as the guy who died outside Tealicious, but I did okay."

"Seifert, right?" he asked. "Wasn't he accused of cheating?"

"I believe so, but nothing was proven." Katie sipped her ginger ale. "I do know the dealer was fired, though."

"Was he in on it?"

Katie shrugged. "I heard the guy had a partner, but I don't know enough about poker to understand how you could cheat like that. Counting cards, maybe? Who knows? I just got lucky."

"Good for you," Jimmy said. "My brother and I aren't tight anymore, but I wouldn't want to be the guy who cheated him at cards, that's for sure."

"I've heard Tony has a bit of a temper," Katie said. "That's one reason I never told Gina the truth about my identity. I was afraid they'd both think I was a big phony."

Jimmy nodded but said nothing.

"Anyway, I really like Gina, which is why I came to you." She leaned forward slightly. "Do you think Gina would understand and forgive me for lying to her when we first met?"

"No way. You'd be better off cutting ties with Gina altogether," he said. "Once your trust is broken with the Solero family, it can never be mended. Trust me, I know."

Katie wasn't easily frightened, but the menace in his voice made her hackles rise.

Jamie was dead. Had he crossed Tony Solero?

Suddenly sleuthing for his killer seemed downright dangerous.

Maybe it was time to let Carol Rigby finish the job.

Again, Katie lamented the loss of her friendship with Ray. And yet....

The waitress arrived with their meals and Jimmy dug in. He charged on, and Katie poked at her salad, only half-listening to his tirade against the family that no longer welcomed him.

Katie knew what it felt like to feel abandoned. And now Margo had declared her her sole heir.

Life had sure taken some strange turns during the past few weeks.

Katie stabbed a grape tomato with her fork and thought about the past. What would she have changed if she could? It was a useless thought. The past was the past, and right now she felt the future was uncertain.

She didn't like that feeling. Not one bit.

CHAPTER 34

*F*eeling rattled after her dinner with Jimmy Solero, Katie remembered the specially blended tea Moonbeam had given her that was supposed to induce a feeling of calm. Brother, did she need it just then.

Upon her return home, Katie removed the pink sachet from her purse and put the kettle on, putting some of the vile-smelling tea into a diffuser. Hopefully, it wouldn't taste as bad as it smelled.

As Mason wound around her ankles, Katie opened a can of cat food and fed him and Della. Then she went into the living room and turned on the television. She used the remote to flip through the channels and stopped on a sitcom she'd already seen. Tonight, she preferred mindless entertainment to anything educational—and she certainly steered clear of the news.

The kettle whistled, and she returned to the kitchen to pour water into the cup. She bobbed the diffuser a few times before letting the brew steep for five minutes. Once she'd removed the diffuser and placed it into the sink, she took her tea into the living room. Curling up on the love seat, she took her first tentative taste of the murky beverage. It wasn't the best tea she'd ever tasted, but it wasn't bad—nowhere near as dreadful as she'd anticipated.

Katie drank the tea while watching the sitcom and listening to the canned laughter—sometimes smiling at the jokes, sometimes not. She felt so very weary.

Upon finishing the tea, she stood to take the cup back to the kitchen. The room spun, and her vision blurred. She sank back down on the love seat and put the cup on the table before it dropped from her fingers.

Obviously sensing her distress, Mason crawled onto her lap and gave a plaintive *meow*. Katie raised her hand to pet him, but her limbs felt as though they were made of lead.

"What...what's...wrong with...me?" she wondered aloud, her voice sounding strange and far off.

She managed to retrieve her phone from the table beside her. Opening her contact list, she called the first name: MARGO BONNER. Katie was fortunate that her former mother-in-law was currently right across the Square.

Margo answered her phone with a cheery, "Hey, there!"

"I...need...help," Katie said. "I feel.... Something is really—"

"I'll be right there." Margo ended the call.

Katie was still sitting on the love seat with her phone in her hand and Mason curled protectively on her lap when Margo and Nick rushed into her living room. For a second, the question of how they got into her apartment ran through her mind, but then she remembered she'd given Nick a spare key in case of emergencies. It was a good thing she had because this definitely qualified as an emergency.

Mason knew Nick well enough that he didn't growl or hiss when Nick hurried over to the love seat to take Katie's hand.

"Girl, you're clammy," he said.

"I feel so dizzy," she said. "And it's...hard...to breathe."

Margo noticed the cup, picked it up, and smelled it. "Phew! What have you been drinking? Sludge?"

"Tea…Moonbeam made…."

"Oh, Katie, you should never straight up trust anything that woman gives you," Margo said. "Doesn't she practice the dark arts or something?"

Katie was too weak to defend Moonbeam, but she did try to shake her head.

Nick plucked Mason off Katie's lap. "We'll take it from here, buddy. You did well."

He and Margo got on either side of Katie and helped her to her feet. They led her to the door, and Nick grabbed her purse on the way out.

"She'll need this," he said. "It has her insurance card in it."

Together, they got Katie down the stairs and into Margo's rental car.

"I'll keep you posted," Margo told Nick.

"Are you sure you don't need me to go?" he asked.

"No, Don needs you this evening," Margo said. "But thank you for all your help."

Nick kissed Katie's cheek. "If you guys need me, call me and I'll be right there."

Once settled in the car, Katie closed her eyes. Margo kept up a steady stream of conversation, but Katie couldn't seem to concentrate on the words. She felt so…lousy.

At the hospital, Margo had an orderly come out and help Katie into a wheelchair. Katie tried to protest but quickly realized it was for the best—she was too lightheaded to walk into the emergency room under her own power.

Unfortunately, there were already two people in line in front of the reception desk and it took nearly ten minutes before Margo retrieved Katie's driver's license and insurance card from her purse to hand to the woman manning the computer.

Once in the treatment bay, Margo paced while a technician took Katie's vital signs. The pacing wore on Katie's nerves, but she had to admit it was rather sweet—she hadn't been mothered since before her Aunt Lizzie had died.

Finally, a woman in a white lab coat entered the cubicle. "I'm Doctor Nakamura. How are you feeling?"

"Awful," Katie said, still feeling woozy.

"Have you eaten or had anything to drink that you'd never tried before?" the doctor asked.

Margo jumped in with an answer. "Yes, she has. She drank some kind of unpleasant-smelling tea."

"I had dinner in a diner a few hours ago, but I only had a salad. I felt fine until after I drank the tea. It was a gift from a friend who blends her own leaves and flowers."

"When was that?"

"An hour or so ago," Katie answered.

"From your symptoms, it's likely you had an allergic reaction. Tea made with hibiscus flowers is known to cause a drop in blood pressure. We'll give you something to counteract that and hopefully, you should be feeling better in no time. If, however, you don't, contact us right away."

After administering a shot, the doctor instructed Katie and Margo to wait a few minutes to make sure Katie was indeed feeling better while she signed the release papers. "A nurse will be in to check on you soon."

It wasn't long before Katie felt distinctly better and well enough to leave and, shortly thereafter, she and Margo were on their way back to McKinlay Mill.

When the women returned to Katie's apartment, they found a police cruiser parked outside. A uniformed sheriff's deputy got out of the car as Katie and Margo were getting ready to climb the steps to the apartment.

"Are you the owners of this place?" the deputy asked.

"I am," Katie told her. "Why?"

"While I was patrolling this area earlier this evening, I saw someone with a crowbar at your door."

Margo gasped. "A crowbar?"

"Yes," the deputy said. "I believe this person was attempting to break into the apartment. I turned on my lights and siren, and the person—whom I believe was a male—fled the scene. I pursued but lost the suspect. I've been patrolling the area since searching for him." She gave an apologetic shake of her head. "No sign. Have you had trouble with anyone—ex-boyfriend, ex-husband, or other family members?"

"No, I haven't," Katie said. "Although there *was* a break-in at my office in Artisans Alley across the Square this morning. I don't know if the two incidents are connected." Of course, they were. They *had* to be. These kinds of coincidences didn't occur—not in her world.

"Please exercise extreme caution and call the Sheriff's Office if you encounter anything unusual," the deputy said.

After the deputy returned to her car, Margo complained the entire way up the stairs about how the woman could have caught the suspect had she not immediately hit her lights and siren.

"Good grief," Margo grumbled. "She might as well have gotten on the loudspeaker and announced, 'Ready or not, here I come!' Of course, the suspect *fled the scene*. What did she expect—a complete surrender? She's probably a rookie. I have half a mind to report her."

"Please don't," Katie said. "I'm sure she was doing her best."

"I'm sure she was, too. That's what worries me." Margo looked over her shoulder at the deserted parking lot. "Why don't we go inside and pack you a bag, and you can stay at Sassy Sally's tonight?"

"No, thank you. I refuse to be scared out of my home." She unlocked the door, and they went inside. Katie was glad they'd left the living room light on. "I have excellent locks and will call the Sheriff's Office at the merest hint of trouble—I promise."

After fussing over Katie for a few more minutes and ensuring she was well enough to be left alone, Margo returned to Sassy

Sally's. Katie hid by the window and watched Margo leave to ensure she was okay. The truth was that she wouldn't have minded staying at Sassy Sally's that night in case she had another episode of lightheadedness, but she was afraid doing so might endanger her friends.

Katie undressed and got into bed, but sleep didn't come easily as she wondered who had broken into her office and then had tried to force his way into her home only hours later. The light *had* been on, and Katie's car was parked in the small lot behind Tealicious when the intruder had tried to enter her apartment. That meant the person who'd tried to break in that evening had believed Katie to be home. It wasn't her belongings the intruder wanted—it was *her*. Katie was the target. But why?

Was it Tony Solero? Given the fact that she'd had dinner with his brother, Jimmy, earlier that evening made it a possibility. Despite Jimmy's complaints of how his family had treated him, he could have used Katie's identity deception as a way to get back into Tony's good graces. But that didn't explain the break-in at Artisans Alley—that incident had occurred *before* Katie had spoken with Jimmy.

If Phyllis had known who Katie and Ray were from the very beginning, other people at the poker game might have known as well. Maybe Tony and Gina had discovered Katie's true identity from someone other than Jimmy. But even if that was the case, why would the Soleros want to break into Katie's office and home? She had nothing to incriminate them or anyone else for Jamie's death. What else could anyone want from her?

Money.

Could it really be that simple? It made sense, or at least as much sense as any other scenario she could imagine.

Jamie had won big at the poker game, and now he was dead. Katie had won a substantial amount of money at an event sponsored by the same group, and now she had a target on her back. It had to be the money. Did the intruder truly believe, though, that

Katie had so little sense that she'd keep a large amount of cash in either her office or her home, rather than putting it in the bank?

Someone that stupid was probably more than willing to make other foolish choices.

And possibly more deadly.

CHAPTER 35

*K*atie awoke Wednesday morning with her mind on a mission. Knowing Brad could handle the Tealicious desserts fine without her, she quickly took care of the cats, bathed, dressed, and headed for Artisans Alley.

Once in her office with a hot cup of coffee, Katie called Ted Roberts, the dealer for Jamie's table who'd been dismissed from his position at the Alexander Street poker club.

"Hi, Ted. This is Katie Bonner," she said when he answered. "I'm sorry to call you so early."

"Not a problem. I've been an early riser all my life. What can I do for you?"

"Could you tell me how much money Jamie Siefert won on your last night at the poker club?" When he didn't answer her right away, she pressed on. "The reason I'm asking is that I know how much Jamie deposited into a new bank account he opened. I want to know if he split the money with his partner before he died."

"How much did Seifert deposit?" Ted asked.

Katie told him.

"Nope. That was the full amount," he said. "I imagine he was going to settle up with the partner later. Maybe he was calculating taxes first or something—I don't know. What difference does it make? Did someone come forward to claim a share of the money?"

"No, but I won around twenty-thousand dollars when I played, and yesterday someone tried to break into both my office and my home," Katie said. "I'm guessing it has something to do with the money that I took home from that game."

"It might. Were you also accused of cheating?" he asked.

"No. But I think it's common knowledge among the other poker players that I had a connection to Jamie."

Ted blew out a breath. "Be careful, Katie. There's nothing more dangerous than a sore loser, especially one who believes he's been cheated."

After talking with Roberts, Katie called Luther Stapleton at Lamberton Conservatory. She realized the conservatory didn't open until ten a.m., but she thought maybe he got there early. He apparently did not, and Katie left him a message to call her.

Finally, she called Moonbeam.

"Hey, Katie. What's up?"

"I was just wondering what ingredients were in that tea you gave me yesterday."

"You won't tell my competition now, will you?" Moonbeam asked and giggled.

What competition?

"Uh, no."

"First up, mint, and a lot of dried herbs from my garden."

"Such as?" Katie asked.

"A sprig of lavender, nasturtium leaf, chives, thyme, tarragon, and lemongrass."

"Is that all?"

"Oh!" She laughed again. "And, of course, hibiscus."

Katie let out a breath. "That's what I thought." She explained about her unplanned trip to the ER the night before.

"Oh, I'm so very sorry," Moonbeam said, sounding stricken. "I should have given you an ingredients list when I gave you the tea. I use it whenever I'm feeling stressed, and it helps me so much. I didn't even think about—"

"I know you didn't," Katie interrupted. "It was simply one of those things. Now I know to stay away from anything that contains that flower."

"While I have you on the phone," Moonbeam said, "there *is* something else I need to tell you."

A feeling of dread crept up Katie's spine. "What's that?"

"I dreamed last night that you were in a mansion," she began.

"Oh." Katie expelled a breath of relief. "That doesn't seem so bad."

"But it was—you were being pursued by Jamie Siefert's killer."

KATIE WAS STILL PONDERING the significance of Moonbeam's dream when Luther Stapleton returned her call.

"Hello, Ms. Bonner. I'm guessing either you or your friend have questions about our wedding packages."

"I'm sorry, Mr. Stapleton, but that's not why I called you." She decided in for a penny, in for a pound. "I'm calling to ask you about Connor Davis."

Sharply inhaling, Stapleton asked, "Who told you I was acquainted with Connor Davis?"

"I met Connor very recently—at a poker game, as a matter of fact." This is where the seed of the idea Katie had upon awakening that morning began to sprout. "Connor seemed sad—like there was something...or someone...missing in his life. Upon learning that the two of you had dated, I thought you sounded like a perfectly matched couple. A conservatory administrator and the owner of a flourishing flower shop bonding over their mutual adoration of plants is utterly romantic."

Mr. Stapleton scoffed. "Connor's shop could hardly be called *flourishing*. *Floundering* is more like it. I wish I had all the money I gave that man to sink into his business. Although now I suspect he didn't put a dime of it into it at all. I believe he squandered all of it gambling."

"Oh, my goodness. That's horrible," Katie said. "I had no idea."

"No one ever does. Connor is charismatic and able to make people believe whatever he wants them to think. If Connor put you up to calling me on his behalf, you've wasted your time, Ms. Bonner." He sighed. "It took me long enough, but I finally saw Connor for who he truly is—a manipulative user."

"I assure you, Mr. Stapleton, Connor didn't ask me to contact you. He doesn't even know I'm talking with you. It's just that the man struck me as being so sad and—" She broke off. "I'm terribly sorry for calling. I've made a dreadful mistake."

"That's all right."

Katie could tell from the tone of Stapleton's voice that it was definitely not all right.

"I won't take any more of your time," she said, "but I do want you to know that I passed the conservatory's wedding information along to my friend Rose, who will likely be getting married soon."

"Thank you."

They ended their conversation, and Katie was satisfied that she got the information she wanted. Connor had an excellent reason for partnering with Jamie to cheat at poker; either his business really was suffering, or he'd merely used that excuse to induce his partner into giving him money.

As an attorney, Seth had connections all around the area. Could he find out if Connor's business was, in fact, struggling financially? Katie dialed his office number and was surprised that she was able to reach him right away.

"Hi, Katie," he said. "I heard about your allergy scare last night. Is everything all right now?"

"Yes. I'm feeling much better."

"You're not calling to start civil proceedings against Moonbeam Carruthers, are you?" he teased.

"Of course not. She can't help that I had a reaction with hibiscus. I didn't even know it myself." She took a deep breath. "But you're aren't going to be happy about why I am calling you."

"What's wrong?" The light tone had been immediately replaced by a serious timbre.

"I think I know who Jamie's partner was on the night he won the money at the poker club downtown," she said.

"You're telling me you believe Jamie cheated."

"Uh, no." She chose her words carefully. "Not definitively. He *might* have cheated because he was so desperate to give you—"

"Cut the crap and give it to me straight," he interrupted.

Katie blew out a breath. "Okay. I believe that if Jamie did, in fact, cheat, then he likely did so with Connor Davis," Katie said.

"Connor Davis? He was at the funeral."

"He was. Anyway, Connor has a flower shop—I visited it the other day. Until recently he was dating a man named Luther Stapleton, who said he put up a lot of money for Connor's failing business. Mr. Stapleton later learned that Connor was a gambler and suspects he frittered away the cash meant to go into the business."

"And you're telling me this because—?"

"Because, as an attorney, I was hoping you could ask around to see if the flower shop's financial affairs are messed up," Katie said. "If it's doing well, then maybe Connor *wasn't* Jamie's partner —if Jamie did, in fact, have one. If it's tanking…." She let the sentence hang.

"Do you think Connor Davis killed Jamie?" Seth asked.

"I doubt it. If he and Jamie worked together to strengthen Jamie's chances of winning—" She was proud of herself for finding a way not to avoid using the word *cheating*. "—then he'd have wanted Jamie to stick around and pay him his share, right?"

"I suppose. Still, if this man *was* working with Jamie on something I knew nothing about, I'll want some answers from him."

"So will I," Katie said.

The pieces of this puzzle were starting to fit together, but it felt like the resolution was still elusive.

Someone was responsible for Jamie Siefert's death, and if it wasn't Connor Davis ... who else could it possibly be?

CHAPTER 36

No sooner had Katie hung up the phone than Rose rushed into her office without knocking. "Come quickly! We have a situation!"

Katie groaned. "Now what?"

Not taking time to answer, Rose darted into the vendors' lounge and out the back door onto the south parking lot. Katie followed Rose to where Vance was lumbering toward them carrying a large cardboard carton—a carton that seemed to be moving...and Katie heard whimpering.

"What's in there?" Katie asked Rose.

Before Rose could tell her, Vance said, "Open the door, please. It's cold out here. We need to get them inside."

"Them?" Katie's eyes flew from Vance to Rose and back to Vance. "What are *they*, and how many are there?"

She'd barely gotten the question out before a fluffy head with adorable brown eyes poked out over the top of the box. Both Vance and Rose ignored Katie's questions as Rose hurried to hold open the door so Vance could take the box of what were obviously puppies inside. Katie followed them into the vendors' lounge where Vance placed the box onto the floor.

Not again, Katie thought. It seemed like every few weeks someone drove up and dumped a litter of kittens or puppies—sometimes leaving the moms, but usually just the helpless babies.

"I suppose as far as emergencies go, it could have been worse," Katie mused. "Where did you find them this time?"

"By the abandoned warehouse," Vance said.

"But now what?" Rose asked.

Katie shrugged. "I'll call the animal shelter and see if they'll take them—"

"No!" Rose interrupted her. "We can't do that! They're so small and helpless."

Katie sighed. "Right. And the animal shelter will be able to do much more for them than we can. That's what they're there for, after all."

"Katie has a valid point, Rose," Vance said.

Rose refused to budge. "No. I don't want these sweet babies to go to any old homes. I want to know they're going to people who are responsible pet owners who'll take care of them." She picked up one of the puppies and nestled it beneath her chin. "Don't just stand there, you two. Give somebody some love."

In the two years Katie had known Rose, she'd never spoken about her love of animals, so her fervent pleas were totally unexpected.

Vance was the first to cave. He plucked a puppy out of the box and laughed when it licked his chin. "Rose is right. I'd also like to know these puppies will be placed in loving hands."

"Fine." Katie looked into the box of cute, roly-poly, tail-wagging balls of fluff. She bent and picked one up, smiling at the grunting sounds it made. It was white with brown-and-black markings. They looked like mutts—adorable, but mutts just the same. "How old do you think they are?"

"They look to be about eight to ten weeks old to me," Vance said. Was he experienced enough to know or was he taking a good guess?

Apparently feeling as though holding one wasn't enough, Rose bent and picked up another of the two remaining puppies in the box. Separated from all its siblings now, the loner began to cry.

"Ah, now, we can't have that." Vance picked up the remaining pup.

Katie felt certain someone was about to get peed on, but she didn't say so. She heard bickering female voices approaching; but before she could turn to see who was there, the voices went from grumbling to squealing with delight.

Sasha and Sadie Davenport rushed over to the group.

"Oh, my gosh! They're so sweet!" Sadie gushed.

Rose handed her one of the puppies. "They're precious."

"Here, Sasha," Vance said. "We can't leave you out."

Sasha eagerly took the pup Vance held out to her. "Where did they come from?"

"Vance found them abandoned outside the warehouse out back," Rose said.

"You know, they *could* belong to someone," Katie said. "Maybe their owner simply left them there for a little while to—" She stopped speaking when everyone else gave her an *oh, come on* look.

"Can we have one?" Sadie asked excitedly.

"That's up to your dad," Katie said. "Plus, I want to take them to a veterinarian and have them checked out first before anyone commits to taking them."

"We'll go ask him right now," Sasha said.

"Wait." Katie's voice stopped the girls in their tracks. "Why aren't you two in school?"

"It's a teacher conference day," Sadie said, rolling her eyes as though that knowledge should have been self-evident. "We were bored over at Dad's shop. Besides, Christmas is coming and this *is* the best place to shop on the Square."

Katie wasn't above relishing the feeling of pride that enveloped her.

As the girls still carried puppies, Katie called, "Bring them back as soon as you can. I'm going to call the vet up on Main Street to see if they can work them in."

Sasha grinned at her sister. "We'll go with you and help."

Katie said nothing. She realized that if she refused to allow the girls to accompany her to a vet's office—provided they could see the puppies that day—she'd only be acting peevish and self-sabotaging. How could she keep her mind on driving if she had to worry about five wriggling puppies in her backseat? Of course, she wasn't sure five puppies *and* two teenage girls would be much better.

"I want one of those pups," Rose said. "I'll help you pay the vet's bill."

"I wouldn't mind having one, either," Vance said. "I'll call Janie and see what she and VJ would think about my bringing home one of these critters. It's been almost two years since we lost our beagle, Babycakes. We're due."

Rose tittered. "Oh, that's right. I forgot I'm part of a couple now. I should probably run the idea of having a dog past Walter as well, since we've been discussing our future together."

Katie inwardly balked at Rose feeling the need to run *anything* by a man she'd only known for a few weeks, but she held her tongue. She returned the puppy she was holding to the box. "I need to make that call."

Vance and Rose reluctantly returned their puppies to the box as well. While the three fluff-balls were looking up at them, Katie snapped a photo using the phone on her camera. She sent the photo to Seth. After all, he'd indicated an interest in adopting.…

As an afterthought, she sent the photo to Nick, as well. These weren't children, *per se*, but a puppy was still a little bundle of joy. Maybe he and Don would decide to adopt one as well.

Sitting at a table near the box, Katie started by calling Mason and Della's vet. Unfortunately, they were booked solid, so she did an internet search for veterinarians nearby, and after a couple of calls, found one who had a cancellation in nearby Greece and who would see the puppies if Katie could bring them right away. Katie said she'd be there as soon as possible.

She was getting ready to text Ray to have him send the girls back with the puppies when Nick burst through the door.

"Ahhhhh! Let me see! Let me see!" Picking up one dog wasn't enough for Nick Ferrell. Oh, no. He had to sit on the floor by the box and pull them all out onto his lap.

Katie laughed and snapped a photo to send to Don. Nick looked like an ecstatic child sitting there with the three canines crawling all over him.

"I want them all!" Nick cried.

"Well, you're going to have to fight Rose and Vance—and maybe the Davenport girls," Katie said.

"Who's going to fight us?" Sadie asked as she and Sasha returned with their puppies.

"There are *more*?" Nick held out his arms. "Add them to the pile!"

"No!" Sasha said. "This one is *ours*! Or, at least, one of them is. Daddy said we can only have one."

"But he did say we can maybe foster them until they find homes," Sadie added.

"I also sent the photo to Seth," Katie told Nick. "So, here's hoping he might want one, too."

"Well, I suppose I can get by with one," Nick said. "That is if Seth doesn't want one of them."

"You guys will have to work everything out among your-selves." Katie began putting the puppies back in the box. "I have to take these wild things to the vet to have them checked out."

"Do you need me to go and help you?" Nick asked.

"No," Sasha said with authority. "Sadie and I are going." The girl was already feeling proprietary about the puppies.

"Great." Nick grinned. "I'm going home and sweet-talk Don. I want a full report on the little angels when you get back."

Katie grabbed her jacket and purse before enlisting help to carry the box of puppies to her car. Sasha and Sadie volunteered to sit in the backseat with the dogs. Katie felt she should've probably rechecked with Ray before leaving the Square with his girls, but they'd said they had his permission, and she didn't want to appear to be undermining them—or seeking an excuse to speak with their father, either.

When they arrived at the vet's office, Katie staggered under the weight of the box and Sasha opened the door.

Counting fluffy heads to make sure no one had escaped the box and was still in the car, Katie announced to the receptionist, "I'm Katie Bonner. I called about the puppies we found."

"Yes, Ms. Bonner." The woman got up from behind the desk. "Right this way."

As Katie turned, she saw Gina Solero sitting in the waiting room with her standard black poodle. "Gina…"

Giving her a tight smile that didn't make it to her eyes, Gina said, "*Katie*. It's so nice to see you again."

CHAPTER 37

*O*n the drive back to Victoria Square, Sadie and Sasha continued to *ooh* and *aah* over the puppies while Katie silently pondered Gina's reaction to seeing her at the vet. The woman had not only expressed any surprise at seeing Katie burst into her veterinarian's office, but she hadn't seemed fazed at Katie's announcement of her name.

Who'd told Gina the truth? Jimmy? Phyllis? Connor? Ted, the card dealer? Or had Gina known all along, just as Phyllis had?

Katie had gone into the exam room and hadn't seen Gina when she came back out. She'd been relieved. What could she possibly have said to Gina that might've explained her ruse or made things all right between the two of them?

She became aware of the girls speaking to her from the backseat. "I'm sorry—what was that?" she asked, glancing up at the rearview mirror.

Giving an exaggerated eye roll at Katie's lack of attention, Sasha said, "I asked if we could stop at a pet store. The puppies need food and stuff."

"Yeah," Sadie said. "You can tell the poor little things are starving."

248

"Of course." The puppies didn't look malnourished to Katie, nor did they to the vet they'd seen only minutes ago. But the girls were right—they did need food.

At the pet shop, the girls protested that the puppies not only needed food, but they also needed toys—*one for each puppy, duh*—collars, treats, and beds. Katie managed to convince them that one big box with a blanket on the bottom would be enough for now.

"After all, they need to stay close to each other for a while," she said.

All of the supplies, in addition to the vet bill Katie had paid, were making for some fairly expensive "free puppies." It was almost enough to make her consider taking Vance and Rose up on their offer to help foot the vet bill. Almost.

KATIE PARKED BEHIND WOOD U, since the girls had told her Ray had agreed they could foster the puppies until they were adopted. Afraid the girls might drop the box if they carried it inside—and also wanting to confirm that fostering was really all right with Ray—Katie carried the staggeringly heavy box of puppies into the building.

"Dad, come look!" Sadie cried as she closed the door securely behind them.

Bending to put the box on the floor, Katie heard a low rumble of laughter. She looked up to see Ray standing in the doorway of his workshop.

"Let's move them into the front," he said, picking up the box. "There are too many dangerous things for them to get into back here. I can keep an eye on them if they're in the front with me."

"That's a good idea, Dad," Sadie said, "but we're going to be watching out for them, too."

"Yeah," Sasha added, "and we need to feed them now. Those poor little things must be *starving*."

"I'll leave you to it," Katie said, with a slight smile. "If you wouldn't mind, would you please check with Rose, Vance, and Nick—and possibly Seth—to see if they'd like a puppy before giving them away? At least three of the four have already expressed a desire to have one."

"Of course," Ray said.

"Girls, would you mind helping me get the supplies from the car?" Katie asked.

Ray smiled at his daughters. "I'll do that. You two get your guests settled in."

An awkward silence fell between Katie and Ray like a heavy blanket. She wanted to say something—*needed* to say something —to alleviate the tension.

"Thank you for fostering the puppies," she said.

"Thank *you*," he said. "Those dogs are the first things my girls have bonded over since—well…in a long time."

"Ray, I have to tell you something," Katie blurted before she changed her mind. "I don't think we fooled anyone at the poker game that night."

"What do you mean? Sure, we did."

"We didn't. In fact, I'm fairly certain we both made fools of ourselves." She resisted the urge to add that for Ray, it was doubly so because he got sloppy drunk. "Phyllis knew all along. I don't think Connor Davis knew, but he found out when Nick and I were at his sister's house." At Ray's befuddled expression, she flicked her wrist. "That's irrelevant. But the girls and I saw Gina Solero at the vet's office, and not even *she* was surprised when she heard my real name."

"Maybe Phyllis told her," Ray said.

"Maybe." She decided it was best not to go into the entire story of what had been going on with Phyllis, Jimmy, the Soleros, and Connor—especially since he was dating the lead investigator who'd already told Katie to mind her own business and to stay out of her way. "I'm probably being paranoid for no reason."

He nodded. "You've been under a great deal of stress. Hopefully, Carol will catch Jamie's killer, and you can feel at ease again."

"Has she mentioned how the investigation is going?" Katie asked.

"Nope. We try not to talk business when we're together."

Katie opened the trunk, got out the sack of dog food, and handed it to Ray. There were two additional bags, and she decided to pile those on him as well. She'd paid for the stuff—the least he could do was carry it inside.

She closed the trunk. "Thanks again, Ray. See you later."

Katie got back in her car and drove away. As she pulled around to Artisans Alley's south lot, she knew one thing beyond the shadow of a doubt—she wasn't being paranoid, and Carol had discovered nothing in the way of real information to aid this investigation. There was no way Ray wouldn't "talk business" when the case involved someone he knew and that had occurred right under his nose.

The whole idea of Carol being ineffectual rubbed Katie the wrong way. She expected far more from the woman. That Ray didn't seemed wrong on way too many levels.

WHEN KATIE RETURNED to her office at Artisans Alley, she was immediately besieged by Rose and Vance.

"What did the vet say?" Rose asked.

"Any idea what breed these puppies are?" Vance asked and allowed Rose to take the seat next to Katie's desk. "I spoke with Janie, and she's excited. We're going to surprise VJ."

"The puppies are most likely an Australian shepherd mix," Katie said. "They're between eight and ten weeks old, so they're ready to go to their forever homes. However, the vet thought it might be best to have them fostered together for a week to ten days in order to let them recover from their ordeal of being abandoned."

"Where are they now?" Although Rose had asked the question, Vance clearly wanted to know the answer as well.

"They're at Wood U." Katie retrieved a peppermint from the jar on her desk. "The Davenport girls are fostering them. I made sure they know to ask both of you and Nick before giving any of the puppies away. I got them puppy collars in different colors at the pet shop, so you can easily distinguish which one you want and pick it out from the litter."

Rose stood and looked at Vance. "Let's go see our babies."

He grinned. "After you."

Katie smiled as they filed out of her office. She didn't know whether or not Rose had spoken with Walter about the puppy, but she got the impression his opinion didn't particularly matter. Good for Rose. And yet ... Rose spent most of her days at Artisans Alley. A dog—particularly a puppy—needed supervision, and the Alley was no place to have a puppy underfoot. If Rose and Walter did get together, would Katie lose her best cashier? Would Rose choose to stay home with a puppy rather than be with her friends and colleagues?

It was a subject that needed to be brought up.

Next, Katie called Nick and relayed all the puppy information to him, and by the time they ended their call, he and Don were also on their way to Wood U. If nothing else, Ray's foot traffic was about to increase.

The phone rang. Expecting it to be Seth, she picked up her phone and looked at the screen.

It wasn't Seth. It was Margo.

"Hi, there," Katie answered. "Please tell me you aren't calling because you're also in the market for a puppy. I've nearly given all of them away."

Margo laughed. "Hardly, dear. I am watching the front desk at Sassy Sally's, so Nick and Don can go make their pick, though."

"How much cajoling did Nick have to do to convince Don?"

"Very little," Margo said. "I believe Don is so relieved Nick dropped the idea of fostering a child that he jumped at the opportunity to adopt a dog instead. I hope they know what they're getting into. My friend, Bethany, got a puppy recently and said it was very much like having a new baby in the house—sleep schedule, potty training, puppy-proofing the home." She scoffed. "Thanks, but no thanks. I value my independence too much to get a pet."

Margo had never had a pet for as long as she'd known the woman, and she hadn't been thrilled with the fact that Katie and Chad had a cat. But Katie knew Margo hadn't called simply to tell Katie she didn't want a puppy. How could she tactfully ask why she'd phoned?

"I'm glad Nick and Don have enough confidence in you to leave you in charge," Katie said, "but they'd better not leave you too long, or else they'll have to give you a discount on your stay."

"Oh, I've already told them that you and I are going to look at that Victorian House at four this afternoon. In fact, I was calling you to make sure you hadn't forgotten."

Katie had, but she wasn't about to admit it. "Of course not. Maybe we can grab dinner afterward."

"That would be great, dear. I'll see you then." Margo paused. "Oh, and I'm sure you'll go home and shower and change after your big puppy adventure this morning…"

And there was the Margo Katie had come to know and tolerate…love was a strong word, but she was working on it.

"Fear not. I won't smell of urine or anything worse," Katie said. She sure didn't need to shower or change clothes, either. And she wasn't going to mention that to Margo, either.

"Do you want me to drive to the house?"

"You know the area better than me, so yes, please." She gave

Katie the address. Katie could look it up on Google Maps before they left for their adventure.

Impossible as it seemed, Katie was getting used to the idea that Margo might be a daily presence in her life. The idea both pleased and repelled her.

Which of those two emotions would gain prominence?

Only time would tell.

CHAPTER 38

K atie had only just finished her conversation with Margo when Seth returned her call.

"Hi," he said. "I got your message, and I'm on my way to Artisans Alley to see the puppies."

"How close are you?" she asked.

"Almost there."

"The Davenport sisters have appropriated the puppies. Can you meet me at Wood U."

"Sure thing. I'll see you in a couple of minutes then," Seth said and the connection was broken.

Katie grabbed her jacket, left her office, and headed over to Wood U. When she arrived, she waited outside for Seth. Soon after, he drove up and parked.

"Hey, there," Katie said as Seth got out of his car.

"Hey, yourself," he said. "So, are they adorable?"

"Eh, if you like wiggly fluff-balls with cottony heads and puppy breath, I guess they're okay," she said blandly.

He laughed. "They sound perfect."

Together, they walked inside the shop, where they found

Vance, Rose, Nick, Don, and the Davenport sisters all crowded into the shop, admiring and playing with the pups.

Rose cradled a puppy wearing a pink collar. "I've named her Lily." She nuzzled the tiny beast. "Two flowers in the garden... that's what we are."

"This is Buddy." Vance walked over to show Seth and Katie the little boy he held. Buddy wore a black collar and was the largest of the litter.

"He's gorgeous," Seth said.

"Our little darling is Ru." Nick brought the puppy wearing the yellow collar over to show Seth. "She's the runt of the litter, but we know she'll make a splash."

"She already has!" Don laughingly pointed out the damp spot on Nick's shirt.

Nick rolled his eyes. "She was simply overexcited to meet me. I nearly peed when I met her, too. So we're even."

Laughing, Seth looked down to see a puppy wearing a green collar sitting by his feet. He bent and picked him up. Cradling the dog like a baby, he looked down into its dark brown eyes. It gazed back at him adoringly. "Is he spoken for?"

Seth had asked the question casually, but Katie could hear the hope in his voice.

"Not unless you don't want him," Sadie said. "If you don't, then Sasha and I are going to keep two."

"Uh, wait a minute," Ray interjected.

"I want him," Seth said. "I definitely do." He turned aside and spoke softly to the puppy. "You and I were meant to be together, Oran. Oran is an Irish name, and it means *green*. Green was Jamie's favorite color. You're my little Oran."

Tears sprang to Katie's eyes, and she had to turn away. Although she was happy all the puppies had so quickly found loving homes, she was most delighted for Seth and Oran.

And then Carol Rigby had to sweep into Wood U and ruin the moment.

"What have we here?" she asked, her voice dripping with contempt.

As Sadie and Sasha cast baleful looks in Carol's direction and moved closer to each other as though to protect their puppy from Cruella De Vil, Ray exclaimed, "Look what was found behind Artisans Alley today. I believe my girls are in dog heaven!"

"Oh, how sweet." Carol's tone didn't exactly match her words. "I'd love to hold one, but I haven't taken my allergy medication today."

"Then maybe you should go outside," Sasha said lightly. "This one is ours, and her name is Belle. Only Sadie and I are holding *her* right now."

The girl ignored her father's warning glare, and her sister openly defied it.

"Yep," Sadie said. "It's too bad you'll be sneezing your head off in a minute. Maybe you should go outside because Belle has four siblings."

"I think I'll be all right for a moment or two," Carol said icily. "How did these orphans find their way from Artisans Alley to Wood U?" She looked pointedly at Katie before turning her attention back to Ray.

"We went shopping at the Alley and they were in the vendors' lounge," Sadie said.

Sasha lifted her chin. "Then we went with Katie to take them to the vet and to the pet shop, and now Dad says we can foster them for a few days until they're ready to go to their forever homes."

Carol managed a smile that more closely resembled a grimace, and pressed the back of her hand against her nose. "How very nice. Katie, may I speak with you outside for a moment? My allergies *are* starting to kick up."

"All right." After sharing a glance with Seth, Katie followed Carol out the door. "What can I do for you?"

Carol's expression was downright menacing. "You can stop trying to interfere with my relationship with Ray."

Katie's eyebrows rose. That was not what she'd expected Carol to say. She'd thought the detective would warn her off the investigation again or maybe ask her some additional questions about Jamie. She hadn't expected Carol to give her the *stay away from my man* speech.

"I have no clue what you're talking about," Katie said. "I'd never butt into your relationship." Silently, she added, *If Ray wants you, he's welcome to you.*

Carol scoffed. "Oh, *really*? Then why are there five puppies that were found outside *your* establishment in Ray's shop?"

"They're there because Sasha and Sadie want them there," Katie answered. "I must admit, however, that having someone abandon puppies behind my building is not at all unique. It happens all too often."

Carol's eyes narrowed. "Just know I'm watching you. I see you trying to win over Ray's daughters and turn them against me, and I'm well aware you're making every excuse you can to visit him."

Katie threw up her hands in mock surrender. "You got me. Ray and I plotted to spend the night at his place so he and I can take turns getting up to take the puppies for their bathroom breaks. They'll have to go out every two hours."

The color rose in Carol's cheeks. "You'd better be kidding."

"And if I'm not, what are you going to do—arrest me?" Without another word, Katie turned and marched back into Wood U.

Carol didn't follow.

"Is everything all right?" Seth murmured to Katie when she returned to stand beside him.

"Absolutely," she said.

Sasha caught her eye and gave her a triumphant grin. The girl seemed to have scored two victories today—she'd gotten herself a puppy, and she'd found a new way to torment Carol Rigby.

Katie smothered a laugh.

"Dad, take another picture of Sasha and me with Belle to send to Sophie," Sadie demanded. "She's going to be so jealous!"

"I bet she'll come home this weekend just to see her," Sasha added, before smiling for the photo Ray snapped with the camera on his phone.

"Maybe we should send Belle back to college *with* Sophie until winter break," Ray teased. "That would be a nice thing to do, wouldn't it?"

"You are *so* not funny," Sasha fumed.

"As much fun as this all is," Katie said, "I, who will not be adopting a pup, have work to do. I'll see you all later." Katie said, gave a wave, and headed for Artisans Alley. She had plenty to keep her occupied before she had to meet with Margo at four o'clock.

"I'll bring Oran right back," Seth promised the girls. "I need to speak with Katie privately for a moment."

They stepped outside onto the aslphalt and Seth urged her to walk with him a few steps away from Wood U.

"What did Carol want?" he asked. "Did she have any new information about Jamie's murder investigation?"

"No," Katie said. "Or, at least, if she did, she wasn't sharing it with me. She wanted to warn me away from interfering in her relationship with Ray. Apparently, she thinks I conjured those puppies up out of thin air to give the two of us an excuse to interact."

"Well, if you did, I appreciate it." He kissed the top of Oran's furry head and then smiled when the puppy yawned. "*Are* you interested in interfering with her relationship with Ray?"

"Not in the least," she said. "And as much as I hate to admit it, I'd probably have never known about the puppies if Vance hadn't found them."

"I'm glad Vance found them, too. By the way, I looked into

Connor's flower shop—the business filed for Chapter 11 bankruptcy last week."

Katie's mouth dropped open. "Isn't that interesting."

"Yeah, the guy needed money and Jamie didn't give it to him."

"Are you thinking what I'm thinking?"

Seth's gaze dropped to the puppy still resting in his arms. "I absolutely hate what I'm thinking."

Yeah. So did Katie.

CHAPTER 39

*L*ater that afternoon, Margo called Katie to remind her of their appointment with her Realtor.

"I have a couple of things to finish up here at Artisans Alley, and then I'll drive over and pick you up," Katie said.

"I'll be ready." Margo gave a nervous giggle. "I'm thinking this house might be the one."

Katie still thought a five-bedroom Victorian was far too big for Margo, but she kept her opinion to herself. She didn't want to burst the woman's bubble. Besides, maybe Katie could change her mind when she saw the house—or perhaps Margo would.

When Katie arrived at Sassy Sally's, Nick met her at the door, grabbed her hand, and hauled her inside.

"Wait until you see the nursery I'm setting up for Ru," he said.

Katie looked from Nick to Don who was shaking his head and giving his husband a loving, indulgent smile. "Nursery?"

"It's actually a small section of our room," Don said.

"Come and look!" Nick led Katie to their suite behind the inn's kitchen. "Are you ready?" He flung open the bedroom door with a flourish.

A credenza-style crate with a bed inside, plus a tufted bed

with crystal tacks stood outside the crate; and an assortment of toys was carefully arranged in a white wicker basket next to the king-sized bed. Food and water bowls stood on a white wrought-iron stand.

"What do you think?" Nick asked eagerly.

"I'm wondering how you managed to pull all this stuff together in one afternoon," she said.

He shrugged and grinned. "I know people who know people."

"Katie, we're going to be late!" Margo called.

Smiling at Nick, Katie said, "Ru is a very lucky girl." As she started for the parlor, she thought about starting a betting pool with Seth, Brad, and Margo on how long it would take Ru to destroy that fancy bed.

Once on their way to the Victorian house, Margo said, "You've caused quite a stir with those puppies."

"You don't know the half of it." She told Margo about her adventure to the vet and the pet store with the Davenport sisters and her encounter with Carol Rigby. "First, she wants to get me as far away from her investigation as possible, and now she's threatened by my friendship with Ray—which is kind of non-existent at the moment anyway."

"She has good reason to feel envious," Margo pointed out. "From what I can see, you've made much more progress in sussing out Jamie's killer than she has. And any fool can see Ray Davenport is in love with you—who wouldn't despise being the second choice?" She patted Katie's arm. "I understand your needing to put some distance between yourself and Ray, but don't entirely throw your friendship away. You'll regret it if you do."

"I know." As much as Katie hated to admit it, Margo was right. She didn't want to lose Ray's friendship.

"Back to the puppies," Margo said. "I'm glad Nick and Don are happy with their imminent pitter-patter of little paws, but I'm afraid Sassy Sally's patrons won't be so thrilled when they're kept awake nights."

"I'm sure Nick and Don will come up with a way to minimize any inconvenience to their guests. As glad as I am for them, I'm especially pleased for Seth."

Margo smiled. "Me, too. And from what Nick and Don have told me, the Davenport girls are delighted with the addition to their family as well."

"They are." Katie glanced at the map on her phone. "Is this our turn?"

"That's it." Margo clasped her hands together. "I see Brenda's car in the driveway."

Yep, Brenda Furnham had her mark all over the property. Not only was her *Brenda Furnham* car parked in the driveway, her *Brenda Furnham* sign was on the front lawn. And Brenda Furnham herself was standing on the porch smiling and waving to them as though she were the newly crowned Ms. Real Estate New York.

"Hi, ladies!" Brenda called, as Margo and Katie got out of the car.

Katie immediately saw that in the light of day, the house was more dilapidated than it had appeared to be in the photographs she and Margo had seen online. A glance at Margo told Katie she was thinking the same thing. Still, Margo plastered a smile on her face and soldiered on.

"Have Gomez and Morticia mentioned why they're selling?" Katie had intended to ask the question softly enough to reach Margo's ears only, but her words were caught by Brenda.

"Oh, you!" Brenda gave a boisterous laugh. "You're a comedienne, you are! Come on in, gals, and fall in love with this beauty."

Katie was already finding Brenda to be a bit much, but she dutifully followed Margo into the house.

"Now, granted, it needs some love," Brenda said. "But that's okay—you can make it more your own with the appropriate upgrades, right?"

As they stood in the foyer, Katie noticed the disappointment settling on Margo's face. She wanted to tell her there were other places—for instance, the mock Tudor house that Katie had preferred to this one all along—but she didn't want to insult Brenda, who was taking her time to be here and show the house.

"This parquet flooring is exquisite," Brenda said, "and look at this cherry woodwork. Isn't it lovely?"

"It is," Margo said.

It *was* lovely, but it was dark. Maybe it would be better with the lights on. Katie looked behind her, saw a light switch, and flipped it on. Nothing happened.

"Sorry! The owners have the electricity turned off right now." Brenda rubbed her arms. "That's why it's a little chilly in here. Wait until you see the kitchen."

They walked through the empty house, their footfalls echoing and the floor beneath them creaking with every step.

The women walked through the arched doorway into the kitchen where they were greeted by white appliances, cherry cabinets, and a horrific floral wallpaper from the 1970s.

"What do you think?" Brenda looked at Margo and Katie as expectantly as though she'd built and decorated the home herself.

"I'm surprised the appliances are so modern," Katie said.

Delighted to have something positive to build on, Brenda said, "Yes, aren't they great? The owners upgraded their kitchen two years ago."

"Did they say why they're selling?" Margo asked.

Katie thought the place was likely haunted, but she waited for Brenda's answer.

"They're moving to be closer to their daughter who lives in Illinois now," Brenda said. "This home was built in the late 1800s, and as you can see, it's built to last."

"When the kitchen was upgraded, was the wiring replaced as well?" Katie asked.

"Oh, that was done long before the kitchen upgrade." A buzzing sound came from Brenda's right jacket pocket. She retrieved her phone and looked at the screen impatiently. "I'm afraid I'm going to have to take this."

"That's okay," Margo said. "We'll go ahead and take a look upstairs."

"What do you think?" Katie asked as she and Margo mounted the cherry staircase.

"It's not for me. The photographs posted on Brenda's site are a bit misleading."

"I agree." Testing the railing, which seemed a bit wobbly, Katie said, "This place would need a *lot* of work."

"More than I'm willing to put into a new home," Margo said. "I believe this house could be stunning, but I'll leave it to someone else—I want a house that's in move-in condition."

"I don't blame you."

They heard a crash downstairs.

Katie's eyes flew to Margo before she called, "Brenda? Are you all right?"

"Fine!"

That faint, high-pitched *fine* didn't sound right.

"That wasn't Brenda." Katie pressed her phone into Margo's hand. "Call nine-one-one."

"But—"

Ignoring Margo's protest, Katie turned and started back down the stairs. She was on the third stair from the top when Connor Davis stepped into view. He was holding a pistol equipped with a silencer.

Since he was staring right at her, Katie froze. "Connor, what are you doing?"

"Tying up loose ends," he said. "You know what I did, or you wouldn't have been checking up on me with Luther and Phyllis."

"I don't—"

"Spare me," Connor interrupted.

"All I know is that you helped Jamie cheat at cards," Katie said. "I'm guessing it was to help you with your business?"

"I helped Jamie because I was in love with him." His expression was a caricature of anger and disgust. "I adored that man, and he did nothing but *use* me." He looked up at Margo. "Drop that phone and get over here with *her*."

Katie winced at the sound of the phone hitting the floor. Was there any way Margo had been able to dial 9-1-1 before Connor caught them? She didn't hear anyone talking on the other end.

"If you need money, I'll give you what I won," Katie said. "I don't think Jamie would have intentionally cut you out of your part of—"

"Then you didn't know him very well," Connor said, ascending the stairs and closing the distance between them.

"But you had to realize that by killing Jamie, you'd never get what was coming to you," Margo said, as she moved closer to Katie and gripped the railing.

Eyes filling with tears, Connor said, "I never meant to *kill* him. I only wanted to punish him. I knew the crushed berries would make him suffer, but I thought that as long as he went to the doctor, he'd be fine. And now I've got nothing. *Nothing!*" he nearly screamed. "Not Jamie, not the money to save my business, nothing."

"You've got your sister," Katie said.

"She doesn't *need* me. I'm only an aggravation and an embarrassment to her," he said.

"That isn't true. She adores you—I saw it all over her face when you walked into her kitchen the evening I was there."

Her proclamation made Connor sob even harder. "I've been such a fool." He placed the barrel of the gun beneath his chin.

"No!" Katie lunged for Connor, grasping his arm and trying to pull the gun away from his body.

"Katie!" Margo screamed.

Connor fought to regain control. He still held the gun but used his left hand to grab Katie and try to push her away.

As they fought, the railing cracked and they teetered before they both fell to the floor below, with Katie landing on top of Connor. A knife-like pain ripped through her chest, the agony increasing with every breath she took. So that's what a broken rib felt like. Not fun.

Connor had dropped the gun when they fell. It had skittered away and lay near the front door where neither of them could reach it.

Connor's eyes fluttered open. His breaths sounded just as painful as Katie's. "Damn," he grated. "This is *not* how I wanted to leave this world."

"I don't think either of us is going anywhere just yet." Katie heard sirens in the distance before she felt Margo's trembling hand on her shoulder.

"Are you able to move?" the older woman asked.

"I don't know," Katie admitted with a grimace. "I'd rather wait for the police or the EMTs to get here before I try."

"You know what this means?" Margo asked.

"Another visit to the ER?" Katie asked.

Margo nodded and looked down at her daughter-in-law, shaking her head. "What am I going to do with you?"

"Keep me, I hope."

"Darling, girl. Of course I will."

CHAPTER 40

*O*n Thursday, Katie was lounging on her love seat with both cats trying to occupy her lap while Margo regaled Brad, who'd brought up a lunch tray, with the story of how *she'd* saved the day.

"We heard that crash, and I knew something was wrong," Margo said. "And when Katie asked if she was all right, it was obvious that it *wasn't* Brenda's voice that answered. Now, I had my phone in my purse, but Katie handed me hers, so I used it to call nine-one-one. They asked what our emergency was, but before I could answer, there stood Connor at the bottom of the stairs!"

"You must've been terrified," Brad said.

"I'll admit it was frightening, but I kept my head long enough to mute that phone hoping Connor wouldn't catch onto what I was doing." Margo mopped her forehead with her fingertips.

Katie hid a smile behind her hand. It wasn't the first time she'd heard this story, and she was certain it wouldn't be the last. Margo had held up well under pressure and she obviously relished the retelling of their frightening encounter with a killer.

"When he put that gun to his chin and threatened to kill himself, I was thinking Katie should simply let him do it!" Margo shrugged. "I mean, we had Brenda to think about. We didn't know *what* he'd done to her."

They later learned that she'd suffered a concussion when Connor had pistol-whipped her, although they hoped the injury wouldn't cause her any long-term harm.

The fall had given Katie two cracked ribs, but fortunately, she hadn't suffered a punctured lung. Connor had sustained a concussion and a chipped vertebra. He had a long road of recovery ahead of him—from physical, emotional, *and* legal standpoints.

Brad had assembled a wonderful assortment of sandwiches, and he took the time to lunch with Katie and Margo. Rose and Walter had been by earlier and brought Katie a nice flower arrangement, and Vance and Janey also came by to wish her well. Even Andy had called to wish her well. She'd kept that conversation short.

The only person Katie hadn't heard from was Ray. She'd gotten an earful from Carol Rigby before the uniformed officers investigating the scene respectfully asked her to wait until they'd processed the scene and taken care of the injured parties to conduct her interrogations. Katie and Margo had driven across the county to the Sheriff's Office and had given their sworn statements that morning.

After Brad and Margo left, Katie stretched out as best she could on the love seat and tried to sleep. She hadn't gotten much rest the night before—partly because of the pain from her cracked ribs and partly because every time she closed her eyes, she relived falling through the stair railing with Connor Davis.

She was awakened from a doze by a tap on her door. Groggily, and with great effort, she got up and answered it. Ray stood on her landing with Belle in his arms.

"Do the girls know you've absconded with their baby?" she asked.

"No. They're back at school today. I have a friend watching the rest of the puppies and the shop while I came to see how you're doing," he said. "I heard you got pretty banged up yesterday, and I thought you could maybe use some fluff in your life."

She didn't bother to remind him of her resident cats, who weren't likely to embrace a canine in their lair. Backing away from the door, she heaved a sigh and said, "Come on in."

As expected, at the sight of the puppy, Della ran and hid in the kitchen. Mason stayed in the living room but watched from a respectful distance.

"Do you wanna hold her?" Ray held out the puppy.

Shrugging, Katie said, "Sure. When I sit down," she amended. She returned to the love seat and Ray handed her the dog. Katie snuggled the puppy against her uninjured side. "How did you and the girls handle your first night with a pack of puppies?"

"It wasn't bad because the litter was together. Whenever the others go home with their owners, it might be a bit rougher." He sat on the chair adjacent to the love seat.

"The *friend* watching Wood U—I'm guessing it isn't Carol," Katie said.

"No. She'd have a conniption if she knew I was here."

"Would you care?" Katie's gaze issued a challenge.

"A little," he admitted. "Carol and I could have a good relationship. We're close in age, we enjoy a lot of the same things, she thinks I'm...attractive." He actually blushed.

Katie noticed he'd said *could have*. She wondered if the friction between Carol and his daughters was the reason they only *could* rather than *did* have a good relationship. Either way, it was none of her business.

"I only want you to be happy," she told him.

"Likewise." Their fingers brushed when he reached out to take the puppy from her. "I'd better be getting back to the store."

"Yeah."

At the door, he turned to look at her over his shoulder. "Anytime you need some puppy love, you know where to find us."

Yes, she certainly did.

Apple Cider Cake

Ingredients

4 cups apple cider

3¾ cups all-purpose flour

1½ teaspoons kosher salt

1½ teaspoons baking powder

½ teaspoon baking soda

¾ teaspoon ground cinnamon

¼ teaspoon ground allspice

1 cup (2 sticks) unsalted butter, melted and browned

1½ cups dark brown sugar

3 large eggs, at room temperature

2 teaspoons vanilla extract

1½ pounds apples, peeled, cored and shredded (about 3 cups)

¾ cup confectioners' sugar

In a medium heavy bottom pan, bring the cider to a boil over
high heat. Cook until reduced to 1 cup, 20 to 25 minutes. Reserve
½ cup of the reduced cider for the frosting.

Preheat the oven to 350°F (180°C, Gas Mark 4). Grease a 12-cup bundt pan with baking spray. In a large bowl, whisk together the flour, salt, baking powder, baking soda, cinnamon and allspice.

In a separate large bowl, whisk together ½ cup cider reduction, melted butter, brown sugar, eggs and vanilla extract. Pour the cider mixture over the flour mixture and stir with a rubber spatula until just combined. Stir in the shredded apples until just combined. Transfer the batter to the prepared pan and evenly smooth the top.

Bake the cake until a skewer inserted into the center comes out clean—about 55 to 65 minutes. Transfer the pan to a cooling rack. Immediately brush the exposed surface of the cake in the pan with 1 tablespoon of the reserved cider. Let the cake cool for at least 10 minutes before inverting onto a wire rack. Brush the top and sides of the cake with more of the apple cider reduction. Let the cake cool for at least 20 minutes before drizzling icing.

For the icing, combine the confectioner's sugar with 2 tablespoons of the remaining cider reduction. Drizzle the icing over the cake and let cool completely.

Spiced Cider Punch
Ingredients
½ cup granulated sugar
1 teaspoon ground cinnamon
1 teaspoon ground allspice
1 bottle (64 ounces) apple cider or juice, divided
1 can (12 ounces) frozen orange juice concentrate
1 liter ginger ale, chilled
Orange slices, optional

Place the sugar, spices and 1 cup cider in a saucepan; cook and stir over medium heat until sugar is dissolved. Remove from heat; stir in juice concentrate until melted. Transfer to a large pitcher. Stir in remaining cider. Refrigerate, covered, until cold. To serve, pour the cider mixture into a punch bowl. Stir in the ginger ale. If desired, garnish with orange slices.

Pumpkin Cupcakes
Ingredients
2 cups granulated sugar
1 can (15 ounces) pumpkin
4 large eggs, room temperature
1 cup canola oil
2 cups all-purpose flour
2 teaspoons baking powder
2 teaspoons ground cinnamon
1 teaspoon baking soda
½ teaspoon salt
½ teaspoon ground ginger
¼ teaspoon ground cloves
1 cup raisins

Cream Cheese Frosting
Ingredients
⅓ cup butter, softened
3 ounces cream cheese, softened
1 teaspoon vanilla extract
2 cups confectioners' sugar
½ cup chopped walnuts, toasted if desired

Preheat the oven to 350ºF (180ºC, Gas Mark 4). Beat the sugar, pumpkin, eggs, and oil until well blended. In another bowl, whisk in the next seven ingredients; gradually beat into pumpkin mixture. Stir in the raisins.

Fill each of 24 paper-lined muffin cups with 1/4 cup plus 1 teaspoon of the batter. Bake until a toothpick inserted the in center comes out clean, 28-32 minutes. Cool 10 minutes before removing from pans to wire racks to cool completely.

For the frosting, beat the butter and cream cheese until smooth. Beat in the vanilla. Gradually add the confectioners' sugar. Frost the cupcakes and sprinkle with walnuts. Refrigerate.

Yield: 24 cupcakes

ABOUT LORRAINE BARTLETT

The immensely popular Booktown Mystery series is what put Lorraine Bartlett's pen name Lorna Barrett on the New York Times Bestseller list, but it's her talent—whether writing as Lorna, or L.L. Bartlett, or Lorraine Bartlett—that keeps her in the hearts of her readers. This multi-published, Agatha-nominated author pens the exciting Jeff Resnick Mysteries as well as the acclaimed Victoria Square Mystery series, the Tales of Telenia adventure-fantasy saga, and now the Lotus Bay Mysteries, and has many short stories and novellas to her name(s). Check out the descriptions and links to all her works, and sign up for her emailed newsletter on her website: www.LorraineBartlett.com

Not familiar with all of Lorraine's work? Check out **A Cozy Mystery Sampler,** which is a FREE ebook download.

If you enjoyed **_DEAD MAN'S HAND,_** please consider reviewing it on your favorite online review site. Thank you!

Find Lorraine on Social Media
www.LorraineBartlett.com

A Look Back

Tea For You (free for download)

Not The Killing Type

Book Clubbed

A Fatal Chapter

Title Wave

A Just Clause

Poisoned Pages

A Killer Edition

Handbook For Homicide

A Deadly Deletion

WITH THE COZY CHICKS

The Cozy Chicks Kitchen

Tea Time With The Cozy Chicks

ABOUT GAYLE LESSON

Gayle Leeson is a pseudonym for Gayle Trent. Gayle has also written as Amanda Lee. She is currently writing the Kinsey Falls chick-lit/women's fiction series, the Down South Cafe cozy mystery series, and the Ghostly Fashionista cozy mystery series, and co-author of several Victoria Square Mysteries (with Lorraine Bartlett). Her book KILLER WEDDING CAKE won the Bronze Medal in the 20th Anniversary IPPY Awards.

Gayle lives in Southwest Virginia with her family and enjoys hearing from readers.

Visit her website to join her email newsletter list! www.-GayleLeeson.com

ALSO BY GAYLE LEESON

Writing as Gayle Leeson
Down South Café Mystery Series
The Calamity Café
Silence of the Jams
Honey-Baked Homicide
Apples and Alibis
Fruit Baskets and Holiday Caskets

Ghostly Fashionista Mystery Series
Designs on Murder
Perils and Lace
Christmas Cloches and Corpses

Kinsey Falls Chick-Lit Series
Hightail It to Kinsey Falls
Putting Down Roots in Kinsey Falls
Sleighing It in Kinsey Falls

The Victoria Square Mysteries (with Lorraine Bartlett)

Yule Be Dead
Murder Ink
A Murderous Misconception
Dead Man's Hand

WRITING AS AMANDA LEE
Embroidery Mystery Series
The Quick and The Thread
Stitch Me Deadly
Thread Reckoning
The Long Stitch Goodnight
Thread On Arrival
Cross-Stitch Before Dying
Thread End
Wicked Stitch
The Stitching Hour
Better Off Thread

WRITING AS GAYLE TRENT
Daphne Martin Cake Decorating Mysteries
Murder Takes the Cake
Dead Pan
Killer Sweet Tooth
Battered to Death
Killer Wedding Cake

Myrtle Crumb Mysteries
Between A Clutch and A Hard Place
When Good Bras Go Bad
Claus Of Death
Soup...Er...Myrtle!
Perp and Circumstance
The Party Line (A Myrtle Crumb Prequel)

Stand-Alone Books
The Perfect Woman
The Flame
In Her Blood (as G. V. Trent)

Made in the USA
Las Vegas, NV
23 February 2021